Availabl

2000 Media

Non Fiction:

No Regrets: How Homeschooling Earned me a Master's Degree at Age Sixteen

Writing for Today

Looking Backward: My Twenty-Five Years as a Homeschooling Mother

Adult Fiction Series:

The Planner

The Chosen

The Kingdom Chronicles

The Fourth Kingdom

The Force

Other Adult Fiction:

The Twelfth Juror

The Warrior

Children's Fiction:

Tales of Pig Isle

The McAloons: A Horse Called Lightning & A House of Clowns

Cover Design: Stefan Swann

Published in the USA by Frontier 2000 Media Group Inc., El Paso, Texas.

http://www.frontier2000.net

ISBN-13: 978-1493524600
ISBN-10: 1493524607

Prologue

One cold January afternoon long before the great fire had destroyed Doppelganger, long before Josef and his father had visited Cornucopia, long before the twins had suffered their great loss, Alexander Sinclair sat dozing in his big leather chair while snowflakes the size of goose feathers filled the sky and floated softly to the ground.

As the logs crackled in the fireplace and Alexander dreamed contentedly, two little boys ran down the stairs, scrambled onto his lap, and wrapped their arms tightly around him. Before Alexander's eyes were fully open, the boys began to talk excitedly, "Daddy, today our Sunday school teacher said that the devil is powerful, and if we don't be good he will get us. We're scared!"

"What?" their father replied, drawing them closer to him. "No! That's not right. You're Christian boys. The devil can't get Christian boys."

"Are you sure?" Jarrod asked.

"Of course, I'm sure," his father replied. "And I'm going to tell you something else: the devil is not powerful; all power belongs to God and to Jesus. The devil uses force, but he has no power."

Joshua looked worried, "It's the same thing! Power and force is the same thing!"

"You're wrong," Alexander assured him. "God's power is unlimited. He created everything there is in heaven and on earth. He has the power to protect us and to help us in every situation. There is nothing that is too hard for God because His power can both destroy and create.

"But the devil is different. He cannot create anything. He likes to destroy things—especially people's lives, but he has never created one single thing because force cannot create."

"I'm still scared!" Joshua exclaimed.

"Don't be," Alexander continued. "Lots of things have force: floods, tornadoes, hurricanes, fires, earthquakes, but they are only able to destroy. Tornadoes have destroyed many towns, but you will never hear of one passing by and creating a town. The earth is filled with destructive forces, but those forces are nothing compared to God's power.

"Now I am going to tell you something else that I want you always to remember: As long as you have the power of God's Holy Spirit in you, the devil can never defeat you, and you never need to fear him. One day God will call you to take a stand against the forces of Satan. When that day comes, remember this: Whenever power and force collide, power always wins the fight."

THE FORCE

SWANN
Alexandra & Joyce

CHAPTER 1

Peter Kessler awakened to the sound of someone pounding on a door. The sound seemed to be coming from a long way away, and Peter's foggy brain had a difficult time processing it. He heard his housekeeper's voice and two male voices that he did not recognize, but the words that floated up to his bedroom were muffled and unintelligible.

Peter turned to face the clock on his bedside table: "1:23 A.M." A jolt of fear and dread surged through his body that instantly rendered him fully awake. He sat up and swung his legs over the side of the bed, waiting for the sound of Liesel's footsteps in the hallway.

Within seconds Liesel had reached the bedroom door. Knocking softly she said, "Herr Kessler, the *polizei* are here. There has been an accident."

Although the night was warm, Kessler's hands were cold, and they shook as he opened the door. "Tell them that I will be right there," he said before shutting the door in the housekeeper's face.

As he pulled on his clothes, he remembered the day twelve years earlier when his wife and daughter had been killed in an automobile accident. The sole survivor had been his four-year-old son, Dieter. Six days after the funeral, Dieter was sent home from the hospital, and since that day Peter had done everything possible to protect him. Dieter was all that he had—his only reason for living. Now, in the middle of the night the *polizei* had come to his door to tell him that there had been an accident.

Peter refused to ride with the police to the morgue. He followed in his Bugatti Veyron, the most powerful, most expensive, and fastest car in the world. Dieter had been thrilled the day that it was delivered to their country home, and when Peter had seen how much his son admired the magnificent piece of German engineering, he had promised to give him one for his sixteenth birthday.

True to his word, Peter had ordered the automobile and arranged for it to arrive during Dieter's birthday party which had been held the previous month. Just as Peter had anticipated, the magnificent gift had delighted Dieter and inspired envy in his friends. Peter had planned every detail of the party so that all eyes were constantly fixed on Dieter; it was a celebration of his son and of the extent to which Peter was willing to go to ensure that Dieter lived a long, happy life.

Now, as he followed the police car to the morgue, Peter felt everything he had worked for slip away, as if someone had silently slit his wrists, and his life's blood were draining from him. Tomorrow headlines all over the world would read, *Billionaire German Industrialist's Only Son Killed in Automobile Accident.*

As Peter stood with the police officers waiting for the body to be uncovered, he gripped the back of a steel and vinyl chair for support. His knees felt rubbery, and it took all his strength to remain on his feet. When the sheet was pulled back revealing his son's face, he spoke, "It is the second time that I have identified my son's body in less than a year. No more," and he turned and walked from the room.

After a quick exchange speculating what Herr Kessler could possibly mean by his remarks, the younger of the two police officers hurried after Peter and asked if they could drive him home; he did not speak but simply shook his head and continued walking to the parking lot where he climbed into his car and sped away.

Twenty minutes later Peter Kessler walked into the library of his country home, pulled his luger from his desk, and shoved it into his mouth. The sound of the explosion brought Liesel running to investigate.

CHAPTER 2

Fred Kowalski was less than one week away from retiring from the New York City Police Department. For the past twenty-five years of his career he had been a detective, and although the job could be both interesting and challenging, most of the time it was simply gory and exhausting. He had witnessed hundreds of scenes that made the acts depicted in horror movies look like child's play. Fred knew from years of first-hand experience that viewing real bodies mutilated by real murderers was neither exciting nor frightening; it was hideous and heartbreaking, and he had never been able to get past the sense of sadness and waste that stayed with him during these investigations.

Today he and his partner were on their way to Fifth Avenue to gather evidence. The mutilated body of a young woman had been discovered in an alley in the heart of New York's most exclusive shopping. Fred thought that was a little curious; the area was well-patrolled and kept as safe as possible for the world's most privileged shoppers. He wondered why anyone would choose to dispose of a body there where it was certain to draw more attention than it would in most of the city's other locations.

Fred saw four police cars with their blinking lights parked at the curb, and he pulled his unmarked vehicle in behind them. One of the officers on the scene recognized him and signaled for him to come forward.

"So, what have we got here?" Fred asked the officer.

"Caucasian female, early twenties, multiple stab wounds, possible asphyxiation. Doesn't look like she's been here more than a couple of hours. She was probably a call girl; she looks like she was a real beauty. Maybe one of her customers got off on torture."

As Fred stood looking at the body, he noticed that there was something familiar about her. She was badly bruised and bloodied, but her platinum hair and pale yellow halter dress stirred a memory. He was certain that he had seen this young woman before. "Any ID?" he asked.

"Nothing."

"Did she have a purse or a shopping bag—anything like that?"

"Nope."

When the photographs of the scene had been taken, Fred squatted to view the body more closely. "Beck," he said to his partner, "she's a dead-ringer for Marilyn Monroe."

Beck, who had just celebrated his twenty-seventh birthday, replied, "I don't know nothin' about those old movie stars. She could *be* Monroe, and I wouldn't know it."

"Well, she's definitely not Marilyn," Kowalski answered. "If Marilyn were still alive, she'd be over a hundred years old, but she sure as heck looks like her. My dad was a big fan. He had every movie she ever made, and he collected her posters. Growing up I probably saw more pictures of her than she saw of herself. Check with all the celebrity look-alike services and see if anyone hired a Marilyn look-alike. After we run her prints we might know more."

Ψ

The next morning Fred visited the medical examiner to see if he had found anything useful.

Dr. Marvin March was obviously puzzled. "She's gorgeous," he said. "No doubt about it, but she's a little too gorgeous. She's perfect. She doesn't have a single life marker."

"Life marker?" Fred was puzzled.

"Yeah, you know, the kind of stuff everybody's got. Babies are born with perfect complexions—soft, smooth, blemish-free, but right away they start to get life markers. A kid falls and has a little scar on his knee. All of the scuffs and scrapes leave little scars and blemishes on the skin.

Most of us never notice them because they're small and insignificant, but they're there. Then there's sun damage. Even someone who uses sun screen his whole life has some sun damage that causes little discolorations, or a little thickening of the skin in certain areas. A person will have a little patch of freckles on his shoulder that resulted from a sunburn that he got as a child. As we age—and by age I mean pass infancy—we develop moles, freckles—all sorts of life markers—but this vic doesn't have a single one. What I want to know is how does a woman get to be twenty-something and not have a single life marker?

"But that's not even the best part," Dr. March continued. "When I examined her organs, I found that none of them had any life markers either. Her lungs were like a newborn's—no damage from twenty-plus years of breathing polluted air, or smoking, or having any illness that might have put some scarring on the lungs. Her heart is in perfect condition—no signs of any stress, ever. Every organ in her body is in pristine condition."

"So, how do you account for that?"

"I don't account for it. I've never seen anything like it. I just don't know."

"We ran her prints," Fred told the examiner. "They didn't turn up in our records, but we've asked the FBI to run them through their data base. Friday is my last day so I won't be working this one, but I'll be checking back to follow up. I have a feeling that there's a lot more to this than anyone suspects right now."

CHAPTER 3

On the Monday morning after his retirement, Fred and his wife Annie put their suitcases into the trunk of their new Ford and began the drive to Chicago to visit their only son, Brian, and his family. Although Chicago was only eight hundred miles away, they had gotten a late start and were planning to stop for the night somewhere around the four hundred mile mark.

Fred felt really free for the first time in his adult life. He and Annie had married young, and Brian had been born fourteen months later while Fred was still in college. To help with expenses Annie had worked at her parents' bakery until shortly before Brian's birth, but afterwards she had to stay home to take care of him. During Fred's final year of college, he had been forced to take on a second part-time job to support his family. He had never forgotten how thoroughly exhausted he had been during that time, working long hours, attending classes, and studying far into the night to earn his degree in criminal justice.

Police work had also taken a toll. Fred was good at what he did, and when he became a detective, he ate, lived, and breathed his cases. He spent many of his off-duty hours following up on leads and tracking down new ones. He could never rest until he was satisfied that he had gathered the evidence needed to put away one of the bad guys.

Now, at age sixty, Fred found himself with no bad guys to put away, no leads to follow, no cases to crack. He and Annie were headed down US-20 with no schedule, no motel reservations, and no reason to hurry. They would eat when they were hungry, sleep when they were tired, and stop to investigate any interesting sights along the way. He reached for Annie's hand and pressed it against his lips. When she smiled in response, he could still see a hint of that blonde-haired blue-eyed girl he had fallen in love with more than forty years earlier.

Late Tuesday afternoon when they finally pulled into Brian's driveway, Fred was relaxed and ready to enjoy himself. When Brian's wife Taylor opened the door she was holding the baby on her hip. She smiled widely and told them that Brian had called to say that he would be home late because he had just been called out on a homicide. It was almost midnight when Brian arrived, and Fred and Annie had already gone to bed.

The next morning at breakfast, however, Brian began telling Fred about the homicide he was investigating. The body of a young woman had been found in an alley on Chicago's Magnificent Mile. "It's really weird," Brian said.

"She had been stabbed multiple times, but there was no ID, no purse, nothing."

Fred felt a tingling sensation at the back of his neck. "Did you see the crime scene?"

"Yeah."

"Did you see the body?"

"Yeah."

"What does she look like?"

"Well, that's the really weird part. She looks like Forever Marilyn, only real and in miniature."

"Was she wearing the halter dress?"

"Yeah."

"Have you run her prints?" Fred questioned his son further.

"Yeah. If her prints are on record, we should be able to ID her this morning."

"I had leave time approved for the next two weeks, but I need to go in today for a while to follow up. You want to come along?"

"I sure do!"

Fred stepped outside and called Beck at the precinct in New York. "Did you get the ID on the homicide vic from last week?"

"Which one?"

"The blonde in the halter dress."

"Yes and no," Beck answered. "The prints matched the ones that the FBI has on file for Marilyn Monroe. Like you said, this girl's not Marilyn, so we told them they made a mistake and to run them again. They did, and they still came back as a match for Marilyn Monroe.

"The FBI has a big file on Monroe because she was sleeping with the president. When she died of the OD, they took blood samples, which they still have. We asked them to do a DNA comparison to see if she's a match for our vic and get us the results ASAP. I know there's no way they're a match, but it's spooky, you know?"

"Yeah, I know. Listen, Beck, I might have something for you here. I'm not sure yet, but I'll be in touch later today."

Fred ended his call just as Brian stepped through the door. "Can I see the body?" Fred asked.

"Sure. We'll swing by the morgue."

An hour later the men were viewing the body and talking to the Cook County medical examiner. "Was there anything unusual about the victim?" Fred inquired.

Consulting his notes the medical examiner read, "White Caucasian female; approximately twenty-two years of age; five feet, five and a half inches tall; one hundred eighteen pounds; blue eyes; bleached platinum blonde hair; forty-eight stab wounds, none of which was fatal; cause of death, asphyxiation. Nothing unusual, but I can tell you that she was gorgeous. A girl like that—you'd think a guy would want to keep her around."

"What about life markers?" Fred inquired.

"What?" the medical examiner responded.

"Life markers."

"I don't know what you're talking about," the medical examiner replied.

"Life markers," Fred persisted, "moles, scars, freckles, sun damage, calluses—the stuff that documents that we were alive."

The medical examiner looked puzzled and then examined the body more closely. "No, there's nothing. She's perfect. Even her teeth show absolutely no signs of wear."

Fred and Brian left the morgue, and when they were outside, Fred took hold of Brian's arm. "You won't find her prints in your data base," Fred advised. "Run them through the FBI data base; they'll have a match."

"And you know this because...?"

"I know this because this same girl turned up dead in an alley on Fifth Avenue last week. She was even wearing the same dress."

"You found Forever Marilyn in New York?" Brian asked.

"Why do you keep calling her 'Forever Marilyn'?"

"Because she looks just like that huge statue in Pioneer Court. I drive past it every day, and I always think that it's just perfect that New York has the Wall Street Bull, and St. Louis has the Gateway Arch, but Chicago has a twenty-six foot tall, forty-thousand pound statue of Marilyn Monroe with her skirt blowing up around her waist standing in the middle of Pioneer Court. It's kind of embarrassing to drive by and see the tourists standing under her skirt getting their pictures taken.

"When they unveiled it thirty years ago, it was only supposed to be here for a year. In less time than that they sent it to Palm Springs for another year. I think the whole country thought it was a monstrosity, so after ten years of wandering from city to city Marilyn ended up right back here in Pioneer Court where she started, and it looks like this is going to be her permanent home."

"That still doesn't explain why you keep calling her 'Forever Marilyn'," Fred countered.

Brian was now becoming irritated, "Dad! That's the name of the statue—'Forever Marilyn'."

Fred was right; the victim's prints matched those of Marilyn Monroe in the FBI data base, and when the DNA comparisons were made, both victims were an exact match for Marilyn.

Ψ

On Friday Fred received a call from Charlie Byrd at the FBI building in New York City. Charlie had seen

Fred's name on the report as the first detective on the scene for the victim who was the Marilyn Monroe DNA match. When he called the precinct, he was told that Fred had retired, but since he had known him on a professional basis for several years, he wanted to talk to him. Searching through his Rolodex, he found Fred's personal communication device number.

"Hey," Fred answered when he saw the caller ID, "what's goin' on?"

"I saw your name on the Marilyn Monroe file," Charlie responded. "Do you have any theories about what's going on?"

"Do you know that a second Marilyn was found in Chicago a few days later?" Fred asked.

"Yeah, I was getting ready to tell you that."

"It just so happens," Fred continued, "that the day I arrived to visit my son, who is a detective in Chicago, the other victim turned up. I went by the morgue with him and saw the body. She's identical to the New York Marilyn. But, as for theories, I have no idea—this is a real head scratcher."

"Well, there's something else," Charlie continued. "On Wednesday a stabbing victim was discovered in a posh district of Miami. We ran her prints, and they were a match for Sophia Loren. Then we ran her DNA and got an exact match.

"On Friday Audrey Hepburn turned up dead in San Francisco. She was even wearing the dress and hairdo from *Breakfast at Tiffany's*."

"How did you have Loren and Hepburn in the FBI data base?" Fred inquired.

"They were both European, and they first came to the U.S. during the hottest part of the cold war—Hepburn in 1951 and Loren in 1957. The FBI kept files on all high-profile foreigners who entered the country at that time. Lucky for us, we never get rid of anything, so we were able to make positive IDs."

"Are you going to call in the Sinclairs?" Fred inquired.

"I called them this afternoon. It takes a lot to shock those boys, but I could tell that they were intrigued. They agreed to consult on all four cases—which we believe are the work of the same perpetrator or perpetrators.

"Since you saw two of the victims, would it be okay for me to give them your number—just in case they have some questions for you?"

Fred had been retired for less than two weeks, and he was already involved in the most intriguing case of his career.

CHAPTER 4

Jarrod and Joshua Sinclair were seated with Fred Kowalski and Charlie Byrd at a small conference table in one of the offices of the New York City FBI building. Fred examined the Sinclair brothers carefully. About forty years old, the twins were identical in every respect. He wondered why they had not followed the example of so many other pairs of identical twins and made an effort to establish their own identities. Their identical haircuts showed off their chestnut hair to its fullest advantage, but it seemed odd to Fred that the brothers would not want to separate themselves from each other in some small ways. Although they were not dressed in "matching" outfits, their conservative suits and ties looked as if they had been purchased by the same person. After nearly three hours of going over evidence from the murders with them, Fred had the impression that he was seeing double.

"Any ideas?" Charlie asked looking at the twins.

"Actually, yes," Joshua replied. "Officially, human cloning has never been successfully done. About twenty years ago, it was attempted in some parts of Asia, but the results were so unsatisfactory that after a few years the labs shut down. Both the physical and mental conditions of most of the clones were substandard to the point that they had to be destroyed; less than ten percent were healthy enough to function as factory workers, day laborers, and domestics. And even for those that were, the labs had the problem of being able to sell them. Wide disagreement existed as to whether clones had legal human status. If they were deemed to be legally human, selling them constituted engaging in the slave trade. Because even those with extreme deformities met the criteria of being human in every respect other than birth, the courts would not agree to assign them a sub-human designation that would allow them to be treated as commodities.

"For about five years human cloning was a hot topic, but during that time it became apparent that, because the rate of successful production was so low, it was not financially feasible to continue. Like so many other things, the cloning debate was settled by financial considerations rather than ethical ones.

"Unfortunately, that was not enough to stop corrupt, ambitious men from doing some pretty horrible stuff. Twenty years ago, a lot of us were concerned that the entire world might end up looking like *The Island of Dr. Moreau.* Some of these ghoulish experiments with cloning and DNA-splicing led to the creation of GenCEN—the Genetic Crimes Enforcement Network—as an international police force to ensure that all genetic research and innovation meet carefully-established international guidelines. We set up GenTECH at about the same time to provide consulting services and assist GenCEN in investigations."

"So these women aren't clones?" Fred looked surprised.

"I didn't say that," Joshua continued. "I'm saying that the possibilities are limited. Josef Helmick is the only person I know of who *might*, and I emphasize *might*, be capable of turning out perfect clones of Hollywood sex symbols."

As Joshua talked, Charlie had input information into his government-issued communication device. Looking up he said, "We have a Karl Helmick in our data base; he was killed in 2021; no Josef. Any connection?"

"Karl was Josef's father," Jarrod interjected. "He owned a beef-cloning facility near Santa Fe that was destroyed by an explosion resulting from a malfunction in the system—at least that was the official finding. Everyone on the grounds was killed instantly. Josef was away at the time, and he was the only survivor."

Fred noted the sadness and anger that was reflected in Jarrod's eyes as he spoke. "How do you know so much about this?" he asked. "That was a long time ago."

"Our father was a botanist who helped pioneer plant cloning for food production. He owned a facility in Missouri where he had managed to adapt all sorts of plants to grow in any climate. Everyone thought that it would be the future of food production. Plant cloning would eradicate world hunger by making it possible to grow any crop under any climate and soil conditions. Theoretically, pineapple plantations would thrive in Alaska. The problem was that while early results were spectacular, after a couple of generations the plants reverted to their natural state. The seeds contained in the adapted species produced plants that were identical to those existing in nature. My father did not live to discover that his life's work in cloning for food production was going to count for nothing, but as we all know, both plant and meat production are now being done the old-fashioned way.

"Our father was a brilliant man, and he began training Joshua and me in genetics when we were children. We worked with him until he died. After his death, we thought that the best way that we could honor his memory was to take everything he had taught us about genetics and cloning and use it to make the world a better place. "

"When did your dad die?" Fred inquired.

"He had a meeting with Karl Helmick on the day the explosion occurred. My mother had gone to New Mexico with him. They were registered in a hotel in Santa Fe; she wasn't supposed to go to the facility, but for some reason she ended up at Doppelganger with my father. They both died in the explosion."

Charlie leaned forward, "What happened to Josef?"

"We never saw him again, but we always believed that he lured my parents there and then deliberately detonated the explosion. As Karl's only heir, Josef became a billionaire at his death."

Fred looked incredulous, "There was that kind of money in beef cloning?"

"No," Jarrod responded. "While working together researching new techniques my father and Karl Helmick discovered a cure for cancer that you know as the Brazilian Extract Treatment. My father was adamant that the price of the drug be kept low enough for everyone to afford, but, even so, he and Helmick both became billionaires."

Fred tried to keep the shock from registering on his face. He had met the Sinclair brothers on a couple of occasions when they had been called in to consult on cases, but he had no idea that their father was the world-renowned Alexander Sinclair. He had never imagined that the rock star of the scientific community who had found the cure for cancer was their father, and he had never dreamed that they were so wealthy. They seemed pretty normal.

Jarrod continued, "Our dad's success in developing a cancer cure has been a source of great comfort for Josh and me. Even though the food cloning didn't work out, he ultimately saved millions of lives with his cancer cure.

"It's because of the money we inherited from our parents that we've been able to devote ourselves to genetic consulting. GenTECH is a non-profit foundation with one hundred percent of the fees we collect going directly to the foundation. The money is used to help families of crime victims. We provide all sorts of services including assistance with mortgages, college educations for the children, job training for surviving spouses—pretty much anything the families need to help with the loss of a loved one. Josh and I know that nothing can make up for losing someone you love, but we can help to some degree by relieving their financial burdens."

"There's another reason why we spend our lives providing genetic consulting for law enforcement agencies," Joshua added. "Jarrod and I have talked a lot about it over the years. My mother was certain that the beef cloning was just a cover for Karl's real work of producing human clones, but my father always insisted that successful human cloning was still a long way in the future. Doppelganger underwent all of the usual inspections, but the inspectors had no idea what to look for. If Karl were cloning humans, he was able to get away with it because the inspection teams did not include geneticists. Because the devastation was so great and the heat so intense, the explosion obliterated every trace of evidence that might have proven our mom's theory correct, but we have never given up hoping that someday we will be able to prove that Karl Helmick was cloning former members of the Third Reich and that Josef was one of his clones.

"Josh and I met Josef several times, and we even visited Doppelganger when we were teenagers, but we never liked him, and we never trusted him. We've always believed that he murdered our parents and used the explosion to destroy the evidence, but we've never been able to prove it. I do know this, however: If anyone could pull this off, it's Josef Helmick."

CHAPTER 5

Fred slipped out of bed, being careful not to awaken Annie. He couldn't sleep, and he wanted to pray, but he was not a man who could bow his head, close his eyes, and pray silently. Fred was a "walker and a talker" who walked as he prayed and spoke in conversational tones. As he stepped through the French doors that led to the backyard he glanced up at the night sky and was immediately overcome by the multitude of stars that filled the heavens above him.

As he began to traverse the yard, he remembered a favorite Psalm, *He counts the stars and calls them all by name*. "Oh, dear Jesus," he said aloud, "when I think about your power, I am completely overwhelmed. No one has any idea how many stars are in your heaven. We think there are billions, but we don't really know. But you know. You know everything. You see every one of them, and you have given each a pet name so that you can call them to you. Yet, even though you own the universe and direct the wind and the seas, you take time to notice someone like me. I know it's true, but I can hardly take it in.

"Thank you for everything. Thank you for taking care of my retirement. You know how worried I've been about what I was going to do with the rest of my life. I've never had any hobbies, and I'm not going to start playing golf or building furniture or doing any of the things other guys my age do. I've always been a cop, and I'll die a cop—even if I am retired. It's the only work that I've ever really understood. I'm good at it, and I thank you for that because I know that you have given me the ability to solve cases that I would never have been able to crack on my own."

As Fred continued to pray, his eyes filled with tears that were beginning to run down his cheeks. "I'm so ashamed that I spent so much time worrying about what I was going to do; I didn't trust that you had a plan for me. But you did. You sent me out on that case the last week that I was on the force. I know they should have sent another detective because they knew I wouldn't be there to complete the investigation, but that was your doing. You had already provided my retirement plan. I believe that this is the most important case I've ever been part of, and if I hadn't been the first detective on the scene, I wouldn't be part of it at all.

"Lord, please help me to do exactly what I need to do to catch this killer. We know that these women are clones, but that's all we know. Show me how all of this fits together. Please show me who is cloning these women, and show me who is killing them. None of it makes any sense to any of us working the case, but you know exactly what's going on.

"Please, Lord, keep me off rabbit trails. I pray that everything I do in connection with this case will be time well spent. I pray that you will direct me and Joshua and Jarrod Sinclair and Charlie Byrd. I have a feeling that this is something much more terrible than anything I've ever been involved in, and I thank you for the opportunity to help stop whoever is doing this. Help me, Jesus, to hear your voice in all of this and to do the best work I have ever done."

Fred spent the next half hour pacing and talking to God—thanking Him and telling Him that he loved Him. When he had finished pouring out his heart, he went inside and crawled into bed where he immediately fell asleep.

CHAPTER 6

Fred was sitting in the Sinclairs' offices drinking a cup of coffee while he waited for them to join him in the conference room. It was a man's room—leather and polished wood, big, comfortable chairs, a stone fireplace dominating the wall at one end. He did not have to wait long. The twins were punctual, and at exactly 10:30 A.M. the door opened and they entered.

Fred placed the mug of steaming brew on the long mahogany table and rose to shake hands. The twins had not told him why they wanted to meet with him, and since their call the previous week Fred had imagined every possible scenario.

Jarrod motioned for him to be seated, and the twins took chairs at the table near him. "Thank you for coming," Jarrod began. "We asked you to come here today because we want to offer you a job."

"A job?" Fred's eyebrows shot up in surprise.

"Yes," Jarrod continued. "We want you to try to solve the Hollywood clone murders. Josh and I know as much about genetics as anyone living. Here at GenTECH we have the world's best crime lab. We employ some of the top minds in genetic research; we work daily to stay on top of new breakthroughs in genetics so that we can anticipate both the philanthropic uses of those breakthroughs and the dangerous ones. We have helped GenCEN stop a lot of really sick people who were trying to do a lot of really sick things. But, what we know about crime investigations you could put in a thimble. We're convinced that Josef Helmick produced the clones, but we don't know how to prove it. Besides, if this is Helmick's work, there are other clones out there. Who knows to what extent he's involved in human trafficking? We can tie him to this if we can find his lab."

"The FBI is already investigating," Fred responded. "They have the resources to do all sorts of things that I can't. I would love to do this, but since I'm retired, I don't think that I can be of much help."

"That's exactly why we want you," Joshua interrupted. "You can devote as much time as necessary to this investigation. There are no conflicts of interest, and you happen to be the best police investigator we've ever worked with.

"We'll pay you fifteen thousand dollars per month plus expenses. Is that agreeable?"

"Yes. No. I mean, it's too much. I can't take that kind of money when it should be going to the victims' families."

"You won't be paid by GenTECH. All consulting fees go exclusively to help the families. You'll be paid by us personally. If we tried, we couldn't spend all of our money in our lifetimes. We'll take care of all the expenses connected to this investigation, but it's really important to us that you agree to do it.

"Our parents died on our twenty-first birthdays, and ever since we've tried to find some answers, but every time we think we have a lead, it goes nowhere. The FBI has a lot of cases to work. If they get a break in this case, they'll go with it, but it's not their first priority. We need someone who can devote his full attention to tracking down Josef Helmick and to finding out what he's been doing for the last twenty years.

"About ten years ago we tracked him to Dubai, but we weren't able to find evidence that indicated he was involved in anything illegal. He has a reputation as a gambler and a playboy, but, unfortunately, that's not illegal.

"The Hollywood clone murders are the first crimes we've found that we believe can be tied back to Helmick. If he's cloning these old movie stars and selling them to wealthy men to use as sex slaves, he's breaking a whole bunch of laws. If he's selling them to be tortured and murdered, he's breaking a whole bunch more. We want to stop him, and you're the only person we know who can help us do that."

Fred drained his mug and set it on the table. "When do I start?"

CHAPTER 7

The next week was a frustrating one for Fred. He spent hours pouring over evidence from the crime scenes, but he found no answers. He spent hours praying, but he felt as if his prayers were bouncing off the ceiling and falling back to earth.

The only useful information that he had been able to obtain was that Josef Helmick's Dubai residence was the top floor apartment at the Burj Khalifa. If he were cloning humans, he was not doing it in Dubai. He found no corporations, no interests in any companies that might have laboratories where he could do his work—nothing.

The only acquisitions in Josef Helmick's name that Fred was able to uncover were a vacation home in the Swiss ski-resort town of Gstaad and a five-hundred acre piece of real estate in the Swiss Alps that had once been a retreat for the world's most privileged—its guest list had included England's royal family, the Rothschilds, the Vanderbilts, the Mellons and the Roosevelts. The retreat included an opulent hotel, various guest "cottages" complete with a full staff of servants and a private chef, tennis courts, swimming pools, a golf course, and a 150-bed sanatorium where those with failing health could take the mineral baths and receive various other treatments. One of the main attractions, however, was an ancient castle which was said to have a dungeon filled with medieval instruments of torture. Although the castle had not been restored to house guests, the retreat provided several tours each day for those guests who wished to tour it.

In 1950 the retreat had been donated to the Swiss government, and for the next fifty years it was operated as a tourist attraction. At the turn of the century, however, interest waned and it was no longer able to bring in even enough revenue to pay for its upkeep. Since it was no longer profitable, the government closed it, locked the massive gates, and allowed it to sit uninhabited and unused.

Fifteen years earlier Helmick had purchased the property from the Swiss government for an undisclosed sum, but no one knew why. The retreat had been deliberately designed to provide its guests with maximum privacy, and even in 2041 the only view available was glimpses of buildings tucked in among the towering forest viewed from a plane. It was known that occasionally Josef Helmick visited the estate, but no one else appeared to live there. Fred was certain that if Helmick were involved in human cloning, his laboratories were on the estate. Legally those laboratories would not exist; therefore, Helmick could operate in total isolation with no government regulations or inspections to interfere with his work.

On Friday afternoon Fred put all of this information into a report and uploaded it to the secure site that Harold Baker, GenTECH's leading IT specialist, had set up for him and sent it to the Sinclairs.

Fred needed a break. In order to take his mind off the case, he turned on the television in his home office just in time to catch Scott Bentley's report on the on-going negotiations between OPEC and the U.S.

Bentley was saying that Prince Abdul something or other had met that day with the president and that the talks were expected to result in the biggest oil deal between the U.S. and OPEC in more than fifteen years.

"After visiting New York, Chicago, Miami, and San Francisco," Bentley announced, "the newly-elected president of OPEC has ended his tour in the nation's capital where it is expected that he struck a deal that will lower gas prices in the U.S. before the year's end. However, the White House has not yet commented on the negotiations or what they may mean for Americans at the pump. That's it for this week. Until Monday, this is Scott Bentley wishing you happy hunting!"

For a moment Fred sat quietly, not taking in the full implications of what he had just heard. The tour had included every place where the body of a clone had been found. It could be a coincidence, but how likely was that?

Fred was reaching for the PCD when it rang. Charlie Byrd was on the other end. "They found another clone this morning. Elizabeth Taylor. In an alley next to the Willard Hotel in D. C.," he said, foregoing any small talk.

Fred's heart was now pounding. "Did you see the new head of OPEC on the news?" he asked.

"No. Is there some reason why I should have?"

"Well, he met with the president today after finishing his tour of several American cities including New York, Chicago, Miami, San Francisco and D.C. Does that itinerary ring any bells?"

"Oh, yeah," Charlie replied. "I'll see what I can find out; I'll get back to you."

Ψ

Early Monday Charlie called back. "Here's something that will get your week off to a good start," he began. "The prince entered the U. S. with an entourage of fifty-seven servants, wives, and assistants, but he left with only fifty-two."

"How can that happen?" Fred was incredulous. "Surely, he has to account for everyone who entered the country with him."

"You'd think," Charlie responded, "but, no. He doesn't have official diplomatic immunity, but he may as well have. If we had video of him killing every single one of those women, we wouldn't be allowed to do a thing about it. It's what we call a 'potentially explosive political situation' so we allow him to do anything he wants, and there are no consequences.

"I'm glad you're working this," Charlie continued. "You can do whatever it takes to find the truth. If I were to look too closely, my next assignment would be in Fairbanks."

CHAPTER 8

The wall of billowing sand blotted out the sun as it crawled across the Arabian desert. Spanning several stories in height, it had a monstrous living quality—as if a huge beast were working its way toward the city, gaining strength as it went and striking fear and dread into the hearts of men and animals alike.

From his penthouse apartment in the Burj Khalifa, a man of about forty stood gazing out the window focused on the storm. He was of medium height—about five feet eleven inches, with thick brown hair, a smooth complexion, and hazel eyes. His face was not classically handsome—his features were too heavy, but any observer would have described his appearance as "attractive." His physique was perfectly-toned and tanned. Every article of clothing was custom made for him by the world's best tailors, so as to fit perfectly. Even his cologne was custom—he had contracted Dior to formulate one scent especially for him, and that scent, which he had named *Eleven*, was his trademark, as he was the only man in the world with access to it.

He wore a white cotton shirt and white cotton pants—casual but well-suited to the intense heat of the Dubai summers. Normally, he preferred to spend the hotter months in Switzerland or Germany or even Scandinavia, so as to avoid the 108 to 119 degree temperatures that were normal for the United Arab Emirates. This year, however, he had not been able to leave because he had contracted to do so much work for one specific client. That was the reason that he stood, legs slightly spread, hands locked behind his back, in a military stance reminiscent of his youth—watching the growing storm through the window and waiting for Anis Shaheen, who was now thirty minutes late for their appointment.

Josef checked his watch again to confirm the time. Yes, it was now 1:30—Anis was scheduled to arrive at 1:00. Josef despised tardiness; his father had drilled into him the necessity for punctuality. One of the hardest adjustments he had been forced to make in working with people of the Middle East was their complete lack of regard for time. Josef had been taught that being late was inexcusable, but here in Dubai time appeared to be fluid; an appointment for 1:00 P.M. meant that the client might show up at 2:00 or 3:00 or sometime the next morning or next afternoon or even a week or two later, and the person's absence might or might not be accompanied by a message or some explanation. This was true of the whole society, but it was particularly true of the royals and even more so of their surrogates, who, although they had no genuine wealth or influence of their own, mimicked their masters as much as possible. Anis was merely a surrogate of one of the wealthiest and most powerful men in the region, and like most underlings to powerful men, Anis spent a great deal of time trying to make everyone believe that he, too, was powerful.

"If he weren't bringing me my money, I would lock him out just to teach him a lesson," Josef silently fumed. As it happened, Anis was bringing him money—he was placing a new order and bringing half the payment in advance as required by Josef's standard contract. The last job had been worth five million Euros—the new one would be at least that. Two and one-half million Euros was worth waiting for, so Josef waited, and as he waited he turned his attention back to the approaching mountain of sand.

He was accustomed to sand storms from having grown up in the Southwestern United States. During his infrequent trips to Albuquerque, New Mexico, he had seen his share of blowing sand, but those storms did not compare to the ones he watched from his 160th story luxury apartment at the Burj Khalifa. He occupied the highest apartment in the 206 story structure—everything above his unit was used for storage and maintenance. The glass window wall of the highest apartment in the world's tallest structure gave Josef a unique vantage point on the world. That vantage point had given him new respect for the wilder elements of the Arabian desert—the sheer force of the wind that picked up the sand and carried it for miles while blanketing everything in its path. No lone person in the path of that storm could stand against it. The Bedouins had learned to lie down beside their camels when the winds came, but no Bedouin would ever attempt to challenge the wind. No one could reason with it; no one could persuade it, and no one could stop it. It was both horrifying and awe-inspiring.

"That would be the essence of power," Josef thought. "The power to control the wind, the sun, the rain, the elements; the power to change the temperature of the sea from its normal July average of ninety degrees, to freezing; the power to make snow fall from the heavens in August. No amount of wealth could compare to power such as that—a man with that power could control all of the wealth and influence of the entire world...."

A bell signaling a new text message interrupted his thoughts. The concierge on the first floor had sent him a text notifying him that his guest was on his way up. "Guest! Try glorified messenger boy. That worm will never be my guest...." By the time Josef had finished his silent rant, Anis was knocking at the apartment door.

Josef stood unmoved while his servant opened the door and ushered Anis into the luxurious apartment.

Anis Shaheen was not originally from Dubai—he was Syrian by birth. He had served in the Syrian military and had chosen the right side of the Syrian revolutionary conflict. His fluency in English had made him useful in his country's government and allowed him to travel to other countries until he had come to the service of his current master. Like all foreigners in Dubai, he was intensely aware of the racial snobbery among Arabs and of the second-class citizenship that extended to all non-native born people. If he had been born in this tiny kingdom rather than in Syria he would have never had to work—his future would have been guaranteed. Instead, he had spent his life laboring for and groveling before his betters, and although he now enjoyed a well-paid position, he was deeply aware of the difference between his station and that of those around him.

Anis glanced around the room with envy. The Burj Khalifa was a decadent, opulent structure, and Josef's apartment reflected its richness. The walls were alternating ruby red and electric blue, with some gold accents. The bar which stood to the left of the entrance was covered in blond onyx; the floor was black granite, and the ceiling was gilded with Arabesques. No expense had been spared; no luxury had been omitted. It was not right, Anis mused, that such wealth and luxury was being enjoyed by this strange German. One day all of these Europeans would be stripped of their riches and power and reduced to their proper role as slaves. In the meantime, Anis was forced to tolerate Josef.

"My brother," he oozed with false enthusiasm as Josef approached. Anis rose to embrace him and Josef, who inwardly recoiled at his vulgar display of affection, remained calm and composed and returned his embrace.

"Welcome home, Anis. How was your tour of the West?" Josef inquired.

"Very satisfactory. The prince thoroughly enjoyed his entertainment. He sent me today to reorder."

Josef held a notepad and a pen as he took a seat on the red leather couch across from the chair where Anis was seated. He never took orders on electronic devices—his work was too sensitive, and electronic devices could be hacked. Anis commented on this. "I find it odd that a man of science makes all of his notes on lined yellow paper like a school boy."

Josef ignored the obvious insult. "My father and I did not agree on many things. He raised me in a Spartan, military environment not unlike the one in which Alexander the Great grew to manhood. As you can see from my surroundings, like Alexander, I have rejected the harsh military life in which I was raised in favor of luxury beyond anything my father ever dreamed. But, even though we virtually never saw eye to eye, he did teach me that sometimes, the old ways are best." He clicked his pen and waited.

"Fifty girls—the same as before except that the prince wants twenty-six of Marilyn. She was his favorite—so pleasing. The other twenty-four can be divided equally."

"When?"

"One week from now. On Saturday, the prince is hosting a party in his palace just outside the city to celebrate the new oil deal. The girls are to be delivered three hours in advance to allow time for inspection—to certify that they are acceptable to the prince and his guests."

Josef laid down his note pad and held out his hand for the money. Anis pulled an envelope out of his jacket pocket and handed it to Josef. Josef counted. "Ten million....there is only ten million here, Anis. The terms are one million per copy—half up front. If you want fifty you need to bring me another fifteen million Euros now and twenty-five million on completion."

"The prince has decided to renegotiate. Ten million for the whole package—that is all he will pay. Consider it a 'volume discount.' He also wants a copy of this." With that Anis took a photo out of his jacket pocket and flicked it across the small table that separated the two men.

Josef picked it up and looked at it. The photo was of a young lingerie model on a fashion runway. The style of her hair and makeup and the condition of her body suggested that this photo was very recently taken.

"What is this?" he stared at Anis.

"The prince saw her at a fashion show in New York while he was purchasing some articles for his wives. He wants you to copy her for him and deliver her with the others. She will be the centerpiece of the entertainment."

"Where do you think you are Anis? Do you think this is some high-end whorehouse? I am a scientist—not some groveling pimp. It takes three months to make a copy—the prince knows that. And you place the order in advance. You don't bring me a snapshot of some girl with no name and tell me to copy her for you." Josef flung the picture back across the table in disgust, but Anis did not pick it up.

"Careful Josef, you have no idea with whom you are dealing or what we are capable of. You are making a lot of money on the prince right now, but the world is full of girls, and the prince has a short attention span. Abdul has imaginative ways of dealing with those who fail to show proper respect—if you don't change your haughty European attitude, you will find yourself begging him to kill you—just like these copies of yours do.

"As for the girl…I am quite certain she has a name. You will find out what it is and copy her for us and deliver her on Saturday with the others. You are staking more than money on this Josef; if you disappoint us you will die worse than these girls of yours."

Josef was instantly hot with rage. "No Anis, you have no idea what *I* am capable of. Don't EVER threaten me, or I will bury whatever is left of you and Abdul so deep in that desert that no one will ever find either one of you, and, then, I will force my copies of you and the prince to lick my feet every morning until I grow tired of you and send you off to sign all of the OPEC oil reserves over to me personally."

Anis stood quickly. He had expected his speech to frighten Josef—he had not expected to see this cold rage staring back at him.

The thought that Josef might actually have a copy of him was unsettling—probably untrue—but very unsettling.

"The prince has invited twenty of the top members of OPEC to attend his party. For that reason, I am going to give you twenty-four hours to reconsider. The prince and I will expect everything we have ordered and a full and sincere apology. If we don't receive the answer we want, the prince will take immediate action to make you wish that you had complied. Do you understand?" With that Anis rose and exited the apartment, leaving Josef sitting alone holding the envelope with the ten million Euros.

Fantasies of cruel deaths he could arrange for Anis and the prince were flooding Josef's mind—he could feed them alive into a wood chipper and then pour them into the sea. He did not really have the surrogates, but he did have enough DNA to make surrogates. That was an appealing thought—he could copy them and then dispose of both of them. Then he could control OPEC through the surrogates.... But it would require three months to make the copies, and with the prince threatening him, he did not have three months. A situation like this one was very volatile and required an immediate response. Josef had been given twenty-four hours, but he knew from experience that he probably really had only about half that time. Fortunately, he did not need much time to plan—he already knew what to do.

Josef had learned one other lesson from his father—to always make extra copies of his work. At the speed at which Abdul was going through girls Josef knew that he would exhaust his supply very quickly, and from his conversations with Anis, he had inferred that Marilyn was a special favorite. A man such as Prince Abdul would not want to be constrained by having to order in advance, and Josef knew that, so he had made enough copies to keep the prince entertained for the next three months without interruption.

From his PCD he called his lab in Switzerland and asked for Heinz, "I need fifty girls here in three days. Twenty-six Marilyn. Eight each of Hepburn, Taylor and Loren. Put them on Helmick I, and deliver them here by Friday morning."

That took care of one problem. He looked at the ten million Euros he was holding. Abdul was getting copies of copies—not that it mattered since he killed them so quickly. Now all he had to do was take care of the other request. He scrolled down on his PCD until he found the number in New York City that he needed. Pressing that number, he waited for an answer.

"Tell Stanley Westbrook that Josef Helmick is calling for him."

CHAPTER 9

At 8:00 A.M. Amanda Sutton had just finished her two-hour workout at her health club in New York City. Two hours each morning of workouts with her personal trainer was only one part of a fitness regimen that included strict dieting and constant weigh-ins. This morning Amanda had been a little under the weather—she was battling a slight head cold, and after putting in a late night working a private party the night before, she had gotten only four hours of sleep before getting up to go to the gym. Still, Amanda was in the beauty business, and her workouts trumped everything else in importance in her life.

Amanda was nineteen and had been living on her own for a little over a year, but she had been modeling and appearing in talent shows and pageants since before she could speak. With her long, wavy medium brown hair and almond-shaped green eyes with gold flecks, she was a stunning young woman. There had never been a moment in her life when she had not been striking—she had won the "You must have been a beautiful baby" contest with its five-hundred-dollar cash prize when only a year old, and that victory had led to appearances in soap and shampoo commercials, and later fast food ads. Her father owned thirty-five casual dine-in restaurants throughout Texas, Oklahoma and Louisiana, and he invested many of the profits from those businesses into sending Amanda and her mother on frequent junkets to New York for work. Melinda Sutton was a typical stage mother—always pushing her daughter forward and constantly maneuvering for space at the front of whatever line they happened to find themselves standing in. Like many child actors and their parent/managers, Amanda and Melinda had a difficult relationship which had become more difficult as Amanda had grown older and had wanted more control over her own career.

At eighteen, Amanda had signed with one of the top modeling agencies in New York, and it was through them that she had been able to secure her contract as the newest model for the country's leading lingerie store. Modeling for the lingerie company was a once-in-a-lifetime opportunity for a young woman in Amanda's position—the job meant not only a steady paycheck but also travel to glamorous locales, frequent television appearances, and the opportunity to consort with wealthy, sophisticated men. Don Sutton was not overjoyed when his daughter landed the contract—he was a little embarrassed to know that his friends would be drooling over his scantily-clothed teenaged daughter. Melinda was overjoyed, but she was less enthusiastic when Amanda let her know clearly that now that she was eighteen she expected her mother to "butt out" and let the agency make her professional decisions. Still, Don paid for half the studio apartment in New York City and the Suttons sent expense money, which Amanda used to supplement her income from her modeling jobs and "professional appearances," such as the party she had attended the previous evening.

As Amanda stepped out onto the warm, muggy street, her PCD rang. The number was blocked; it read "Private." Amanda was intrigued; a couple of the men at the party had asked for her number the previous evening. Maybe one of them was calling to ask her out. She answered.

"Amanda, how are you this morning?"

"I'm okay," she didn't recognize the voice. "Who is this?"

"This is Stanley Westbrook, Amanda. I want to have lunch with you today. I represent a man who wants to hire you for a very special job."

"Uh, you need to call my agency. I can give you the number…."

"My client does not work through agencies, Amanda. This is a very special private job. Look, meet me for lunch at The Four Seasons and hear what I am offering. I am authorized to give you one thousand dollars cash just for showing up…whether you take the job or not. Can I expect you at 12:00?"

"Uh, sure. I'll be there."

"Fine. The table has been reserved under your name. I will see you there."

Amanda disconnected the call. That was the downside of modeling—there were always low-life types trying to take advantage of a girl. On the other hand, one thousand dollars was good money just to eat lunch and hear what he had to say—too good to pass up.

She decided that rather than stopping in at the agency she would just call and see if they had any assignments for her. As it turned out, they didn't, so she went back to her apartment to get ready for her lunch date.

At 12:00 she was at The Four Seasons. Her long hair curled softly on her shoulders. She wore a small amount of well-applied eye makeup to accentuate those amazing green eyes and a little bronzer on her cheeks. In her blue jeans, knit top and sandals she looked young and fresh and completely lovely.

Stan was already seated at the table when she arrived, and he rose to shake her hand. He was about forty-five and balding but not unattractive. He had large dark eyes, thick dark brows, and an olive complexion. He seemed pleasant and cultured and smooth. As they talked, Amanda thought that he might be interesting company—if he had a lot of money.

She ordered water with lemon and fish with steamed vegetables. After the waiter left the table she studied the card that Stan had given her. "So who are you, and what do you do?"

"I am a purveyor of beautiful things," Stan answered smoothly.

"Huh? You mean like an agent?"

"I am an agent, but not in the sense that you are probably thinking. I work with highly-specialized clients from all over the world to help them find exactly what they want when they want it. Currently I am doing a job for a particularly discriminating client. He saw you at the lingerie fashion show you did three weeks ago, and he was very impressed. He wants to hire you."

"I have a contract; you need to talk to my agency."

"I told you this is a very special job, and my client is not working through ordinary agencies. I have been hired to find exceptional models for a private Armani fashion show in Dubai. This is an exclusive show—the models are being hired individually. The guests will include the world's wealthiest men from Europe and the Middle East. The show lasts two days—you will fly to Dubai on a private jet and stay at the Hotel Armani. As part of your assignment you will also attend a private party at the Armani Club in the world-famous Dubai Tower. You will mingle with the fashion show guests —along with the other models, of course. When the weekend is over, the private jet will fly you back to New York City."

"Dubai—on a private jet?" Amanda was very excited. This was the kind of offer that the top models usually received; women like her who were just starting out were normally passed over for these opportunities.

"But…if I take a job outside of my contract, I can get fired immediately. That is one of the conditions—I can't take other work without written permission from the agency."

"This is a private show in Dubai, Amanda. Who's going to tell them? All you have to do is call in sick for a couple of days. Tell Marjorie that you caught that summer flu that's going around, and you need a few days off. You'll fly out Thursday, and you'll be back on Monday. This is an amazing opportunity—not only will you be in the same room with the world's most powerful men, but you will be very well compensated for your time."

Amanda looked at him expectantly, "How much?"

"Fifty thousand dollars in advance and fifty thousand dollars when the show is over."

"One hundred thousand dollars? For a weekend…." Amanda's fork still had a steamed carrot attached to it when it fell to her plate. What an offer! Dubai, the Armani Club, a private show—this was exactly what she had dreamed of when she first signed with the agency.

Trying not to sound too excited she asked, "How do I get paid?"

"Give me a voided check. If you agree to my terms, I will wire transfer the fifty-thousand-dollar advance to your account on Wednesday. I will call you after the wire has gone out so that you can check with your bank and verify that it has been received. I will send a limousine for you at 6:00 A.M. Thursday morning to take you to JFK, and you will fly out on the private jet. When you return, I will wire transfer the other fifty thousand."

Amanda's heart was racing. "This sounds incredible. Can I think it over? I might need to talk to someone."

"Sorry, darling, but you can't think it over, and you can't tell anyone. This is a once-in-a-lifetime job for an exceptional girl. If news that I am putting together opportunities like this got out, I would be mobbed by a million would-be starlets. This deal is conditional upon your not telling anyone—if you breathe one word of this to anybody, the deal is off and you must return our money. And, Amanda, if you tell anyone, we will find out. It's now or never, yes or no."

"You know what, you're right! I don't need to talk to anybody. My answer is 'yes'. I'm in." She was opening her purse to get the check.

"Wonderful! Welcome to our team, Amanda. My employer will be so pleased."

"And when will I meet him? This guy you're working for, I mean?"

"You'll meet him in Dubai. He's looking forward to it." Stan rose from the table."I have another appointment, my dear, so I must leave you, but take your time and finish your lunch. I have already taken care of the check." Reaching inside his jacket pocket, he produced an envelope and placed it in her delicate hand. "I will call you on Wednesday. Thank you for having lunch with me."

"Thank you, Mr. Westbrook." She opened the envelope carefully and counted ten hundred-dollar bills. Placing the envelope into her purse, she finished her lunch alone and then hurried back to her apartment.

She was too excited to take a nap now. For the next two days, all Amanda could think about was her impending trip to Dubai. She wanted to tell everyone, but she was afraid that if she told anyone Stan would find out and rescind his offer, so she kept quiet. Finally, on Wednesday about noon, she received a call on her PCD from a number marked "Private." When she answered, she heard Stan's voice on the other end. "Check your bank account, dear. I just wired the money."

Amanda used her PCD to access her bank account and, sure enough, she was fifty thousand dollars richer. It was real—she was going to Dubai!

The next morning she was up at 4:00 getting ready for her trip. At 6:00 she was standing outside her building waiting for the limousine. When the car stopped at the curb, she did not even wait for the driver to help her; she opened the door, put her own bags inside, and climbed in. When the door closed, the driver pulled back onto the street and headed for JFK.

CHAPTER 10

The limousine transporting Amanda Sutton pulled up to the entrance of the Burj Khalifa, and the chauffeur opened the door for her. After a thirteen-hour non-stop flight she was feeling the jet lag—Dubai was nine hours ahead of New York City, so after flying all day she had arrived about six in the morning. Fortunately, Amanda was still young enough to have the reservoir of necessary energy to rebound quickly from such a demanding trip. Her hotel suite was amazing, and she had gotten to take a little nap and freshen up before going to the Burj Khalifa to meet her mysterious employer. Local time was now 2:00 P.M.

Amanda was doing her best to appear more sophisticated than her nineteen years, but she was overwhelmed by the opulence of the lobby of the Burj Khalifa. She had done a lot of modeling, but she had never been further away from the United States than Cancun, Mexico. Nothing in her travels had prepared her for the sights that confronted her now—from the marble floors with their wavy design, to the rich reds and purples, to the elegantly-dressed cosmopolitan staff representing people of all nations. "Wow, it looks so different from the movies," she gasped quietly. Rashid, the concierge, ignored her comment as he pressed the elevator button for the penthouse.

In a matter of seconds the door opened, and Amanda was standing in front of the door of the man who had hired her. She had been told only that he had asked to meet her and that she would be spending about thirty minutes with him before being taken to her fitting for the party she was to attend the next day.

She had not had a chance to knock when the door opened for her and a man with dark Mediterranean coloring wearing white linen slacks and a white shirt motioned for her to enter. "Come in, please, Miss Sutton. Mr. Helmick will be with you shortly."

Amanda took a seat on the couch. For this meeting, she had dressed in a black sheath dress which showed off her figure to its best advantage. Her five-inch platform strappy sandals accentuated her beautiful tanned legs. Her long brown hair hung in soft waves against her shoulders. She smoothed her dress as she waited—first impressions were important, and she wanted the man who had hired her to be pleased.

As she looked up from arranging her dress, she saw him standing in front of her. Funny, she had not heard him enter the room—it was as though he had just appeared. Her first impression was that he was a very good looking man. He was wearing a beautifully-tailored khaki-colored cotton shirt and perfectly-fitting khaki cotton pants. His cologne was warm and musky, very masculine and very sexy. She smiled her most alluring smile and stood to shake his hand. "I'm Amanda, so nice to meet you." As she said it she tossed her head a little to show off her hair. Just at that moment she looked into his hazel eyes and saw the coldest most calculating look she had ever encountered. It was not that his eyes were unattractive—far from it—but as she looked into them she saw no warmth, no humanity—only a labyrinth of darkness.

Amanda had met many men, and she had learned early on that their opinion of her was a great deal more important to her success than her opinion of them, so she never allowed her personal feelings to interfere with her professional conduct. In this particular case though, as she stood with him still holding her hand, she wanted to give the money back, run from the apartment, and flee Dubai.

"I am Josef Helmick. So good of you to come on such short notice. I promise you that just by your presence here you have made my entire weekend." Still holding her hand, he pulled her close and gently kissed the side of her face. Amanda tried to control her breathing, but she was so repulsed that she could hardly bear for him to touch her. Working hard not to change expressions, she waited until he withdrew his hand, and then she sat back down on the couch. She smiled that flirty smile again.

"I am so excited to be here, Mr. Helmick. I am very flattered that you wanted me in the show tomorrow." She sounded nervous—she could hear it in her own voice. She thought about the opulence of her surroundings and the magnitude of the opportunity before her. She really needed to calm down.

"You seem nervous, Amanda. Did you have a good trip?"

"Oh yes, it was wonderful."

"And your hotel accommodations? Are they satisfactory?"

"It's all…just so beautiful. Everything is wonderful. And now I am here and ready to get started."

"Good. Tell me about yourself, Amanda."

"Well, I'm from Louisiana, originally…Baton Rouge, but I've been in New York City for over a year now. I've been a model since before I could walk. And, of course, now with my contract I'm doing runway shows, which is very exciting and a dream come true for me. Stan said that you were in New York for my last show."

"Not me personally. One of my associates. But he brought me back your picture, and I was instantly smitten. I knew that I had to bring you to Dubai for the party that we are hosting tomorrow."

He had picked up Amanda's hand as he talked and now was holding it in his. She was starting to wonder whether there really was a legitimate job here or not.

"Stan said that it was an Armani show. Do you work for Armani?"

Instantly he dropped her hand, stood and walked to the bar. "Armani works for me," he answered coldly as he poured each of them a glass of wine. "Last year I bought fifty-one percent of the company, so I am the majority stockholder."

"Wow! So how long have you been in the fashion industry?"

"Fashion is a recent acquisition for me. I have numerous holdings here and throughout the world. My ownership in Armani allows me to meet beautiful women and enjoy diversions from the stresses of my work."

"So you're like an investor? Or something?"

"Or something. I am a scientist."

"A scientist?" Josef Helmick did not look like Amanda's idea of a scientist, and he certainly didn't act like one. Was it possible that he was putting her on?

"What kind of scientist?"

"I bend the laws of the universe. I transform fantasy and desire from mere thought into tangible reality. I make it possible for my clients to attain their deepest desires—their darkest fantasies, their most heartfelt wishes, their most passionate dreams. I am the master of life and death. That's what I do."

Amanda had no idea what he was talking about, but she was quite certain that he was the biggest liar she had ever met. For a girl who had met as many liars as she had, that was quite a statement. Still, she did not wish to sound ignorant or uninterested, so she answered, “Awesome.” She did want to direct the conversation from its current strangeness back to the show, so she tried to change the subject. “Tell me about the party tomorrow.”

“Yes, tomorrow. Tomorrow at 6:00 you will attend a party at the palace of one of the most powerful men in the world. He lives right here in Dubai. Twenty of his colleagues and fifty of the world’s most beautiful women will be in attendance…and, of course, you. You will arrive at the palace at 4:00 for check in.”

“Uh, Stan said that the party was at the Armani Club.”

“We had a change of plans…the party will be held at the palace. And you will arrive at 4:00.”

There it was again—that same ice-cold tone that made her afraid to ask any more questions. “And the fashion show?”

“The fashion show will be held on Sunday. Immediately after it ends, my car will take you back to the jet, and you will return to New York.

“I wish that I could go with you to the fitting this afternoon, but, unfortunately, I am detained with other pressing matters. I have personally selected the dress that you will wear for the party. You will go this afternoon to be fitted. The dress and the accessories will be delivered to your hotel suite tomorrow morning."

Josef was standing over her again staring that same cold stare. "You truly are a stunning woman. I just have one small request of you. I hope that you won't mind."

She looked up at him.

"I am very sentimental. When I meet a remarkable woman, I always ask for a lock of her hair as a keepsake. Would you mind very much if I took a lock of yours? I can promise you that I will cut very discreetly. No one will be able to tell."

"Of course…of course you may have a lock of my hair." Secretly she was thinking that she hoped he did not ruin her hair, but she could not say no. She saw that he was already holding the scissors. She stood and turned her back to him, and he lifted up her hair. Within seconds she felt a little snip and her hair and his hand were resting against her shoulder.

That appeared to be the end of the meeting. Amanda picked up her handbag and turned to say goodbye to her strange host. "Will I see you again?" she tried to muster her flirty provocative look, but all she could manage now was an odd smile at the strangest and most truly frightening man she had ever met.

"I can absolutely guarantee it. Not tonight, though. I really am held up with a pressing matter to which I must attend." He kissed the side of her face again, and his servant opened the door. Amanda felt weak as she rode the elevator to the first floor—not in a giddy romantic way but as if she had just been in the presence of a force that had drained the life from her. She hoped with everything in her that she would never see this man again. She was still shaking when she stumbled into the limousine.

Josef carefully took the lock of hair he had cut and placed it in a small sterile bag. He then poured the wine remaining in her glass into a small sterile container and secured her used wine glass in a separate sterile bag. Every trace of DNA would be important and highly useful—later. Amanda Sutton was a spoiled, stupid American girl, but she was beautiful, and Josef always had both personal and professional uses for beautiful women. For the moment, however, he had much more important concerns and not much time.

The same day that Anis Shaheen had come to visit him, Josef had sent him a couriered message with a note that said only, "I have reconsidered and will comply with all your requests." That message bought him the time he needed to locate Amanda and bring her to Dubai, but it did not begin to rise to the level of humility that Prince Abdul and Anis were expecting. Now that he had all of the pieces in place, Josef must send an appropriate apology. He had the girls—all he needed now was a gift.

The same private jet that had transported Amanda had also brought Josef's peace offering—twenty-four

Jeroboams of Dom Pérignon White Gold—the world's most expensive champagne in the world's most expensive bottles.

The champagne would be delivered to the party along with the girls. Opening his desk, Josef took out a piece of his personalized cream-linen stationery with his black initials, JH, and neatly and meticulously wrote his note of apology to Abdul.

"I spoke in haste in my recent meeting with Anis Shaheen. I am honored by your long patronage of my company, and I humbly ask your forgiveness for having offended you.

"As a token of my remorse, I am sending you all of the girls you ordered, along with Miss Amanda Sutton of the USA, the model you requested. Miss Sutton is not a copy; I have flown her here from New York City for your enjoyment.

"As a final expression of my obeisance, please accept these cases of Dom Pérignon White Gold for your opening toast. I am sending my personal wine steward, Lutz Von Hess, to pour the opening toast for your party. He was born in Germany, but he trained in Paris and is regarded as one of the world's foremost wine connoisseurs. I remain your humble servant, Josef."

He put down the fountain pen and smiled as he re-read the flawlessly-penned note. Personal notes in beautiful penmanship were a lost art. Abdul would be flattered. Anis would be jubilant.

He folded the note carefully, placed it in an envelope from the stationery set, and called down to the concierge. A courier from the Burj Khalifa would hand deliver it to Anis within the hour.

Walking to his wall safe, Josef opened the door and carefully removed a pair of specially-designed latex gloves. Karl had formulated these for handling highly-toxic substances. After placing them on his hands, he reached into another locked compartment of the safe and carefully removed a hypodermic needle and a small black bottle with an orange mark on its label.

Each bottle of champagne had to be treated—one drop injected through the cork with the hypodermic needle. One drop of *Diablo* was all that was needed. It was very tedious work requiring special care not to spill even one drop. For all of his technology, for all of his inventions, for all of his breakthroughs, Josef had still never discovered any poison as effective as this primitive one from the Brazilian jungles bottled by his father more than a quarter of a century before. "Sometimes the old ways are best," he thought as he finished his work.

After several hours all of the bottles were ready for transport. He had received a photo from the design director at Armani of Amanda in her dress. It was perfection—a sensuous sleeveless gown fitted perfectly to her exquisite figure. Even in a room with the world's most beautiful women, all eyes would be on her. Everything was ready.

At 3:00 the following afternoon, the limousine picked up Amanda to take her to the palace. She was wearing the champagne-colored Armani gown fitted with a draped neck and a long slit up each side to reveal her shapely legs and gold high-heeled Armani sandals designed specifically to complement her dress. It was the most beautiful dress she had ever worn. Diamond earrings dangled gently from her ears, and she carried a small clutch that completed her outfit. On her right hand she wore the only item that belonged to her—a simple band completely encrusted with cubic zirconia cut to resemble pavé diamonds. It was the first piece of jewelry she had purchased after moving to New York and firing her mother as her manager, and she wore it tonight as she always did, "for luck".

The drive to the palace, which was just outside the city, took forty-five minutes. From the exterior, the palace appeared to be a huge rectangle with a series of domes and spires protruding from the top—Amanda thought that it looked a little like the palace in Disney's *Aladdin* that she had watched over and over as a child. The excitement of being here, of visiting a real palace in the Middle East, eased the anxiety that still lingered from her meeting with Josef the day before. The chauffeur escorted her to the door which was opened by a male servant.

The rooms were massive—gray marble floors were inlaid with colored marble mosaics to mimic Persian rugs. Amanda stood drinking in the sights. On her first trip to New York, her mother had told her that she should always look up when entering old buildings because the most remarkable architecture was usually in the ceiling. That was true here—from tray ceilings with intricate mosaic marble designs hung massive crystal and gold chandeliers. The pale gold light reflected off the gray marble walls. She walked along behind the man who had beckoned her to follow. Even in the intense heat, the marble made the room feel cool.

At one end of an almost empty room was a massive spiral staircase with walnut colored wooden banisters and patterned gray and brown marble stairs. Amanda walked carefully up the stairs—the stairway was very long and difficult to navigate gracefully in her long dress and high heels. She would feel so foolish if she tripped as she made her entrance.

At last they came to the stair landing, and she paused to take in her surroundings. Above her was another story, another intricate tray ceiling—this one with an elaborate mural. Below her she could see the full view of the room they had just left. It was so beautiful—and yet so cold. This palace reminded her of something—someplace. What was it? Suddenly she had a memory of being at her grandmother's funeral in Louisiana when she was eight years old and of seeing her grandmother laid to rest in a mausoleum. That's what it reminded her of—it felt like a tomb. As the thought came to her, the same icy fear that she had felt the day before returned. She wished in that moment that she had not come here—that she had told Stan Westbrook to keep his money.

"Follow, please," her guide curtly interrupted her thoughts. It was too late now. She told herself that she was being silly. She had never been so far away from home, and she had not been able to tell anyone where she was going—not even her mother. All she needed was to breathe deeply and relax. She was going to a party, and then a fashion show, and then home.

They walked through a hallway lined with gilded chairs upholstered in rose pink velvet. The hallway was so wide that even with the large chairs on both sides, two people could easily walk unobstructed down the center. Still, she wondered why anyone would line a hallway with chairs. It was like walking through a massive waiting room. At the end of the hallway a man dressed in a linen suit was waiting for her.

"Welcome, Miss Sutton. I am Anis Shaheen, the personal aid to Prince Abdul, by whose invitation you are here in Dubai. Allow me to show you to your room." Amanda was accustomed to having men stare at her; she was used to having men leer at her, but normally when this happened she was safely out of reach on a runway or at a party supervised by her agency. Considering that she was alone and friendless in a foreign country, she found Anis' lustful stare particularly unsettling, and she felt her own apprehension increasing. He opened a door at the end of the hall, and when she had entered, he locked it behind her, leaving her alone and trapped.

Ψ

Lutz Von Hess arrived at the palace at 5:30 to begin setting up for the party, and Anis came downstairs to oversee the preparations. He leaned against the wall with his arms folded while the wine steward painstakingly unpacked the bottles.

"I was expecting you. I received your master's note. Who writes handwritten notes these days, even among pretentious Europeans?" Anis sniffed.

"Herr Helmick said to tell you that his father taught him that sometimes the old ways are best. He sends me and the champagne with one final gift: German lead crystal flutes for the toast—one for each of your guests and attendees. They are his gift for you to keep."

Anis smiled. "He has finally learned his place. I think going forward we will to have a much different relationship. Get everything ready and don't loiter. I want you out of here before the prince arrives."

"No," the steward answered firmly. "I must pour the champagne and make certain that each guest is served personally. Those are Herr Helmick's terms, and he is very firm on them."

Anis stared at the steward. He was a little over six feet tall, but he might be wearing lifts. He had blond hair and a blond mustache, and sky blue eyes. He was out of shape and slightly overweight—under his white coat small bulges of fat were visible. Still there was something familiar about him—and Anis knew what it was. He had that same proud disdain for the world as Josef. It must be a German trait.

There was no time to find a new steward, and Prince Abdul would probably be amused by Josef's deference. At any rate, Anis was not about to spend the early part of his evening pouring champagne, so he might as well let the steward stay and finish.

"Fine. Be done with it. Prince Abdul will arrive within the half hour."

Lutz continued setting up the bottles and the flutes—seventy two in all, including Anis. Lutz knew that he was not officially counted in the party numbers, but Josef had counted him during his preparations. By the time he was finished with his meticulous preparations, it was almost 7:00 P.M. Now he would wait. Two more hours passed before a crier announced Prince Abdul's arrival.

Ψ

Amanda had been sitting on the chair in her locked room for almost six hours. There was nothing in this room except a chair and a bed. The room had grown dark; and she had groped around unsuccessfully to find a light switch. She did not have her personal communication device with her, and even if she had, from this country, she would not have been able to make a call to anyone she knew. She was seriously wondering whether there was a party after all or whether she had been kidnapped for some terrible purpose.

Finally, the door opened slowly, and she nervously looked up to see who was there. The light from the hall hurt her eyes, and the man standing in the doorway was backlit so that she could not see his face. Fortunately, it was not Anis—it was the same servant who had escorted her to him. "Follow, please," he beckoned. She rose and walked down the hall with him and slowly descended the stairs. The previously empty room was now filled with women. A majority were platinum blondes wearing yellow halter dresses. Others were stunning brunettes with amazing violet eyes wearing white halter dresses, and still others were cool brunettes in black sheath dresses. They were beautiful but so dated—in their fashions, their hairstyles, and even their demeanor. Yet, they looked familiar—like people she had seen in pictures. Like people she had seen in movies—old movie stars! She looked more closely at them—yes, they were celebrity lookalikes. Most of them were Marilyn Monroe. They were amazingly good lookalikes, she thought. She had seen a lot of Marilyn impersonators, and these were really good. What was even more amazing was that they all looked exactly like each other—none was prettier or less pretty, or heavier, or thinner or older or younger. They all looked the same. She did not recognize the brunette with the short black hair and the violet eyes, but she did recognize the women with the piled-up hair in the black sheath dresses. They were impersonating that lady in the *Breakfast at Tiffany's* poster. They all looked the same too. The other lady looked earthy and Italian—Amanda wasn't sure who she was, but all of her impersonators looked exactly like each other. What agency could have provided these women?

The women in the room stared back at her, but none of them spoke to her, and she did not speak to any of them. Soon Prince Abdul entered the room, and the crowd bowed deeply to him. Abdul and his twenty male guests surveyed the room, and then Abdul walked over to Amanda. Lifting her face upward he studied her carefully. "You were in the fashion show in New York City last month?"

"Yes, Your Majesty," she answered nervously.

He smiled coldly, "Welcome to Dubai."

At that moment Anis appeared at his side. "As a token of his remorse for his arrogance, Helmick has made us a gift of his personal wine steward, along with two cases of Dom Pérignon White Gold champagne and German lead crystal flutes for our opening toast. He sends the gifts along with his personal handwritten apology."

"Good. The steward will stay then. You will tell Helmick that everything that enters my palace is my property to be used and disposed of as I please, and he will do well to hold his tongue in the future."

Lutz Von Hess was standing nearby, and he now bowed deeply to the prince. "It is an honor to serve you, Lord Prince. May I present you with the first glass."

The second flute of champagne went to Anis, and from there Lutz made his way carefully around the room until every person held a glass. The last person he served was Amanda. As she took the glass from him she looked into his eyes, and when she did, she felt the same icy cold darkness she had seen in Josef's eyes the day before. "A gift from Dr. Helmick to you, Miss Sutton. He says to tell you that he looks forward to seeing you again."

When the glasses were served, Lutz tapped an empty crystal flute lightly. "Herr Helmick sends this champagne and his wine steward to honor the house of Prince Abdul, and he proposes the following toast, 'Long life and health to Prince Abdul. May your subjects and slaves revere you forever.'"

All of the guests, the women, Anis and the prince lifted their glasses and drank their toast as Lutz watched. Within thirty seconds he heard the first of the champagne flutes shatter against the marble floor as the bearer—one of Josef's Marilyn copies—sank limply to her knees and then collapsed. Immediately there was another, and then another, and another. Amanda watched in horror as those around her collapsed; she wanted to scream but she could not because her own breathing was constricting. She was losing all sensation in her hands and feet, and her chest was so tight that she could not inhale. It was as though the life was being squeezed out of her. Within seconds she, too, was on the floor, and seconds after that she was engulfed by deep darkness. All around the room the OPEC leaders, Anis, and Prince Abdul lay dying. Lutz walked to Anis and bent down over him. "I told you never to threaten me, you maggot." Anis' final breath was a gasp of horror.

Lutz walked through the room surveying the dead and dying and carefully removing souvenirs from the twenty OPEC leaders, Anis and Amanda. From Prince Abdul he took an intricately-carved ivory pipe; from Anis he took a heavy gold bracelet. From Amanda, he took her "good luck" ring.

Gathering all of the bottles, the wine steward carried them to the van that he had arrived in. He did not need to worry about the flutes—after twelve hours of exposure to the air *Diablo* was untraceable. By the time the bodies were discovered in the morning, there would be nothing left to detect.

He drove the van three miles into the desert where he buried the empty bottles in the sand. Loading the unopened bottles into the Lamborghini that was waiting for him, he removed his blond wig, false nose, mustache and blue contact lenses. From around his waist he unfastened the padded suit he had worn to make himself appear twenty pounds heavier. Then Josef Helmick drove back to his apartment at the Burj Khalifa.

CHAPTER 11

Melinda Sutton had been trying to call her daughter for the past five days, but the calls would not go through. Always they had gone straight to voice mail. Even though she and Amanda had plenty of disagreements, they talked at least every other day; it was not like her daughter to ignore her calls. Melinda was beginning to be genuinely concerned when her personal communication device rang. The number was blocked, but when she looked at the screen, she felt something very much like fear spring up in her chest.

"Is this Melinda Sutton?" the man's voice on the other end of the line asked.

The question startled her. She had not used "Melinda" since she had graduated from high school. When she had started college she had become "Mel". Mel had such a cutting edge. A masculine name for a feminine, sexy woman put men off balance. That slight name change had given her the advantage of seeming smart, savvy, and in control. All of her credit cards, her driver's license, her bank accounts—everything was in the name of “Mel” Sutton. The only person who still called her “Melinda” was her mother.

“This is Mel Sutton,” she answered defensively.

“You are not Melinda Sutton?” the voice inquired.

“That’s my legal name. I never use it.”

“Is Amanda Sutton who resides at 1654 North Hampton, Apartment 6A, New York City your daughter?”

Mel’s knees went weak, and she sat down on the couch. “Yes, Amanda’s my daughter.”

“I’m calling from the State Department. I am sorry to inform you that your daughter was killed in a demonstration that took place in Dubai on Saturday. Her body has been cleared for transport back to the United States. If you will tell us where you want the remains shipped, I will make the arrangements immediately.”

“What? What are you talking about! Are you crazy! My daughter’s not in Dubai. I’m going to call the police and have you arrested, you sicko,” and with that Mel ended the call.

Immediately, Mel contacted her husband who was in a meeting with the franchise owners finalizing the purchase of four more restaurants. He was in a great mood; his fortunes were increasing; Amanda was settled in New York, Mel was preoccupied with her own life and pretty much leaving him alone. He had finally achieved everything he had hoped for. He was surprised, therefore, when he saw Mel's number come up on his PCD, and he almost didn't answer, but he knew that she wouldn't be calling if it were not important.

The moment he heard Mel's voice he knew that something was wrong. He had excused himself and walked away from the booth in his Baton Rouge restaurant to take the call, but he was unprepared for the barrage of words that poured out of his wife. "Mel! Stop! You aren't making any sense. No, I don't believe it. Have you called her agency? Give me the number. I'll call them now and get back to you."

With shaking hands Don Sutton punched in the agency's number where he quickly discovered that they had not heard from Amanda for more than a week. "When you talk to her," the woman on the line informed him, "tell her to call us at once. Her contract requires that she be available for all assignments and that she check in with us once every day. She has failed to meet those terms and is in danger of being terminated for breach of contract."

The woman's tone infuriated Don, but he did not want to burn any bridges—if Amanda called the agency, he wanted to make certain that they would tell her to call home. "I'll tell her," he said before ending the call.

Don immediately put in a call to his local Congressman, and while he was waiting for him to pick up, a call with a blocked number came in. He answered it immediately. “Is this Donald Sutton?” the man’s voice on the other end of the line asked.

A week had passed since those calls. Seven short days, but those 168 hours had changed everything. The Methodist minister from their church was saying something about Amanda’s being in a better place and reading a scripture about the hope we have in Christ, but Don Sutton was not listening; he was remembering.

He had been married to Mel for twenty years. She had been so beautiful when they met. She was still in college, and he had just opened his first Steak and More franchise. He had loved showing her off to his friends, and he had loved the prestige he achieved from having her on his arm. He was not sure that he had ever loved Mel, and he often thought that he probably would not have married her if she had not become pregnant, but less than six months after they met she had told him that she was going to have his baby. Don had been taught to accept responsibility for his actions, so he had never really questioned whether he should marry her.

In spite of the circumstances, Mel had insisted on a huge formal affair, and Don had spent every cent he had saved on it. Everyone had said that it was a “beautiful” wedding. No one who did not know her well would have suspected that she was almost four months pregnant by the time the ceremony took place, but Don was nervous. He had been raised in a very conservative home where that sort of thing was frowned upon, and he did not want her parents to know that she was pregnant until after they were married.

For a while Don had imagined that he and Mel were happy—as happy as married people can be. But it soon became apparent that Mel was restless. When Amanda was born, she took little interest in her daughter. By the time she was six months old, however, Amanda was an uncommonly beautiful baby, and Mel began to plan her daughter's career as an actress/model.

It was then that Mel began to talk about her own aspirations to be an actress that had been cut short by her marriage to Don. "I gave up my career for him," she often said. The truth was that she had never had any aspirations to do anything except marry a man who would pamper her and lavish her with gifts.

Don hadn't even minded that. He had a gift for making money, and Mel was able to spend extravagantly even while he was growing the restaurants. But with each passing year Mel became more obsessed with Amanda's career. Don suspected that Mel didn't care about Amanda at all. She was living vicariously through her daughter, and she constantly tried to position herself so that the spotlight would fall on her. Don was nothing more than a means to finance Mel's dream of fame and adoration to be supplied via their little daughter.

Unlike his parents, Don was not a religious man. He felt that he had been taken advantage of by a wife who saw him as nothing more than a bank account. He never considered divorce—he was not about to divide up his assets—but by the time Amanda was two years old Don was turning to other women for the attention he craved. He was never serious about any of them. They were casual, short-lived affairs that he ended within a few weeks. Thus, he enjoyed the thrill of the pursuit and the excitement of a new affair without the downsides of a long-term relationship.

Mel was beautifully turned out in a black designer dress and huge sunglasses. Her perfectly-groomed blonde hair glistened in the sunlight, and her large diamond rings sparkled. She looked like a not-so-grieving widow from central casting, but her tears were real. She was unable to hold back the deep sobs that came from her innermost being, but, ironically, it was not for her daughter that she wept. She was mourning herself; she was mourning the death of her own dream.

From the moment she had realized that she could turn Amanda into a star, Mel had used her daughter as a means to put herself on the Hollywood A list. She had never actually been able to do that, but she had always believed that it was just around the corner. When Amanda had gotten the lingerie contract and fired Mel as her manager, Mel had been only a little daunted. She was certain that she would be able to make Amanda see that no one could take care of her the way Mel could. Amanda would realize her error and beg Mel for forgiveness. Mel would accept her apology and sign her to an air-tight contract drawn up by her lawyers. Anyone who wanted access to Amanda would have to come through her.

Mel was thinking that it was ridiculous that Amanda was the one who had been sought after when she was the one with the beauty and talent. Mel had to admit that Amanda was pretty—by some standards even beautiful—but she had never been as beautiful as Mel. Mel had class and charm. She was the one with the magic—not Amanda. Yet, she had devoted nineteen years to making this ungrateful, ordinary girl into a star. She had allowed some of her own light to spill onto Amanda, and now, without warning, Amanda had robbed her of her dream.

Mel had stayed married to Don so that she could devote her full time to making her dream come true. Don who had never appreciated her, who had never deserved her. Don with his Steak and More franchises whose main concern was the price of rib eye. Boring, predictable, Don who had stolen her youth. At the thought of what he had done to her, Mel's sobs became uncontrollable. Six weeks later she left him and moved to California.

CHAPTER 12

Fred was sipping lemonade in a garden at the American Embassy in Dubai. Peacocks wandered among the trees and lush flowering plants tucked in among numerous fountains. The sky was hot and blue, but skillfully-placed misters among the foliage kept the guests cool and refreshed. This was *Shangri-La*, *Lawrence of Arabia*, and *A Thousand and One Arabian Nights* all rolled into one. Fred felt like pinching himself to make certain that he was not dreaming.

"When I talked to Charlie Byrd, I told him that I would give you whatever help I could, but you must understand that if you find yourself in trouble, the Embassy will make an official statement that we had no knowledge that you were in the country. We'll leave you twisting in the wind," Ambassador Walter Wainwright said as he glanced nervously about as though he expected to find someone eavesdropping on the conversation.

"Of course," Fred replied. "Whatever happens I won't involve you or the embassy. I just appreciate any information you can give me on a local by the name of Josef Helmick. We know that he's retained his American citizenship, although he also holds citizenships in both Germany and Switzerland. We think he's been in Dubai for the last fifteen years. That's all the information we have on him."

"Charlie said that you think Helmick's involved in the murder of Prince Abdul and the other OPEC leaders. That's pretty high-level stuff. I don't think you can uncover anything that the combined police forces of the OPEC nations can't do a whole lot faster."

"The truth is," Fred replied, "they're not going to be able to tie anything to Helmick, although we're one hundred percent sure that he orchestrated the whole thing. Oh, the investigators will arrest some poor schmuck and announce that he was part of a terrorist group who is trying to get control of the world's oil, but none of it will be true. I'm not here to impede their 'investigations.' I'm here to find out the truth about Helmick.

"We believe that he furnished the movie-star lookalikes for the murders in the U. S. a few months ago. And we believe that Prince Abdul was the one who slaughtered those five women. Obviously, Prince Abdul is no longer a threat to anyone, but we were able to discover that fifty of the fifty-one women attending the party were movie-star lookalikes. The other one was Amanda Sutton, a nineteen-year-old lingerie model who also happened to be an American citizen. Two days before she arrived in Dubai, she received a fifty-thousand-dollar untraceable wire transfer into her bank account. We believe that Helmick used those funds to lure her to Dubai to sell to the prince as a sex slave. I want to keep a low profile, and I won't interfere with anyone else's investigation. I just want to get to the bottom of this."

"Who do you work for, exactly?" Wainwright asked.

"It's probably better that you don't know. Officially, I'm not even here, and the less I tell you the less you'll have to deny if anything does go wrong."

The ambassador shifted uncomfortably in his chair. "Right, right, that's good. You're not even here. I like that.

"I'm going to give you the name of a local who can help you. He's a native and very well connected." Handing Fred a business card, Wainwright continued, "His name is Hadad. I suppose that he has a first name, but I have never heard it. Everyone calls him Hadad. His number is on the card. Don't tell him who gave it to you."

"I thought the citizens were paid by the government to do nothing. Why is this Hadad guy so desperate for money?"

"It's not about need; it's about greed. Hadad would sell his own daughters for the right price. In fact, he might sell them for the wrong price if it were the only price he could get. Watch out for him because he'll rob you blind if he can, but he knows everything that's going on in the city."

The ambassador stood and extended his hand to signal that Fred's time was up. Fred shook his hand, thanked him for his help, and left the embassy through the back gate.

When he stepped through that gate, Fred entered a strange, hostile world. In spite of the soaring temperatures, the sight of the dry, dusty street and the ancient adobe houses in the distance sent a chill up his spine. The opulent garden of the embassy had made him feel secure. The foreign land into which he had just stepped made his heart race.

Fred immediately called the number on the card and connected with a woman who spoke heavily-accented English. When she determined that Fred was an American, she told him that he could come to their offices that same afternoon at 2:00. That gave him less than thirty minutes to find a taxi and drive to his meeting.

Fred headed toward what appeared to be a main cross street which he reached in a little over two minutes. As he scanned the street for a cab, he happened to notice that the building directly in front of him was the one that housed Hadad's offices. He felt that arriving early was not a good idea, so he took a seat at a sidewalk café and ordered coffee. His stomach was churning, and he did not want the strong brew that the waiter delivered—he wanted a place to wait for his appointment. He paid the waiter for the coffee, gave him a generous tip, and shut his eyes.

Praying silently was difficult for Fred, but he did not want to draw attention to himself, so he pretended to be resting his eyes and began his unspoken prayer, "Oh, Lord, please help me. I don't know what to do. I know that I shouldn't be afraid, but I am. Please give me wisdom, and give me the courage to do what I need to do. Help me to be as wise as a serpent and as harmless as a dove. Guide me, Jesus, so that I will know who to trust and who to avoid. Please put the people in my path who can give me the answers I need to find out exactly what Josef Helmick is doing and to give me the evidence I need to prove that he is involved in the cloning of these women.

And, Jesus, help me to be a good witness for you in everything I do. I pray that in this foreign land I will glorify you with my life and with my lips. Thank you for being with me." Fred opened his eyes, and surveyed the street. A group of boys was kicking a ball in what appeared to be a game of street soccer. As Fred watched them his mind traveled back to Omar.

He was only twenty-two when it happened. Like so many other young Americans, Fred had joined the army within weeks after 9/11, and he had ended up in Afghanistan. Life there was hard; being quartered in a tent in 110 degree temperatures was reason enough to count the days until he would be sent home. The worst part, however, was living in circumstances where it was impossible to identify the enemy. The woman walking down the street clad in a burqa might be wired with explosives. The teenaged boy standing in the doorway might be wearing a suicide vest. No one was what he appeared to be.

The afternoon it happened Fred was working at a checkpoint monitoring traffic. Five or six boys ranging in age from ten to thirteen were kicking a ball in the hot dusty street, and for a few seconds the sounds of their laughter had diverted Fred's attention. Thirty-eight years later Fred could still see the scene as if it were frozen in time. A skinny boy of eleven was laughing loudly after having scored, and Fred turned to look. For an instant Fred forgot that he was in a hostile land, and a smile spread across his face as he shared that very human moment that transcended cultural and ethnic differences. He was simply a young man watching a group of boys at play, and his spirit soared. Instantly, the calm was shattered by the sound of a bomb exploding in a car waiting in line at the checkpoint. Before Fred could react he saw the child who had scored the point tossed into the air, his mouth open and a look of horror on his face.

Instinctively, Fred had lunged toward the boy hoping somehow to save him, but his limp body hit the ground with a thud. Civilians were running and screaming, and a man appeared from a nearby shop and picked up the boy. He caught sight of Fred and ran toward him holding his son in his arms. "Help me!" he pleaded.

Fred had taken the man and the boy to the combat hospital where the doctors began working to save his life. From the man Fred learned that the boy's name was Omar, and Fred silently prayed for him before he left the hospital. Each day Fred checked on the boy's progress, and after a few weeks he was surprised to learn that Omar was going to make a full recovery.

When Omar was able to talk, Fred began visiting him, and whenever he had the chance he told him about Jesus. Omar was silent when Fred mentioned Jesus, but he could see something in the boy's eyes that led him to believe that one day Omar would become a Christian.

Fred's tour ended before Omar left the hospital. He returned to the states and tried to put Afghanistan out of his mind, but occasionally, he would think about Omar and wonder what had happened to him. With the passing of time Fred thought about Omar less often—sometimes several years would pass without his giving Omar a thought, but then something would trigger the memory, and Fred would send up a quick prayer for the boy who had been the victim of a car bomb.

As Fred watched the boys, he once again sent up a quick prayer, "Please help Omar wherever he is, and, Lord, if it's okay, I'd sure like to know what happened to him." Fred checked his watch, and rose from his chair. It was time to cross the street and meet with Hadad.

Ψ

Hadad's office was of medium size, dingy, and brown. Although Wainwright had implied that Hadad had a great deal of money, it was apparent that he did not spend much of it on rent. The building, which was situated in a low-rent district, displayed peeling plaster, grimy tiles covering the floors, and dirt in every corner. Hadad's private office contained a few shelves displaying statues of camels in brass, plaster, wood and various other media. The scuffed wooden desk and few straight-backed chairs were old and dusty. The view from the single window was of the wall of an equally old building with cracked stucco about ten feet away.

Hadad was smiling and talking—sizing Fred up to determine just how much money he might be able to get out of him. "As you can see," he said as he gestured around the room, "I am a businessman. I have extensive real estate holdings here in Dubai as well as in Europe, Asia, and the United States. Others of my countrymen choose to live lives of idleness, but not me. I build my fortunes because one must always be prepared for the unexpected."

Fred thought that Hadad must have spent a considerable amount of time in the United States. His English was flawless, and there was barely a trace of an accent. About fifty years old, he was not really fat, but his body was soft, and his hips were wide. His hair was black and thick, but his hairline was receding. His large brown cow-like eyes peered at Fred from behind wire-rimmed glasses which he removed from time to time to mop his facc with a stained handkerchief. He was dressed in a white short-sleeved button-up cotton shirt, khaki pants, and tan canvas shoes with no socks. Fred thought that Hadad looked as if he did his shopping at the Dubai equivalent of Wal-mart.

"How may I assist you?" Hadad was asking.

"I am looking for information on Josef Helmick. I think he has lived here in Dubai for at least fifteen years. Have you heard of him?"

"Ah, yes. Herr Helmick is…infamous, as they say. One hears a great deal about him, but who can say how much of it is true? He is like a shadow. He disappears and reappears without warning, and no one seems to know where he goes or why."

Fred was growing irritated. "Can you help me or not?"

Hadad sensed his impatience and immediately changed his tone. "Of course, but information is an elusive commodity. Real estate is different—it is what it is. Not so with information; you cannot put a price on it."

"Yet, I'm betting that is exactly what you're about to do, so why don't you jump right in and give me a figure?"

Hadad looked at Fred out of the corners of his eyes, trying to judge how much he could get from this naive American. "Five thousand to start."

Fred returned his stare, "Fifteen hundred."

Hadad was surprised that the American was haggling over the price, but he had started high to hedge against that happening, "Twenty-five hundred."

"Done," Fred counted out the bills and handed them to Hadad along with his card containing his PCD number. "Let me know when you have something."

Hadad smiled broadly. Only an American would have paid twenty-five hundred. He was already thinking about how much he should demand for his next payment.

Ψ

When Fred entered the street, the soccer game was breaking up. One of the boys was headed in his direction, and Fred spoke, "Do you speak English?"

The boy smiled and nodded. He was a handsome youth of about fourteen. His eyes were large and dark, and his hair hung almost to his shoulders in soft black curls. Fred felt encouraged.

"Would you like to be my translator? I'm here on business, and I need someone to translate for me. I'll pay you, of course."

The boy's smile broadened. "I'm your man! What do you need?"

"Right now, I need lunch," Fred responded.

The boy motioned for Fred to follow and took off down a side street. Fred hesitated for only a moment before following him to a dilapidated café.

The boy looked so pleased with himself that Fred asked him to order lunch for both of them. The boy spoke to the owner in Arabic and then turned to Fred. "Sit at one of the tables. The food will be here soon."

Lunch was an indistinguishable mass of shredded lamb and vegetables that tasted like a combination of spices and dirt, but Fred made a show of pretending it was delicious—a move that apparently pleased the boy very much.

As they ate, Fred asked the boy about himself. He learned that his name was Walid and that both of his parents were dead. He lived with his grandfather not far from the café. He did not go to school because his grandfather would not allow him to attend classes at the mosque. Afshin was a follower of Pluto, the god of the underworld, and he was waiting for Pluto to rise from the bowels of the earth and reestablish his kingdom.

Fred wanted to know more about Walid, and he felt that the best way to find out about him was to meet his grandfather. "Do you think your grandfather would agree to meet me?" Fred asked.

Walid looked thoughtful. "I think so, but there is a problem."

"What kind of problem?"

"Well," the boy continued, "I am your man; I would serve you without charge, but my grandfather will not speak to you unless you pay him. To him you are the infidel."

"How much?"

"I think two hundred dollars American," the boy responded. As he spoke his eyes searched Fred's face for his reaction.

"Two hundred dollars it is," Fred replied. "Take me to him."

CHAPTER 13

The old man's eyes that met Fred's were clouded with cataracts, and it was apparent that if he could see at all it was only shapes and movement. His hair was long and matted and his robe was stained and streaked with dirt. Fred thought that Afshin should have been an object of pity, but a spirit of such evil and darkness came out of the old man that when Fred looked into his eyes, he took an involuntary step backwards.

"Grandfather," Walid said, "I have brought someone to meet you."

Afshin's sightless eyes darted about and his head moved in quick little jerks like some ancient bird of prey waiting for an unsuspecting animal to scurry by. "Why are you here?" Afshin asked in a hoarse quavering voice. "I do not serve your God."

Fred remained silent and the boy spoke, "Grandfather, he wants to know about the Gate to Hell."

"Ahhhh," the sound that came from the old man's throat was like a stream of putrid air gushing forth from a grave. “So, you want to know, do you? First you pay,” and he held out a trembling, wrinkled hand with gnarled fingers and long thick nails.

Fred handed Afshin the two hundred American dollars that he and the boy had agreed on, and Afshin smiled as he turned the bills over in his hands, feeling their surfaces with his calloused fingers. When he was satisfied, he tucked the bills inside his robe and leaned back against the crumbling wall.

In the dimly-lit room with specs of dust drifting thickly through the rays of light filtering through the single window, the old man’s hoarse voice had an almost hypnotic effect. “For many years those of us who still practice the ancient arts were scoffed at. We were told that the Gate to Hell did not exist—that it was only a myth for fools, but we knew better. We knew that the time for the god of the underworld to reign was at hand. We knew that the stories of the Plutonium were true because we had experienced the power of the underworld in our ceremonies. We knew that there was a place where Pluto’s breath pours forth from the deep recesses of the earth, destroying all who mock him. We had our ancient manuscripts that told us times and times and half a time need pass before Pluto would rise from his place in the underworld and inhabit his throne on earth.

“I was sixty years old when the Italian made the discovery. He was conducting an archeological dig in Turkey, near Pamukkale, when he uncovered some ruins of the ancient city of Hierapolis. As his team dug they came upon some fragments of Apollo's temple where the pilgrims came to bathe in the sacred pool and receive his blessing.

"Near the pool they found the Plutonium—the most sacred of all places. At first look it appeared to be only a small cave, but when one ventured closer he could smell the warmth of Pluto's breath emitting from the earth. The space was filled with a vapor so misty and dense that one could scarcely see the ground. Any animal that passed inside met instant death.

"In ancient times when pilgrims came to worship, small birds were given to them to throw into the cave so that they could experience the power for themselves. The priests breathed the vapors and were made to see visions as they led bulls into the cave as a sacrifice to Pluto."

Afshin's eyes glittered as he spoke, "I, myself, made a pilgrimage to the Gate to Hell where I threw sparrows into the mist. They immediately breathed their last and fell to the earth. The sweet scent of death was everywhere."

The old man suddenly stopped speaking and turned toward Fred. "Why have you come here? You are no friend to me. You have come to learn our secrets and destroy the portal to the underworld. The infidels came by night and filled the portal with stones. They set explosives to wipe it from the earth, but they could not destroy it. The god has hidden it from your eyes, and one day he will send forth his mighty breath to destroy all who oppose him. On that day you will die, and Pluto will rise to claim his kingdom. I curse you!" he screamed.

Fred was not frightened, but such a sense of horror engulfed him that he retreated from the stifling room into the bright sunlight outside.

Walid watched him with interest, but it was impossible to tell what he was thinking.

Finally, Fred spoke, "Do you also practice the ancient arts?"

"No," the boy replied. "Those are the old ways for old men."

"Do you believe in God?" Fred persisted.

The boy looked down and shrugged, and Fred felt a thrill of excitement. Perhaps he would be able to share his faith with this boy. Perhaps he would see him accept Jesus before his time in Dubai ended. "Would you like to know God?"

The boy looked into Fred's eyes and smiled. In that young face so full of trust and hope Fred saw his first opportunity for evangelism in this dry hostile land.

CHAPTER 14

After Fred had arranged to meet Walid the following morning, he walked aimlessly about the streets. He could not stop thinking about his meeting with Afshin. The old man had such a presence of evil about him that Fred wondered how Walid was able to endure life with him. Walid was still a child with a child's dreams; Fred had looked into his eyes and seen something that set him apart from the other street boys—an expectancy, an optimism, a kind of raw faith that his life would one day be better.

Fred did not know how long he had walked when his attention was drawn to a small store front with a wooden sign that read "Yeshua Ministries" printed in Arabic, French and English. He stopped and tried the door. To his surprise, the knob turned and the door opened.

Fred found himself inside a small room with a few uncomfortable-looking chairs. Sitting at a worn wooden table was a young woman working at a computer. She looked up and smiled, "The pastor is not here," she said in accented English.

Fred looked uncomfortable, "I'm sorry to interrupt you. I saw your sign, and I was just wondering what Yeshua Ministries does. I can come back another time."

"No, please," the woman replied. "I am happy to talk to you. You are American?"

"Yes." Fred felt very foolish. He had barged into the offices of Yeshua Ministries to satisfy his curiosity. It had not occurred to him that he might be acting rudely.

The woman did not appear to be offended. "I am Fatema," she said, "the wife of Pastor Saeed. He is visiting those in the church who are sick, but he will be back in time for services this evening. You are welcome to attend."

For the first time since arriving in Dubai, Fred felt welcome. He was staying in a luxurious hotel suite where his every need was met. The service was impeccable; the employees were gracious and smiling, but Fred did not feel welcome. Yet, in this hot, dingy building he felt peaceful and relaxed. "Will you tell me about your work here?" Fred asked.

"We are a Christian ministry working to bring Jesus to Muslims," Fatema answered. "We provide Bible training for hundreds of believers every year. We have much teaching in the UAE, but it is dangerous because evangelism is not allowed in Islamic countries. We have our offices in Dubai because Christians are allowed to have home churches and other churches here too, but not evangelism. We train here and then send missionaries to Islamic countries to work secretly under the covers."

Fred struggled to suppress a smile at the young woman's choice of words.

"That is how you say it?" Fatema asked when she saw the hint of a smile play around his lips. "Under the covers?"

"Yes," Fred replied. "They work undercover."

Fatema smiled broadly and continued, "Some of our pastors are arrested and sent to prison, but they continue to preach the Gospel while they are in chains. We have taken 2 Timothy 2:9 as our scripture for those who are in prison for their faith: *And because I preach this Good News, I am suffering and have been chained like a criminal. But the word of God cannot be chained.* Much good is done by our Christian brothers who suffer for Christ. They will not be silent, and they have brought many to Jesus as they sit in their cells.

"We also bring the Bible to the people. Yeshua Ministries has printed more than one million New Testaments, and we are now printing a second million. But it was not always so, and still there are not enough Bibles to meet the need for the Gospel. I work with believers in Iran because that is where I am from. I could tell you many stories of the things God is doing there. Do you have time to hear about the work?"

Fred nodded, and Fatema continued, "A young Iranian girl named Elham lost her father when she was only thirteen years old. He was arrested because of his Christian ministry and taken to the police station. Elham's family could get no information about him for three weeks, and then they were informed that he had been hanged.

"Elham was so sad that she could not think of how she would go on living, but one day she decided that she would honor her father by following Jesus, and she began her own ministry. Elham's father had been an evangelist, and she, too, wanted to evangelize for Jesus. In the Middle East Christians are called 'People of the Book' because they spend so much time reading and teaching the Bible, but Elham had only one Bible—the one that had belonged to her father. How could she share the Bible when she had only one Bible?

"After much prayer Elham felt God leading her to copy scriptures and leave them in public places. She and a Christian friend began to write short scriptures out by hand and leave them in taxis, restaurants, doctors' waiting rooms—wherever seemed good to them. All that time she prayed that God would send Bibles to Iran so that her people would hear the Gospel and be saved.

"Elham worked always to spread the Gospel with her scriptures, but when she was seventeen she felt the need to copy the Gospel of John by hand. It took her one month of working every night, and when she finished, she wrapped it like a gift and walked through the streets until she felt God lead her to leave it on the doorstep of a strange house.

"Nine years after her father was martyred Elham came to Yeshua Ministries to study and prepare for ministry. She was full of surprise when she found that a team here was translating the Bible into modern Persian. When the translation was finished, ten thousand copies were printed and distributed to the people of Iran. It was a dream come true for Elham."

"Is Elham still with Yeshua Ministries?" Fred asked.

"Oh, yes. She is the leader of our women's television ministry that is broadcast into Iran."

"So, your workers have been protected here?"

"Yes, but we had one thing happen that is still a mystery. Four years ago Rashin, a young girl who did women's street ministry, disappeared. She had gone out to talk to women as she did every day, and she simply vanished. We did much inquiry with the police and talking to women in the area where she usually went to speak, but we were never able to find anything. We believe that she was arrested and imprisoned, but we have never been able to find the smallest bit of information of what happened to her."

"How did you come to Yeshua Ministries?" Fred inquired.

"If it will please you, I will tell you my story," Fatema replied.

When Fred nodded, Fatema began.

Ψ

"I was born into a Christian family in Iran. When I was five or six years old, my father was imprisoned and executed for sharing his faith. After that my mother lived in fear that one day the police would again come to our door and take away other family members.

"I was never allowed to go outside during daylight hours. Sometimes at night my grandmother would take me into the small patch of dirt surrounding our house and allow me to look up at the stars and feel the fresh air on my face, but she was always watching and listening, always afraid that the police would come and snatch me away. I did not go to school, but my mother taught me to read, and together we studied the Bible every day.

"Always I could feel Jesus in my heart, and when I was alone in my bed I would ask Him to help me serve Him. Perhaps it was because I was the only child that I drew near to Him; I only know that day and night I dreamed that I would leave our small house and travel into the world beyond to tell people about Jesus.

"When I was twelve years old, my cousin Maryam came to live with us. She had lost both her father and mother to the fighting in the South, and she was full of sadness. Maryam and I were the same age, and, even though we had not met before, we instantly became like sisters. I knew that God had sent her to me so that we could take away each other's loneliness. Maryam had the same love for Jesus that I held in my heart, and we soon began to plan how one day we would go together to tell the people of Iran about our faith.

"When we were sixteen, Maryam and I began to leave the house without permission and go into the streets where we talked to people about Jesus. The first time my mother cried and begged us not to go again, but I told her that God had called me to serve Him, and I must obey. Maryam said the same things to her, and, finally, my mother agreed that we must obey God. She was still very much afraid for us, but after that she did not try to stop us.

"Nearly every day Maryam and I ventured into the streets, and when we were not arrested, we grew bolder. By the time we were nineteen, we were openly proclaiming the Gospel to anyone who would listen.

"One afternoon as we ministered to a group of women and children, the police appeared from out of nowhere and arrested us. I was more afraid of being separated from Maryam than I was of being arrested, and I prayed and asked God to let us stay together. He answered my prayer, and Maryam and I were put into the same cell where we were to wait to stand trial for prostitution.

"I was always strong, but Maryam was frail, and she soon developed a fever and a cough. As the days passed, I knew that she was getting weaker, and I prayed fervently for her to become well. I prayed that we would be released so that we could return to our family, but many days passed and we were still locked in our hot, filthy cell.

"Maryam and I were without knowledge of men. We had never been alone with a man, and we knew nothing of the ways of a man with a woman. We were unprepared for the cruelty of the prison guards. They called us horrible names and said disgraceful things to us. Often they beat us—sometimes with their bare hands and sometimes with a rod. Every time they subjected us to such cruelty they would taunt us and ask us where was our Jesus now? Why did He not come to save us?

"Maryam did not become bitter. She prayed for our captors and asked Jesus to forgive them and help them accept Him as their Lord and Savior. I was not like Maryam; I felt myself become bitter. When she would return to our cell bruised and bloodied, her body covered with running sores, I would feel hatred burning in my chest. I wanted to kill those men for what they had done to us.

"In Iran there is a saying that if we are bitten enough times by the snakes of this world, we are filled with poison, and we become like them. In Iran revenge and unforgiveness are believed to be virtues, so this saying is often repeated. It is the Iranian way of saying, 'If you harm me, I will turn on you and sink my fangs into your body and fill you with my deadly poison!'

"One day as I tried to wash Maryam's sores with the little water we had been given, I repeated this saying to her, and she began to cry. 'Do not do this!' she begged. 'If you do not forgive these men, you will become like them.

You will be filled with the poison that will drive Jesus from your heart, and you will become the servant of the evil one.

"'No, Fatema, I beg of you; do not let this thing happen. Forgive these men so that their poison cannot make you into a poisonous snake. God has much work for you to do. That is why the devil has attacked us. Last night God spoke to me in a dream and told me that I will not leave this place, but He will deliver you from the hands of the enemy so that your work can continue. If you allow yourself to hate these men, they have won. Forgiveness will deliver you from their grip.'

"Eleven months after we were arrested I gave birth on the dirt floor of that tiny cell. It is a miracle that the baby and I survived. We had no water to wash, and we had no one to help us deliver the child. No guards came to discover the cause of my screams as I suffered hours of blinding pain.

"During all that time Maryam was very brave. As she looked at my tiny baby girl her face shone with joy, and for the first time since we had been arrested I thought that Maryam seemed stronger. At that moment I was certain that she would survive our ordeal. 'A gift from God,' she said as she held my daughter up for me to see.

"The next morning Maryam did not awaken; I named the baby after her and made a promise to God that I would not allow the poison of my captors to infect me. I would live for Him and for my child.

"Three days later I was released from prison. My attorney had kept our case before the public, and Maryam and I had many people all over the world praying and petitioning for our release. The official story was that we had been arrested for prostitution, but all who knew us knew that this was not true. Since I had been in prison for eleven months when my child was born, they could not say that I was pregnant as a result of prostitution. I had simply become an embarrassment to the government of Iran, so the prison door was thrown open, and I was pushed out into the street with my baby in my arms. Neither my attorney nor my family had been notified that I was to be released. I walked to the home of a Christian family that I knew held secret church meetings in their house, and they took me to my mother.

"Some people from the United States helped me to leave Iran with my mother and baby—the only family I had left to me. They offered for me to come to America, but I could not do that. I knew that God had called me to bring Christ to the Muslim nations so I came here to Dubai and joined Yeshua Ministries.

"It was here that I met my husband Saeed. I did not believe that I would ever be able to marry. I felt disgraced, and I had learned to fear men, but when I met Saeed, I knew at once that God had sent him to me. He is gentle and good—a true man of God. And he loves my daughter as if she were his own child.

"My body has healed, and my mind has also healed. But most important, my spirit has healed. The poison is gone from my veins, and I am filled with the joy and peace and love of the Holy Spirit. I refuse to hate those who hate me. I refuse to be stung by them. I choose forgiveness; I choose life; I choose to serve Jesus."

CHAPTER 15

Through the towering, multi-story windows, the nine-hundred foot lighted fountains of the Burj Khalifa appeared to dance magically to Middle-Eastern music. Against the deep darkness, the sparkling lighted waters took on the quality of spirits or water genies out of *A Thousand and One Arabian Nights*. A crowd was gathered outside to watch them, as they did every night, but from this special, private meeting room at the world's most exclusive hotel in the heart of downtown Dubai, the spectators could watch the show while enjoying their meal.

Amanda Sutton had a spectacular view of the fountains from her table, and though she was transfixed by their beauty, she was also acutely aware that her fascination with the fountains was irritating her date for the evening.

She had met this strange man just this afternoon after she arrived in Dubai. Amanda was supposed to be here for a private party at the club Armani, followed by a fashion show the next day, but when she had met Josef at his apartment that afternoon he had told her that there had been a change of plans, and the party was being held in a private meeting room there at the hotel and that she would be his companion for the evening. The way he stroked her hair and her shoulders left no doubt as to exactly what he meant by 'companion', but he had promised that he would introduce her to Francesca Giovanni, the current head of the house of Armani. Amanda was no prude; she knew that in the fashion world sometimes a girl has to play along to get ahead. Still, the loathing she felt for this man at first sight had made his offer a hard one to accept—if she had not been thousands of miles from home in a strange country she might have actually refused him.

In her beaded, shell-pink dress she was a vision. Amanda had been amazed when the concierge had delivered it to her hotel room; it fit as if it had been made for her. The dress was knee length and showed off her beautiful, tanned legs, which were further accentuated by the metallic stiletto heels. She wore only one piece of jewelry—her pavé zirconia "good luck" ring which everyone assumed was diamonds. The Dubai Tower Salon had coiffed her hair into a sophisticated upsweep which showed off her eyes to their best advantage. Her softly-applied makeup was flawless, and the touch of pink on her lips was the exact shade of her dress. When she entered the room on Josef's arm, every man turned to look at her, and many of them continued staring throughout the evening.

Josef was reveling in the attention. His own suit was custom-made by the house of Armani especially for this occasion. Amanda and he were seated at the head table, and he was surveying the room with a sense of both pride and power in the moments before he stood to make his opening speech. Every moment of the evening had been planned to the smallest detail, and, as with all of Josef's plans, everything was proceeding perfectly.

The gathering assembled in this private meeting room overlooking the fountains represented all walks of the world's elite—monarchs and prime ministers, the greatest scientific minds, the captains of industry, and the titans of finance. For over three quarters of a century, the men in this organization had been formulating public policy on myriad issues—world governance, environmentalism, population control, currency manipulation, trade, and control over international resources. The ideas that flowed from these gatherings filtered down to the United Nations and then to national governments where they were messaged to individual people groups through carefully-crafted promotional campaigns. Yet, for all of their power and influence, the Club conducted most of their work in secret. Tonight, they were gathered for their annual assembly to induct their 2041 secretary-general.

Josef rose and stood at the podium; all eyes were on him.

"I want to begin this evening with a toast. The wait staff is presenting each of you with a glass of wine from my newest acquisition—Italy's oldest and most prominent vineyard. I have purchased this vineyard with a new commitment to sustainable agricultural practices in the production of the world's premier wine."

As he spoke, the wait staff placed a flute of sparkling white wine in front of each attendee. With his usual meticulous planning, Josef had made certain that there would be enough staff to serve every person at exactly the same time so that by the time he had finished his introduction, all of the flutes would be in place. Lifting his own glass he proposed the toast:

"We drink tonight to a new, sustainable future, to equality of all human beings, to a renewed respect for the earth, and to a reorientation of government and social systems which will enable these processes to begin. To the New World Order."

"To the New World Order!" repeated his audience, who stood to drink the toast and then returned to their seats.

Josef continued, "More than three quarters of a century ago, the Club of Rome was founded to bring social order out of chaos—to ensure a cleaner, fairer, safer, more equitable world. I am long familiar with the Club and its inner workings. Many of you know the work of my father, Karl Helmick. He introduced me to the Club of Rome when I was thirteen. My regularly-assigned readings were the writings of its intellectual members. When I was fifteen years old, my father took me to Sweden to one of the general meetings and introduced me to then Secretary-General Laurence Wilcott and after that I attended the general assembly meeting every year. Over and over I heard speeches not unlike my own tonight about the need for a new global paradigm and how this must be enacted by 2052. Yet, here we stand today, just eleven short years away from that benchmark, having accomplished substantially none of our original goals. The sovereign nations of the world still govern their own peoples in their own way; free markets still permit a supply and demand system of economy; the West is still fat and rich and consuming a disproportionate percentage of the earth's resources, just as they were when I was a boy.

"So my question to you tonight is this 'How many of you here in this room are truly, fully committed to the goals of The New World Order?' Please raise your hands."

Every hand in the room went up, except Amanda's; she had no idea what he was talking about. He caught her eye and glared at her, and she reluctantly raised hers also.

"Excellent. The 150 of you represent the world's elite—the Guardians of Mankind. You have just told me that you are fully committed to the New World Order, so I am going to ask that you lead by example in ushering in this New Order.

"Many of you know that my father was an extraordinary man of many inventions. He discovered and patented the cure for cancer. But he was introduced to the Club of Rome through some of his other scientific breakthroughs in reversing death and aging—breakthroughs of which some of you in this room have availed yourselves over the years. My father had one other discovery—his greatest and most secret which I have never disclosed to any person until now. He learned how to bend the laws of space and time in such a way that he could erase the past and transform the future. Tonight, I propose that we use this discovery to begin to remake our world right now—here in this room.

"At the top of each place setting is a small crystal prism. This prism is the portal to the beginning of a new world. Take it into your hand, and you will feel it grow warm in your grasp. As you look into its facets you will experience your past, your present and your future. You will look upon your deepest desires, your most intimate memories, your most passionate aspirations. When you are ready, gently rub your thumb over the prism and repeat these words, 'I renounce my wealth, my status, my family, my fortune, myself—all that I was, all that I am, all that I could be. I surrender myself as a servant to the New World Order to no longer rule but to serve in whatever capacity I am instructed. I give myself to this cause freely and without reservation.' As you say these words you will disappear from this room, and you will cease to exist in your present state. You will still be alive, but you will be working at whatever assignment you are given by the masters of the new state. You will live wherever you are assigned without question; you will consume a new sustainable diet of 750 calories per day for the rest of your life. Your memories of your present life will disappear, and all memories of you by those who know you will also disappear. The space that you occupy in the universe will close, and it will be as though you had never existed."

As Josef spoke, the prisms on the table had begun to sparkle in the light of the chandeliers. As the guests watched, the prisms slowly began to change color—first they were the color of pale sparkling champagne and then they became a dazzling pink. Josef's suggestion was, on the surface, revolting to the men in the room, and at first they resisted the urge to comply, but the prisms seemed to call out to them to be held and caressed. One by one, each of the men picked up the crystal directly in front of him.

His Royal Majesty of Spain, King Luis Carlos, was the first. The prism warmed in his hand, and suddenly Luis Carlos was no longer in the room. He was alone, suspended in an ethereal mist holding the glittering object. As he gazed into the facets, he was suddenly a little boy of about four years of age, walking on the beach on a warm day as the gentle waves tickled his sandy toes. He held a shell to his ear. "Mama, listen. I can hear the ocean."

His mother was walking beside him, "Of course you can, my love," she laughed. He could hear her voice, her laugh. The sun had made her fair skin pink and left a few freckles on her bare shoulders. His aunt Cristina was at her side, and they were talking about a school for him….

Now he was older—a young boy playing soccer for his country on the Olympic team. He was at the university….he was at the funeral of his best friend Enrique who was killed by a car bomb….He was attending his own state wedding to Patricia—how young and slender she looked. Had she ever been so young and beautiful? Paparazzi from the entire world were photographing the ceremony. Patricia's embroidered white silk dress was exquisite—custom-made for her by the house of Vera Wang.

When he turned the prism slightly and looked into another of its facets, he could see his present. His mistress, Ines Jimenez, the most sought-after actress in Spain, had made dinner for him and was opening the door to greet him. Her long tresses were the color of a raven's wing, and they fell softly down her back. Her eyes were as black as pools of tar, and they glinted with love and passion whenever she and the king were together. Every man in Spain wanted her, but although Luis Carlos had just celebrated his sixtieth birthday and Ines was a mere twenty-eight, she whispered to him that he was the only man who excited her. He could hear her soft laughter and smell her jasmine-scented fragrance; she was so close that he could almost touch her....He was again on the beach, and he could see Ines' three- year-old son Carlitos squatting on the sand, shaping the wet grains into a cone with a toy. Legally Carlitos was the son of Spanish cinema heartthrob Eduardo Quiñones, but their affair was merely a cover to hide the open secret of her passion with Luis Carlos. Carlitos was the monarch's only son, born to him in his golden years, and though the boy could never be his heir, he was his father's pride and joy.

One more turn of the prism in Luis Carlos' hand, and suddenly he was transported to the future....It was Patricia's funeral; none of the people in her family lived past sixty-five. Heads of state worldwide had come to pay their respects....Ines was moving into the presidential palace. They would never marry, but she would be his constant companion until his death. He would never acknowledge Carlitos publicly, but behind the scenes he would open every door so that his only son would be a man of wealth and prominence....He could see his own funeral, four decades into the future, as heads of state again paid their respects, and a still stunning Ines mourned the love of her life.

If he rubbed the prism and repeated the chant, he would cease to exist. Ines not only would not mourn for him—she would not be conscious that he had ever lived. He could see her cavorting playfully with Quiñones in their publicity shoots. Ines would belong to him. The life that Luis Carlos had lived would vanish—his presidential palace, his friends from school, his travels, his three daughters with Patricia, even his precious memory of walking with his mother and his aunt on the beach—all would be gone in an instant. No, no, he could not bring himself to do that. He tried to release his hand from the prism, but he was unable to let it go.

Across the room, bioethicist and Harvard professor Kevin Leeds sat transfixed as he held his shimmering prism. He had scoffed at the notion of bending time and space until he had looked into the facets and once again become a boy in New England in a cold empty house waiting for his parents to come home. Kevin's parents were ACLU attorneys who had time for every cause but their son. Day after day he returned from school to a lonely, messy house where the heat was seldom turned on because heating and cooling were bad for the environment. Tall for his age, pallid and lanky, Kevin was not athletic, and he did not make friends easily. As he looked into the prism, he could once again feel the sting of the rejection and mockery that he experienced every day at school and the anger and resentment he harbored toward his more popular classmates who had friends and siblings and relationships. He relived the awful loneliness of turning the key to an empty house day after day. His mother did not think television was a good pursuit for her son, but she did leave him a stack of approved reading materials, and his one joy was the afternoons that he spent reading Jane Goodall. Her writings transported him to Africa—a continent of exotic people, animals and locales.

Now he was graduating with his bachelor's degree. His parents were there, of course, but he remembered feeling that they were more interested in how his achievements reflected on them than in his future. Willow, the girl he lived with in college, was graduating too. She was barely pregnant, but soon she wouldn't be; they had both decided that they were not ready to start a family.

Now he was working on his doctoral thesis—a five-year case study on the effects of family-planning techniques on a control group in Nairobi. During the five years of his research, Kevin had found himself. In Massachusetts he was still the skinny, pallid twenty-something with an old hybrid that barely ran and not enough money for dates, but in Nairobi he was a god among mortals. He had shared most of his five years with Anasa, a young Kenyan woman who had agreed to be sterilized to participate in the case study. Anasa's name meant "joy" in Swahili, and his relationship with her and his life in Nairobi had been the closest thing to joy Kevin had ever experienced. He had left when his research was over and never contacted her again, but barely a day passed when he did not think of her and his five years in Africa.

The prism moved in Kevin's hand, and he could see his present. He was walking toward his office on campus. On his way, he stopped at the shop where he bought his daily cup of coffee from Nadine, the owner and his long-term part-time lover. Nadine was his age and had been married three times, so she was more than content with their casual relationship, which perfectly suited Kevin. They took trips together and dined together a few times a week. Though not intellectual, she shared his core beliefs in environmentalism and socialism, and she made a suitable sounding board for his ideas. She was the ideal companion for a man of his intellect who did not want a more demanding relationship but was still haunted by the loneliness of his youth.

Now Kevin was on campus. The walls of his office at Harvard were lined with awards he had received for his work in international population control and environmentalism. He still loved the smell of a classroom on the first day of school, the way the chalk felt in his hand, and the fresh faces of the students taking their seats. With Kevin's credentials he did not need to teach a freshman class; yet, he requested the opportunity to teach "Bioethics, Population Control, and the Future of the Human Race" every year to another freshman class. For many of these students this was their first time living away from home, and Professor Leeds was one of the first voices they would hear who would help them unlearn any superstition or religious influence or archaic sense of national pride left over from their parents. Every semester he began with the same goal—to ensure that no student attending his class completed it without experiencing a radical transformation of belief so great that they could never again relate fully to any belief system other than Leeds'. Whether that transformation came through belittling students in class who dared to argue with him about his beliefs, or encouraging them to shed their outdated ideas about morality, or punishing dissenters with failing grades, Leeds could see the transformation he wrought in the eyes of his students at the end of every semester, and he rejoiced that a new crop of young people had been indoctrinated.

The prism turned again in his hand, and he could see himself five years into the future, receiving the Nobel Prize for Bioethics. This was the one award that had eluded him, but he had been working steadily toward its achievement. Kevin once again had international recognition...He saw himself going to visit his father in the long-term care facility where Douglas Leeds had lived for many years as Alzheimer's destroyed his mind. Douglas looked up in shock to see his son standing there after nearly a decade without a visit. Kevin explained to his father that he had won the Nobel Prize and that he had just returned from Sweden. As Douglas looked at his son, for a split second the fog that shut out his surroundings lifted, and he viewed Kevin with a combination of envy and admiration that the younger Leeds had never before seen.

If Kevin rubbed his thumb across the prism and renounced his life, he would be making the ultimate sacrifice for the good of nature. He would be eradicating himself—his past, his present and his future. Yet, in doing so he would also be erasing his research, his work. The hours that he had spent initiating thousands of students into global environmentalism would be gone. How would their lives be changed if Leeds' influence was suddenly eradicated? He thought of his walks on campus; he would never again see the vibrant fall colors as he strolled among the paths. He would never drink coffee with Nadine or take another trip to Europe with her as his companion. He would never explain to another coed that by pleasing her professor she could improve her GPA just enough to make it into that vital top five percentile so critical for a student's future in the modern competitive world. In less than a moment, all of his work, his ideas, his contributions to society would disappear. He could never do that—that was a sacrifice to be made by a lesser intellect. The universe could not afford to lose Kevin Leeds.

Two tables to the left of Professor Leeds sat Hemraj Ambani. Hemraj's name meant "King of Gold" and it aptly described his financial situation—Ambani was one of the world's leading industrialists and currently occupied the number one spot as the richest man in the world.

Ambani studied mysticism and world religions as a hobby, so he felt more curiosity than contempt at Josef's suggestion to pick up the prism. If the prism could bend time and space and act as a portal to a changed reality, Hemraj knew that the secret did not lie in some scientific discovery but rather in the dark arts. That fascinated him, and he picked it up carefully and looked into it deeply.

Immediately, he was ten years old at boarding school in London. It was winter, and he was being bullied by the British boys. He hated these boys. His family was immensely wealthier than any of them, but they mocked and ridiculed him relentlessly. The intense anger that he carried toward the West had grown in this school until it had overcome everything else in life. During his visits home on every holiday, he begged his father not to send him back, but his father flatly refused and said that his son must have a Western education.

Now he was at home in Mumbai. The family was celebrating his sister Vasana's engagement to Ishan Pai. Vasana did not attend school in London. She was educated at the Scottish Presbyterian School in Mumbai where she received a Western education and achieved fluency in English, but her socially conservative parents did not trust their daughter outside of the country. Hemraj and Vasana had never been close—she was badly spoiled and petted by both parents, and it always seemed to her brother that she got the best of everything. In accordance with centuries of tradition, Vasana's father had arranged her marriage, but she had been allowed to meet Ishan prior to the wedding and apparently had liked him. She was spinning around the room like a dervish showing off the jewels he had given her for a wedding gift and boasting about the dress she would wear and the world cruise they would take for their honeymoon trip. Hemraj did not meet Ishan until his sister's wedding, and he hated him on sight. Forty years later, his opinion of his sister and brother-in-law had not changed.

Suddenly he was at his own wedding marrying Ramita, the bride his father had chosen for him. Ramita—in English it means "pleasing," and she was pleasing in every way. Her marriage to Hemraj was the merger of two of India's most powerful families. Like Vasana, Ramita was educated in India for primary school, but unlike Vasana, Ramita's parents had sent to her to the University of Edinburgh in Scotland. She was beautiful, graceful, fluent in English and gracious to everyone. Hemraj was once again standing in front of her on their wedding day knowing with a certainty that at that moment he was the envy of every man in attendance, including Ishan. It had been one of the rare moments of happiness in his life.

The prism glinted in his hand, and now he was sitting in the office of his father's chief business manager and his attorney for the reading of the will. Hemraj's mother had died from cancer while she was still in her forties, and his father never remarried. He had buried himself in his work and his mistresses and barely acknowledged his son. Hemraj was in New York on business when he received the call that his father had suffered a massive stroke and was in a coma. The elder Ambani died before his son arrived. Hemraj did not feel grief about his passing—his emotions were more akin to disbelief and shock. At thirty years of age, he had become the head of a billion-dollar conglomerate and one of the richest men in the world.

Hemraj's father left his vast business and financial holdings to his son and his daughter and son-in-law. Hemraj owned fifty percent, and Vasana and Ishan each owned twenty-five percent. His chest was hot with anger and humiliation as he left the office and stepped onto the crowded streets of Mumbai where his driver awaited with an armored car. Silently, he cursed his father for dividing the holdings in such a way that he was permanently chained to Vasana and Ishan.

The prism turned in Hemraj's hand, and he was in present-day Mumbai in the palatial home he had built for himself, Ramita, and their two children. His personal residence was the most lavish and expensive in the history of the world—a writer for *Forbes Magazine* had joked that the private estate of Hemraj Ambani had replaced the Taj Mahal as India's greatest tourist attraction. Ramita was the ideal companion—still beautiful and a flawless picture of grace and culture. She understood and embraced Indian culture without hesitation—she never challenged her husband on any point. She accepted his romantic dalliances without confronting them. For his part, Hemraj knew that he could never find a substitute for her, so though he frequently enjoyed other women's company as a diversion, he rewarded Ramita's discretion with the largest, most expensive private jewel collection in the world. Every piece of her clothing was custom-made by the world's top designers. She traveled frequently to her luxurious homes throughout the world where she entertained the world's wealthiest families at her lavish parties.

Now Hemraj was standing in his office arguing with Vasana and Ishan. Hemraj was chairman of the board of the family enterprises, but Vasana wanted that title for her husband, and she constantly schemed and plotted against her brother. The newest coup was an effort to persuade the board of directors of some of the Western corporations to replace Hemraj as CEO with Ishan on the grounds that Hemraj was embezzling from his own companies to support his lavish lifestyle. Vasana was standing in front of him yelling at him. She was wearing western clothing and much too much make up, and he thought how he hated her and her fat, bloated worthless husband.

The prism turned in Hemraj's hand and two more years had passed. He was now at Ishan's funeral. Ishan had been the unlucky victim of a random shooting in the street. Vasana was weeping inconsolably at the loss of her husband, but Hemraj was quietly overjoyed. Under the terms of his father's will, Ishan's interest in the family's holdings had now passed to Hemraj, giving him seventy-five percent control and leaving Vasana with only twenty-five percent. She had no more power to start a coup. Hemraj's first official act would be to lock her out of the building. He was only sorry that she had not been on the street with her husband when the shooting had taken place—he had, after all, paid to have them both assassinated.

If Hemraj rubbed the prism, he would cease to exist. In the present reality, Ishan was still alive, and he and Vasana would become the sole heirs to the billion-dollar conglomerate. Ramita would be the wife of another man. All of the wealth, the prestige, the fame that Hemraj had accumulated would pass to others. The thought of his wife belonging to another man, of Ishan sitting as chairman of the board of his companies, of Vasana boasting about her husband's business savvy, was more than Hemraj could bear. He could never give up this life—and why would he? The present world was home to nine billion people. Let those who had nothing to live for disappear.

Amanda Sutton had not intended to pick up her prism, but somehow, the piece of crystal had made its way into her delicate hand. She, too, found herself transported from the room, but when she stared into its facets, everything looked fragmented and hazy, and if she were viewing it through a mist. She could see small shards of memories—a fleeting image of herself as a child with a tiara on her head as she was named the winner of a pageant. A woman was next to her, but Amanda could not see her clearly. Was that her mother? She had an impression of being on a rollercoaster on a blazing hot day. She was seven or eight years old at the time. She could not see the faces of anyone around her. She could not remember the name of the amusement park or how long they stayed.

She felt the prism turn, and she could see briefly a shouting argument that she was having with her mother. What did they argue over? What was said?

The memories sharpened a little as they became more recent. Now she had a hazy recollection of sitting in a restaurant with a man who was giving her an envelope containing one thousand dollars and asking her to take a job—somewhere. She could see his face; she could even hear his voice, but she couldn't quite make out what he was saying. When the prism turned again in Amanda's hand, she saw only mist.

Josef had said that if she rubbed the prism with her thumb, she would disappear. She had not done that, but as Amanda stared into the crystals, she had the disturbing sensation that she was already disappearing—that the space she occupied in the universe was already beginning to close and that she would soon simply vanish.

A loud crack from the front of the room broke the trance. Immediately, all 150 participants in the conference were seated in their chairs with their dinners in front of them.

Josef lowered his hand from snapping his fingers into the microphone. He had watched the experiment with intense interest. As each person had disappeared into his or her own reality, Josef had been able to study their reactions and their fascinations with their personal visions. When he was ready, he was able to call them back.

Now he spoke again, "Thank you for taking part in my little experiment. I observed that not a single person in this room elected to sacrifice himself for the greater good. Not one of you rubbed the prism and repeated the chant. Why not? What did you see when you looked into the crystals? The passionate embrace of a lover?" his eyes fell on Luis Carlos, and the monarch felt his own face color with embarrassment, "the pride of accomplishment of academic achievement?" now he was looking directly at Kevin Leeds, who stared back at him coldly, "wealth and possessions?" now he was gazing at Ambani. The men shifted in their seats—surely he could not see their memories—their fantasies. Each man felt a vulnerability he had never before experienced, as if Josef had forced him to expose his most secret thoughts.

"Would anyone like to volunteer to tell us what you saw? Would you Amanda?" he was now staring at her.

Amanda shook her head, looked down, and sat silently turning the ring that she hoped would bring her good luck.

Josef continued, "I submit to all of you that this is the very reason why after more than seventy-five years we have never been able to achieve our goal of a sustainable world. We ask residents of democracies to vote for laws and governments that will make their wealth, prominence and professional achievements vanish—that will remove from them the joys of family and the relationships they treasure. Not one of you chose to sacrifice yourself because when you stared into the crystals you saw elements of your past and present and hopes for your future with which you could not bear to part. But I would have you understand that every person who has ever been faced with the decision to erase himself, his work, his life for the greater benefit of society has felt the same way—no matter how menial or meaningless his life would appear to us. The plumber who works long hours performing the most noxious tasks and then sits in his usual place at the neighborhood pub waiting for the waitress to finish her shift so that they can be alone together; the first grade teacher who congratulates herself that she is shaping the next generation and then goes home to an empty apartment and fills her hours reading romance novels while she dreams of one day meeting her fantasy lover; the accountant who works a seventy hour week and every year plans a new marketing campaign in the hopes of growing his tiny business into one that will someday support him without such grueling effort and will give him a retirement worthy of the years that he has invested—to each of these people and billions more just like them, life as they presently experience it is precious. They will never vote to erase themselves.

"We have long known that global environmental goals cannot be achieved through democracy. They must be achieved through force. Yet, how can the few force the change that is needed on the many? History teaches that even great military might is not sufficient to permanently quell the desires of the majority—for examples we have only to look at the failed Soviet military occupation of Afghanistan at the end of the twentieth century or the failed Western colonial exploits of Africa and the Near and Middle East in the eighteenth and nineteenth centuries. Though the occupying powers possessed greater military strength, weapons, and training, they never impacted the will of the people, and over time their grip on the places they occupied slipped away. That is the way military occupation always ends—with the conqueror being rejected by the conquered.

"No, what I am proposing tonight is that we must advance our goals using a different type of force. The New World Order can succeed only when we are able to shape the desires and will of the people to conform to global environmentalism. When we are able to manipulate the thoughts, the desires, the ambitions of the plumber, the teacher and the accountant, as well as the monarch, the professor and the industrialist, then and only then will we be able to persuade the billions who occupy this planet to embrace the changes that are necessary to save it—even if in that embrace they must cease to exist.

"This is my pledge to you as your new secretary-general: In less than a decade, I will accomplish what this organization has failed to do in the past three quarters of a century. I will persuade the world's population to make the necessary changes, to embrace sacrifice and the loss of everything they value—every comfort, every luxury, every pleasure. I will bring the world into submission to the ideals of a New World Order unlike anything it has ever experienced. I invite each of you to join me as we redefine what it means to be a citizen of the world."

As he concluded his speech, Josef's audience applauded more enthusiastically than they felt. For many, the experience of staring into the crystals had been a disconcerting one. Now he had essentially promised to further the goals of environmentalism through mind control on a global scale. That was fine—as long as he limited his techniques to plumbers and teachers and accountants, but what if he unleashed these techniques on them? After what they had just experienced, they were not at all certain that they trusted this strange German. Still, he had assured them that he could achieve what no one else ever had, and they were confident that no force was powerful enough to shield him from them if he became too much of a problem.

As dinner ended, Josef and Amanda made their way outside. He was being stopped by various members of the Club who were calling his speech "brilliant" and "masterful". Amanda was watching the midnight show of the Fountains—the last one of the night in which the waters danced to Andrea Bocelli and Sarah Brightman singing *Time to Say Goodbye*.The Fountains had concluded their performance to this duet for over forty years, and Amanda had seen videos of it on YouTube. Normally, she would have been thrilled to be here, but tonight the song and the dance seemed so melancholy—as if she were the one who was saying goodbye. From the remarks of the other people who had attended the dinner she could tell that they had experienced vivid memories as they stared at the crystals. Why could she remember so little?

Josef appeared at her side. "You seem sad, my darling. Can I do anything for you?" She looked up at him. His voice was low; his tone was warm and reassuring. This was a side of him that she had not seen. Tears came to her eyes. "I…I'm sorry. I just left New York suddenly. The man who hired me, Stan, said that I couldn't tell anyone where I was going so I didn't. I was just wondering if my mom's worried about me…She didn't know I was going away…"

"Shhh." He drew his arm around her. "I have just the thing. When we get back to my apartment, call your mother and tell her that you are here with me and that you are working. That will set her mind at ease—and yours. I don't want you to worry. You are going to experience the most amazing night of your life, and I want you to enjoy it."

Taking her hand in his, he lightly kissed her knuckles, and they walked back to the room together. His confidential tone reassured her, and the warmth of his hand holding hers calmed her. When they entered the apartment, he pointed to an old-fashioned telephone on his desk. "I have to go back downstairs for a few minutes. I took the liberty of having your mother's number pre-programmed into this phone along with the international dialing code. All you need do is press 1, and you will be connected. Call her and let her know where you are. I will return in five minutes."

He kissed her gently, and she watched him leave and close the apartment door behind him. She could not entirely shake her feelings of apprehension, but she was glad he was gone and that she was going to talk to her mother alone.

Standing at the desk, she picked up the phone and pressed 1. She could hear clicking on the line as the long series of numbers needed to make an international call from Dubai to the U.S. were entered; then she heard her mother's PCD ringing and, finally, her mother's voice on the other end.

"Hi, Mom. It's Amanda. I wanted to let you know that I took a job in Dubai this weekend. I left Thursday morning and flew here on a private jet, and now I'm in the apartment of the guy who hired me, and....Mom. Mom...." The line was dead. She felt a hand on her shoulder and her blood turned cold. She did not need to turn around to know who was standing behind her.

CHAPTER 16

It was 8:00 the evening after Josef's induction as secretary-general. He was alone in a private dining room with Hemraj Ambani, who had requested the meeting immediately after the conclusion of Josef's speech the previous evening. Ambani had been both fascinated and appalled by Josef's demonstration; he had to know more. Josef had watched Ambani closely during his experiment, and he relished another opportunity to make him squirm. Besides, Josef suspected that what Ambani really wanted was a personal introduction to Amanda.

As the men sipped their champagne and ate their lobster, each engaged in a mind game intended to manipulate the other.

"That was quite a show you put on last night," Hemraj began. "For a moment I almost believed that I was living out my past, my present and my future in another dimension. Would you care to share how you did it?"

"The powers that allow me to bend space and time are not to be shared," Josef replied coolly.

"Really, Josef? The powers that you claim would give you the status of a god; we both know that you are just another purveyor of parlor tricks," Hemraj pursued, knowing full well that his remarks would incense his host. Josef's eyes flashed. Hemraj persisted, "It was an entertaining show, of course, but did you stop for a moment to consider what would have happened if anyone in the room had actually rubbed the prism and recited your incantation? What then?"

"Of course I considered it," Josef snapped. "If anyone had repeated the incantation and rubbed the prism, he would have instantly ceased to exist, and today the Club of Rome would have a vacancy. However, there was no danger whatsoever that anyone in that room would actually do so because all of you are much too selfish to sacrifice yourselves for any higher purpose. Your collective narcissism insured that all of you were quite safe."

Hemraj stared at Josef. He had assumed that in private Josef would admit that this was a cheap magician's trick; instead, he was insisting that the prisms really were the gateway to another universe. That was preposterous—unless it was true. And if it were true—what would that kind of power mean to a man like Hemraj? If Josef actually possessed such power, what would it mean for all of them? The thought was exhilarating…and terrifying.

"It is one thing to use a sort of mass hypnosis on one intimate gathering of unsuspecting people, Josef. What you promised last night was something vastly greater. You indicated that you are in possession of a means to control the thoughts of billions of people—to persuade much of the world's population to abandon its own ambitions, to relinquish its own right to exist. No such force exists—you and I both know that. So what is your real plan?"

"You are quite wrong, Hemraj. Such a force does exist. It is the power to command armies, to control the minds of men, to corrupt the virtuous, to transform otherwise decent, educated, ordinary people into mass murderers. It is the power to cause loving families to kill and betray each other, to cause mothers to kill their own babies, to cause neighbors to turn on each other without any reward for doing so. I will use it to transform the world." Josef stared coldly at Hemraj, "You think I relied on a carnival trick last night when, in fact, I performed an experiment—for demonstrative purposes only. I wanted to prove my point—that the basic inclination of people is to protect their own stations in life, regardless of how meager or grandiose those may be. However, I can also promise you this," Josef's tone became more confident, "if I had wanted to do so, I could have induced every one of you to eradicate every trace of yourselves from off this earth."

Hemraj put down his utensils. "This is what everyone is talking about today, Josef. I have come to you tonight as your friend, but I will not do so again. Many members of the Club perceived a veiled threat in your remarks last night—as if you could and would eliminate us at will. I told them that it was merely your flare for the theatrical, but now I see that I was wrong. I am warning you: Any mind control or mass hypnosis that you choose to unleash on the world's population or its leaders has our consent as long as you can accomplish what you claim. We must reduce the world's population from just over nine billion people to just short of one billion in the next eight years; no action that accomplishes this goal is too over-reaching, but do not make the mistake of thinking that you can hypnotize and control us. The 150 of us in the Club of Rome are the true Guardians of mankind's future. You have built most of your personal fortune through your connection to us. Your station in the world is due to our influence. We made you, and if you turn on us, we will destroy you."

Josef did not answer, but he looked directly into Hemraj's eyes and smiled. Ambani felt his own blood run cold and the hair on the back of his neck stand up as his eyes met Josef's. In that moment, he was convinced that Josef really did have the power to do anything he chose.

"You are amused?" Hemraj tried to steady his own voice and to keep Josef from seeing the terror that was consuming him.

"I am. My father also used to tell me that he had made me. Now he is dead, and I am here. You and I have done a lot of business together, so I am going to pretend that you did not just make that last speech. You may deliver this message to your 150 Guardians of Mankind: Do not ever threaten me, or I will force each of you to disembowel yourselves as I watch. Do you understand?"

Hemraj pushed his chair back and stood to go. His legs were weak and his stomach was churning. He could barely speak. "Good evening, Josef," he gasped.

"Good evening, Hemraj. Get some rest; you look as though you need it," and Josef finished his meal alone.

As he left the dining room, he was greeted by Luis Carlos. "How good to see you, Josef. Where is your exquisite companion this evening?"

Josef returned the monarch's greeting with a charming smile. "Ah, my young companion needed her rest this evening. As I am sure you can imagine, we had a very exhausting night together."

The two men laughed knowingly, and Josef headed back toward the lobby and took the elevator to his apartment.

Ψ

At that same hour Paolo Castro, a Filipino kitchen worker at the Club Armani, was carrying some refuse to a trash receptacle in the alley behind the hotel. The stench was so terrible that he could hardly approach the dumpster; even in a land of intense heat such as Dubai where a few hours of exposure to the elements reduced all waste to an almost instant state of putrefaction, the stench was both unusual and unbearable.

As Paolo neared the dumpster, he caught sight of the source of the stench. A badly-burned female body had been thrown across the top of the dumpster so that it was partially in the receptacle and partially out. Flies covered her. Most of her clothing had been dissolved, but he could still see remnants of a shell-pink beaded dress. Her face and body were so mutilated that he could not tell her age or even her ethnicity. Paolo vomited in the alley before running back into the kitchen and reporting the body to his supervisor.

Within an hour the Dubai police had arrived and were reporting back to the chief inspector. The woman had been burned with acid poured over her face and body, and she was apparently covered from head to foot with numerous lacerations. The body had probably been in the alley less than twelve hours when it was discovered, and the massive damage indicated that she had suffered for a long time before she had died. She had no identification, and thanks to the acid, she did not even have fingerprints. It was a grisly crime, and without victim identification it would be nearly impossible to solve.

The chief inspector appeared uninterested. "Where was she found?" he asked his subordinate.

"With the trash, in the alley behind the hotel, like the others," answered the officer. He already knew what the chief inspector's answer to this problem was going to be—the same as it had been for the other dozen or so women who had been found tortured and discarded at this same site over the past year.

"She is a prostitute. There is nothing to investigate. Send the body to the landfill with the rest of the trash, and don't come back to me with another of these cases."

CHAPTER 17

Mel was lying by the pool of her Malibu rental house when the call came in. She was still trying to come to grips with Amanda's death four months earlier. Everyone had assured her that after the funeral things would begin to return to normal. That was ridiculous! Her life would never be normal again. Mel had invested everything in Amanda's career, and when Amanda's life ended, so did hers.

It was true that when she moved to New York Amanda had fired Mel as her manager, but Mel was working on that. Before her death Amanda had called her mother nearly every day. It would have been only a matter of time until Amanda realized how much she needed Mel. Mel had secretly planned to move to New York to live with Amanda when their relationship improved. She would persuade Don to buy her an apartment with a view that she and Amanda would share. As soon as she made the right contacts, Mel would arrange for the two of them to have their own reality show.

Mel would finally have her place in the sun. She would be known as the woman behind Amanda Sutton. Amanda would achieve supermodel status—of that Mel was certain—but she did not have Mel's business savvy. Mel would emerge as the true star of the family—a smart, sophisticated businesswoman who knew how to make things happen.

She would remain married to Don for a while—until she got a better offer. She could imagine herself married to one of New York's elite—a true socialite. To have that dream snatched away from her was almost more than Mel could bear. She could not help feel that Amanda was a selfish, ungrateful girl to get herself murdered just when Mel's plan was starting to come together.

Mel had partied the night before and was still dealing with a slight hangover when her PCD rang. She almost didn't answer it, but she was hoping to get a callback on the idea she had floated to a movie executive at the party. Without opening her eyes, she picked up her device and said in her most sensual voice, "Hello."

When she heard the voice on the other end of the line, Mel sat bolt upright. It was Amanda! She had longed for this—to find out that Amanda was not really dead, that the girl they had buried was only an imposter look-alike. Now, she was living out her fantasy, only it was real, "Hi, Mom. It's Amanda…." and the line went dead.

"Amanda! Amanda! Amanda!" Mel screamed into the device, but the only sound that came back to her was the hum of a dial tone. With trembling fingers she punched in Don's number. "Amanda just called me!" she screamed.

"Mel, are you drunk?"

"No! You pig! I'm not drunk!"

Mel blurted out what had just happened and told Don that he needed to do something.

"What? What would have me do? Amanda is dead. We went to her funeral."

"That's what you want me to think, isn't it! That's what everyone wants me to think! But I know better! She called me. You didn't count on that, did you? You always tried to come between us, but it didn't work! She needs me, and she knows it. You had better find my daughter, or you'll be sorry!

"The only thing you care about is your stupid restaurants and your cheap little girlfriends. You think you're a big man, but you're not! You're a loser! You've always been a loser!"

Don sighed, and said, "Tell me again, slowly, what happened."

When the call ended Don called a friend who was a detective in the New Orleans police department and asked him if he could find out who had placed the call to Mel.

Three days later Detective John Breaux called Don with a report. "I ran every call that came in on Mel's device during the twenty-four hours before she called you. Just the usual stuff. The last call that she received before she talked to you was from a call center in India; that's why it was blocked. I talked to the supervisor; it was just a routine sales call for PCD service. I even talked to the guy who made the call. His English isn't very good, and he's hard to understand; maybe that's why Mel freaked.

"I don't really know how to ask this, but is Mel having mental issues? I know that Amanda's death was hard on her, but I've never heard of anyone doing something like this."

"I don't know," Don replied. "Six weeks after the funeral Mel rented a house in Malibu. We haven't talked much. The only time she calls is when she needs something. I thought that getting away from here would help her get herself together, but, apparently, she's not doing so well."

Ψ

During the course of the next four months Mel received five more calls. They were all some variation of that first call:

"Mom, it's Amanda. I'm sorry I left without telling you...."

"Mom, I'm scared. I'm in Dubai and...."

"Mom, don't be mad at me. I want to come home but...."

"Mom, please help me...."

"Mom, I don't know what to do. There's this creepy guy...."

With each call Mel became more hysterical. She could neither eat nor sleep; she was certain that Don had arranged this hideous hoax because he hated her, and he wanted to keep her from Amanda. She was convinced that he was holding Amanda hostage and that Amanda was trying to escape. Detective Breaux investigated the calls each time they came in, but there was always a logical explanation for every call.

A week after the last call came in Don persuaded a judge to have Mel committed to a mental institution. "I really don't want to do this," Don had told the judge, "but if I don't, she's going to end up killing herself."

CHAPTER 18

Walid was stationed outside Fred's hotel, just as he had been every morning for the past several weeks. As Fred stepped through the door into the stifling heat he caught sight of Walid loitering near the entrance, and Fred smiled. He had grown very fond of the boy and had been entertaining the possibility of sponsoring him to go to the United States and attend school there. Walid had no future if he stayed in Dubai. His grandfather did not appear to have any love for or interest in him. Fred thought that if he paid the old man enough, he would be willing to let him go.

Fred had not said anything to Walid about his plan, but this morning he felt that the time was right to broach the subject. After they had walked a few blocks Fred asked, "Do you think you might like to come to America to go to school?"

Walid stopped short. Fred could not tell whether the boy was pleased or offended. For the first time that morning Fred looked at Walid's eyes. The pupils were slightly dilated. Suddenly, Fred thought that the boy was ill.

He looked—odd. "You don't have to," Fred quickly added. "I just thought that you might like to go to school in New York where I live. My son is grown. He moved to Chicago, so his room is empty. My wife and I miss having a boy in the house. We would be very happy for you to stay with us, but if you don't want to it's okay. Just think about it; you don't have to decide right now."

Without a word Walid began running through the crowd, putting as much distance as possible between Fred and him. As he maneuvered through the sea of people he seemed unsteady on his feet. Then just as suddenly as he had begun running he stopped. The explosion threw produce from the vegetable stands high into the air. People were screaming and running; a shower of blood and glass and debris covered everything in the immediate vicinity.

Fred watched in horror and then began running toward the boy. Even in all the turmoil, he could clearly see the suicide vest strapped to Walid's lifeless body.

Fred knew that he should not wait for the police to arrive. He turned down an alley, hailed a cab and went directly to Hadad's office. Hadad was sitting at his desk drinking coffee when Fred arrived.

"Find out what happened," Fred ordered.

"Of course, of course, but these things must be done delicately."

Fred could hardly believe his ears. That line was straight out of an old movie. Surely, Hadad did not believe that he was as gullible as that.

Hadad had extended his hand palm up as if he expected something.

"Yes?" Fred inquired.

"My informants must be paid."

"So far, you've gotten twenty-five hundred dollars from me, and I've gotten zip from you!" Fred exclaimed. "You can put your hand back in your pocket, because unless you come up with something I can use in the next few hours I'm going to find a new informant!"

At 3:00 P.M. Fred's PCD rang. It was the woman from Hadad's office telling him that Hadad wanted to see him immediately.

Hadad's attitude had changed; he was no longer playing the part of the clever schemer. "Sit down," he said. "I have information for you. I believe that you will agree that it is worth far more than the small sum you have paid for my services." Hadad was angry and defensive; his pride had been pricked, but he knew that Fred would continue to pay him well for his services so he chose his words carefully.

"My informants tell me that the boy—Walid—was working for you," Hadad paused.

"Go on."

"Yes, well, the leaders at the mosque have been watching you since your arrival. They instructed one of the boys who plays soccer with him to find out what he was doing for you. Aziz has been following the two of you for the past week. He and Walid were friends so he persuaded Walid to talk about you. He told Aziz that you and he were going to attend a Christian meeting today, and Aziz reported that information back to the head of the cell. Yesterday, when Walid was on his way home they abducted him and told him that he must restore his honor by killing everyone at the meeting. They strapped him into the vest and drugged him to keep him calm. This morning they sent him to your hotel while they watched from a distance. They followed the two of you to make certain that Walid did as he was told. Evidently, he deviated from the plan."

The color had drained from Fred's face. "Is that all?"

"For now."

Fred rose from his chair and walked out into the afternoon sun. The heat shimmered off the pavement and washed over him like a hot blue wave. It was 3:45; the meeting would begin at 4:00. Fred felt that he had to talk to someone. He needed to be with other Christians who would help him make sense of what seemed to him to be senseless.

He hurried down the street toward the building that housed Yeshua Ministries. He wanted to talk to Fatema and

Saeed. He knew that they would be preparing for the meeting, but he had to talk first.

He arrived too late. When Fred entered the small room that served as the chapel for Yeshua Ministries, Saeed had just finished introducing their guest speaker, and Pastor Soodmand was telling the sixty people who were tightly-packed into the small hot room that he was privileged to be able to share his testimony with them.

Fred found a spot near the wall and stood with his back against the rough plaster. "I am here today," Pastor Soodmand said, "to tell you about the one who is the King of Kings and the Lord of Lords. He is the beginning and the ending. He created all that there is, and then he came to earth to die as a sacrifice for all who will come to him so that we can live forever. His name is Jesus Christ, the Son of God, but the Bible gives him other names too. He is *El-Shaddai*—the all sufficient one; He is *Jehovah-Jireh*—the Lord who provides; He is *Jehovah-Rophe*—the Lord who heals; He is *Jehovah-Shammah*—the Lord who is there; He is *Immanuel*—the God who is with us.

"My story begins thirty-eight years ago on my eleventh birthday. I was playing with my friends near a military checkpoint where some American soldiers were working. It was a happy day for me because my father had given me a new soccer ball, and my friends and I were showing off for the soldiers hoping that they would give us some candy, as they often did. The last thing I remember about that day is seeing a young soldier turn to watch. He smiled, and I believed that he was going to give us a treat. Then everything went black.

"I did not regain consciousness for several days, but when I opened my eyes, my father told me that a bomb had exploded in a car waiting in line at the checkpoint. A soldier had taken us to the military hospital and the Americans had given me much care that saved my life. I did not understand this because although I knew that the soldiers were good to the children, I also knew that many of my people considered them to be our enemies. Why would the American doctors work to make their enemy live?

"The next day a man came to the side of my bed. He was the same one who had smiled at me when the bomb exploded. I asked him did he take me to the hospital, and he said, 'Yes'. He reached in his pocket and pulled out a Snickers bar and gave it to me. I was so happy to see that Snickers that I forgot about everything else. While I ate, the soldier told me that Jesus had saved my life. I did not know about Christianity, so I thought his name was 'Jesus'. The next day when he came to see me, I said, 'Hi, Jesus.' Then he said, 'No, no, I am not Jesus, I am Fred.' I was thinking that this soldier was very strange.

"Every day Fred would visit me at the hospital and tell me about Jesus. He told me Jesus loved me and had saved my life. He told me that Jesus died for me. This was strange to me because in Islam the best thing anyone can do is strap on a suicide vest and give his life so that others will die. But in Christianity the best thing anyone can do is give his life so that others can live. I wondered, 'Why would anyone die to save another?'

"One day Fred came to the hospital and told me that he was going home. I was sorry because of the Snickers; I knew that I would not get any more. But I also did not want Fred to leave me. I liked to hear about Jesus, but when Fred was gone no one else at the hospital ever mentioned Jesus to me.

"I was in the hospital for many days, but finally I was well enough to go home. Eventually, I recovered completely, but I never forgot the things that Fred had told me about Jesus. It was Fred that opened the way for me to become a Christian years later when I was twenty-five years old."

Fred's head was spinning, and with his back against the wall, he slid down so that he was sitting on the floor. His mind was racing, and he did not hear how Omar became a Christian. When he was able to focus again, he heard Omar saying, "People say to me, 'You were a Muslim from your birth, and you have become a Christian.' But I tell them, 'No! That is not correct. My family was Muslim, but they did not know that Christ had already chosen them to be Christians. He chose us from before the foundations of the earth. Jesus said that we did not choose Him; He chose us! He made His plan before the creation of the universe. When I understood this, I said, 'I am a Christian!' and I believed in the Lord Jesus Christ.'"

Pastor Soodmand spoke for a long time, but Fred was so overcome with the grief of Walid's suicide and the awe of having found Omar after so many years that he heard little of what the pastor said. When the service ended, Fred waited until the congregants had left before he approached Omar.

Extending his hand, he said simply, "Omar, I'm Fred."

Omar knew at once that something was deeply troubling Fred, and after the two men had embraced and exchanged greetings he led him to one of the folding chairs and told him to sit. When Omar was seated across from him, he asked, "What is wrong, my friend?"

Fred told Omar that he was in Dubai on business and that on his first day there he had reminded God that he would surely like to know what had happened to Omar. "You can't begin to imagine how significant it is that God would bring us together tonight," Fred said. He fell silent for a moment, but Omar waited for him to continue.

"Did you hear about the suicide bomber this morning?" Fred inquired.

"Of course, everyone is talking about it, but it is very strange. Did you see it happen?"

"Yes, I saw it; I caused it."

Omar searched Fred's face before he spoke, "Tell me about it."

Fred spent the next hour telling Omar about Walid—about how they met, about his grandfather, about his affection for the boy, and about his offer to have Walid come to New York to live with Annie and him. "I told him about Jesus every time we were together," he said. "I really thought I was reaching him. He listened and even asked questions, but today he was prepared to kill me and everyone at tonight's meeting."

"Did you teach him the Bible?"

"Yes. From the first day I began to teach him about Jesus' love for him. I didn't know how much time I might have so I started with the Gospel of John. We finished chapter 15 last night."

Omar was nodding his head. "I am not surprised. When I was a boy, you persuaded me that Jesus loved me."

"Well," Fred responded, "apparently I wasn't as successful with Walid."

"You don't understand," Omar responded. "The moment they strapped that vest on Walid he was already a dead man. He knew that. His only decision was how he was going to die.

A bomber always kills as many infidels as possible. That is why he was told to come to the meeting tonight to detonate the bomb. Instead, he ran away from you and away from the crowd in the street—straight to the vegetable carts. Because of the time of day, people were not gathered around the carts. There was much property damage, but only Walid died. If he had not made that choice you and every person in this church would now be dead.

"Tonight I said that in Islam the best thing anyone can do is strap on a suicide vest and give his life so that others will die, but in Christianity the best thing anyone can do is give his life so that others can live. Walid chose chapter 15."

"What?" Fred looked genuinely confused.

"Last night you taught Walid about the love of Jesus Christ. John 15:13 says, 'I demand that you love each other as much as I love you. And here is how to measure it—the greatest love is shown when a person lays down his life for his friends.'"

"Don't you understand? Walid got it. I have been a pastor since I was a young man, and sometimes I work with people for years who never get it. But Walid heard the word and believed it. He did not commit suicide, he laid down his life for love of you and for love of Jesus—his friends."

CHAPTER 19

Fred spent the next week tracking down information on Josef Helmick and relaying it back to the Sinclairs. A lifetime spent in the NYPD had taught him the value of well-placed informants. Their information was not always reliable, and they could never be trusted, but paid informants were an endless source of bits of information that could not be obtained through any other means.

Based on this principle, Fred had chosen the Burj Khalifa for his Dubai stay. He had been careful to give Ambassador Wainwright little information, and, to his surprise, Wainwright had asked him few questions. Fred was certain that Wainwright had given him Hadad's number because Hadad was a low-level informant who might provide Fred with some useful information but would not have access to anything that might prove embarrassing to the United States government. Thus, by working through Hadad, Fred had ensured that Wainwright would have virtually no interest in his activities.

Although Fred was working through Hadad, he was not relying on Hadad, and he had immediately begun to set up a network of informants. When he checked into the Burj Khalifa, the concierge had insisted on showing Fred to his room personally. Fred knew that Rashid thought that, as an American, he would be willing to pay outrageous prices for anything he might require, and he wanted to be first in line for any money that might exchange hands.

When Rashid had placed Fred's bags in his room, he had smiled eagerly and said, "If there is *anything* you wish to have, let me know. I am a purveyor of delights who can fulfill your darkest desires."

Fred had returned his smile and replied, "What I desire is information."

Rashid had looked uncomfortable, "The Burj Khalifa ensures our guests utmost privacy. I am limited in the type of information that I can provide, but if you desire girls, or young men, or drugs that will take you to heights that you never knew existed, I can fulfill your every fantasy. Our sources of entertainment are without equal."

"I desire information about Josef Helmick who occupies the penthouse apartment of your residential tower."

"Ah," Rashid was visibly nervous, "Herr Helmick is a very private person. No one can provide you with such information."

"And, yet," Fred replied, "something tells me that you can provide me with a great deal of information about Herr Helmick," and as he spoke he pressed a one-thousand dollar bill into Rashid's palm.

When Rashid looked at the bill, his hands began to tremble, and Fred knew that he would prove to be an endless source of information. He also knew that a great deal of that information would be unreliable, but Fred was certain that when the time was right, Rashid would give him something that would prove to be very valuable.

Ψ

Since his arrival, Fred had been working twelve-hour days, but as tired as he was, each night when he crawled into the bed in his luxury suite at the Burj Khalifa, he was unable to sleep. Every time he shut his eyes the image of Walid running through the crowd and then being thrown into the air by the force of the bomb was replayed. The guilt Fred felt was overwhelming. If only he had not talked to Walid that day at Hadad's office. If only he had not offered him a job as his interpreter. If only he had not told him that they were going to a home church that evening. If only…, if only…, if only….Fred was ensnared in an immense web of regrets from which he was certain he would never escape.

It was Wednesday, and Fred had decided to quit work early so that he could attend the weekly meeting at Yeshua Ministries. He was hoping that Omar might be there so that he could unburden himself to him. When he arrived, however, Fred discovered that Omar and Saeed had left that morning on a mission's trip and would be gone for ten days. A pastor Fred did not know led the service, and although it was a good service, Fred was unable to concentrate. When the pastor had finished the closing prayer, Fred walked across the room to ask Fatema if he could talk to her after everyone was gone.

Now the two of them sat in the small dingy offices while Fatema waited for Fred to speak. After a long pause, he looked up and smiled a very faint smile. "I feel so guilty," he began, and when he spoke those words it was as if a floodgate had opened. His chest heaved and great racking sobs took control of him. Fred was embarrassed, but he could not control himself. His sobs grew louder until he feared that people on the street would hear him, but Fatema sat quietly and looked as composed as if this were an everyday occurrence.

When Fred was finally able to quiet his sobs, Fatema spoke, "Why is your heart so troubled?"

"Walid. It's my fault that he's dead. "

"Did you kill him? I thought that the leaders of the mosque strapped him into the vest."

Fred felt himself growing irritated. "Of course, they did. But it's my fault that they strapped him into the vest in the first place."

"How is that so?" Fatema pressed.

"If I had not befriended him and witnessed to him, he would never have made plans to come to this church. And he would not have died."

"So," Fatema continued. "If you had never told Walid about Jesus, he would still be alive. He would play street soccer with his friends from the mosque, and he would grow up. Then one day he would strap on a suicide vest all by himself and willingly blow up as many people as possible; because, Fred, that is what street boys with no families do. They allow themselves to be recruited by the mosque leaders, and they kill themselves and as many others as possible while shouting 'Allahu Akbar!' This is what you wanted, yes?"

"No!" Fred snapped. "Don't twist my words. I wanted Walid to have a good life. I wanted to take him to New York to live with my wife and me. I wanted him to go to college, and get married, and have a family."

"Oh, I am sorry," Fatema responded. "I did not understand that you know more than Jesus. Your plan was better than His. He was probably busy watching someone else when Walid died."

Fred was so angry that he would have liked to slap Fatema, but he clenched his teeth and said nothing.

"Fred, do you believe that Jesus died for Walid? But I know that you do. The Bible says that God wants everyone to be saved. Walid was like the hearer in the parable of the sower; he heard the Word and he believed it, but only Jesus knows what the outcome would have been if he had lived. Perhaps, Walid would have been like the seed that fell beside the path and was eaten by the birds; perhaps, he would have been like the seed that fell on rocky soil or that which fell among the thorns. He would have believed for a little while, but when persecution came, he would have fallen away. We will never know, because Jesus took him quickly. But this we do know: Walid is safe with Jesus, and nothing can change that.

"You are mourning Walid's salvation and entrance into heaven. Stop it!"

Fred was stunned. He had expected Fatema to be sympathetic—perhaps to cry with him. He had not expected to be lectured. He thought that after today he would never speak to this heartless woman again.

Fatema continued, "When Maryam died, I felt so guilty. She was the one with the pure heart. She was the one with the strong faith. She was the one who forgave her captors. She was the one who gave me the courage to survive our ordeal. I could never be the strong woman that Maryam was. She was love in the midst of hate; she was light in the darkness of our prison; she was what I wanted to be but knew that I would never be able to achieve. Even so, God took Maryam and left me. God also took Walid and left you.

"Have you thought that, maybe, He took them because He knew they were ready? Maybe God looked down and saw that they had completed their work, and so

He took them away from the sickness and pain and sorrow that is this world.

"Maybe he left you and me because we still have more to do here. Only He knows."

Silently, Fred rose from his chair and walked out into the darkness. His anger had passed. For the first time since Walid's death, he felt deeply peaceful. That night, almost as soon as his head hit the pillow, he was asleep.

CHAPTER 20

Heinz Felhaber was watching the vast expanse of desert beneath him as Helmick I coasted to a landing on the private airstrip outside Dubai. He stared with curiosity at this strange barren land; when he had left his lab in the scenic Swiss Alps that morning he had seen expansive forests and mountains disappear far beneath him. Now, he might think he was landing on another planet if he did not know otherwise.

Heinz was a plain man—unimpressive in every sense of the word. He was of average height and had average non-descript thinning hair which had once been light brown but was now so salted with gray that the exact color would be difficult to describe. His small pale eyes, heavily-lined by age, were hard to detect beneath his thick black-rimmed glasses. His weight was average for his age—he was pudgy and out of shape but not fat. In short, there was nothing about Heinz Felhaber that would make anyone look twice.

In spite of his ordinary outward appearance, however, Heinz was, in fact, a very special individual. First, he was one of the only individuals in the Helmick Empire who was organic—Josef's term for men and women who had been conceived and born through natural means rather than artificial cloning. This accounted, in part, for his plainness—Josef liked for the men and women around him to be beautiful, so he frequently fixed any imperfections he found in his clones, and he periodically exterminated and remade them so that they were always the perfect age and perfect weight, with good complexions free of wrinkles and age spots and clear bright eyes with no bags or sagging—in other words, they generally had the "right" appearance to represent Helmick. In Heinz's case, there was no fixing anything—the man was, as he liked to boast, exactly as "God" had made him. Of course, he did not believe in God, but he knew the reference annoyed Josef. In fact, being organic made Heinz feel special in a world of perfect, beautiful clones, and when he looked in the mirror and saw his own plain visage staring back at him, he felt empowered.

The second quality that made Heinz truly special was his mind. As a young scientist, Felhaber had developed extraordinary breakthroughs in chemistry. More than any other living person, he understood the power of narcotics to enhance the human experience, not just for pleasure but for mind control. Heinz understood that "better living through chemistry" was not merely an advertising slogan—chemistry was the means to remake the world into utopia.

In his post graduate school days he had worked for major pharmaceutical companies, and for a time he had enjoyed a very promising career. Increased scrutiny of narcotics and mind control in the 2020s had forced him out of his job and onto the Genetic Crimes Enforcement Network (GenCEN) watch list. No one on that list was employable by any major company. Fortunately, at the lowest point in his life, when he was in a state of true despair, a far-thinking innovator named Josef Helmick had visited him in Berlin and hired him to be the chief chemist for Helmick Laboratories.

Officially, Heinz's name appeared nowhere—officially Heinz Felhaber was buried in a cemetery in Berlin after having died in an explosion in a homemade lab in the basement of the rundown apartment building where he had lived after being relieved of his previous position. Of course, officially Helmick Laboratories did not exist either. Unofficially, Felhaber was the mind behind most of Helmick's genius. He lived in luxury in a six-bedroom guest cottage on Josef Helmick's Swiss estate; he went to work every morning in a car driven by one of Josef's staff, and he enjoyed the companionship of his choice of the exquisite copies—the left-over clones from the beautiful women he produced for Josef to sell to wealthy men worldwide. Life was better than he had ever imagined—except for one thing. In spite of the fire and official story of his death, Heinz had remained on the watch list. Jarrod and Joshua Sinclair were a major source of funding for GenCEN, and they had never confirmed to their satisfaction that he had actually died in the fire. Because they suspected he was alive, they kept his genetic information and insisted that he remain on the watch list as "possibly living." This fact, combined with Josef's general paranoia about the possibility that his existence would be discovered, made it impossible for Felhaber to see the world. His universe was confined to the Helmick estate where he lived and worked. Every few months he flew on Helmick I to this private airstrip in Dubai, and there he met with Josef on the jet, but he was never allowed to disembark. Therefore, although he had traveled this route dozens of times, his feet had never actually touched the ground in Dubai.

The door of the jet opened and blinding light flooded the aircraft. Heinz stood but did not move toward the door. He had made the mistake of doing that once, and he had never forgotten the blinding rage he had seen unmasked on the face of his employer. Josef had beaten Heinz back from the door with his fist, breaking the scientist's glasses, bloodying his nose and blackening his eyes, until he collapsed in a heap. When Helmick began kicking him, Felhaber feared that his explosive new master might actually kill him, but, fortunately, Josef regained his composure and allowed the scientist to crawl to a corner before any real damage was done. There he had remained, curled up in a ball, until Josef reviewed his reports and exited the aircraft. From that time on, when the jet landed, Heinz rose and stood by his seat waiting for his employer to enter.

Now he stood in front of his seat in a slouchy form of attention as air so hot it seemed to come from a blast furnace flooded the cabin. Felhaber waited for a long time—twenty minutes—and still Josef did not appear. He knew better than to approach the door; he had observed that after a "lesson" such as the one that Josef had administered to him, Helmick would often "test" the subjects by setting up another situation to see if they would repeat the behavior that had warranted the initial punishment. In the cases of the "enhanced" employees—his clones—these tests normally resulted in death. In the cases of the organics, by the time their master had finished with them, they often wished they were dead.

Thirty-five minutes passed before a strong figure darkened the door of the jet. Josef sauntered casually toward Heinz, but his sardonic smile seemed to confirm what Heinz had quietly suspected—he had made him wait so long in the hope of finding another excuse to beat him. No matter—it was not for no reason that Felhaber was widely considered one of the greatest minds of the twenty-first century; Josef could direct his cruel tricks and traps at some of the many lesser intellects he employed.

"Herr Doctor," Heinz greeted Josef with more enthusiasm than he felt.

"Heinz, so good of you to wait for me," Josef responded. "Welcome to Dubai." His expression and tone grew serious, as if he were just now remembering why they were there. "Show me what you have for me."

From a sealed case, Heinz produced the reason for today's trip—a small black vial of liquid.

"This is the second generation of Labyrinth," he proudly displayed his handiwork and then carefully handed it to Josef.

"The properties?" Josef questioned his chemist as he carefully handled the small black glass bottle.

"The first generation—level you might say—of Labyrinth enhances and stimulates the memory sectors of the brain. Our studies in enhanced subjects demonstrate that implanted memory sectors grow much faster with the drug than without. Memories become more vibrant and vivid. Sounds, sights, smells and impulses are recalled with a level of intensity that would not be possible without the drug. The first generation of Labyrinth also made those taking it very susceptible to suggestion; because the drug stimulates the sensory perception areas of the brain, the subject loses track of time and of any connection with reality. As desires and impulses become magnified, and as inhibitions disappear, the subject can be told he is looking into the future when he is actually only viewing his own desires and fantasies magnified by memories. Labyrinth blocks and confuses the way the brain tracks time and perceives reality, thus, giving the impression that the recipient is traveling through time. When we conducted our studies, the enhanced subjects believed that they had traveled back and forth through time and that they were able to look into both the past and the future with equal clarity. In reality, they were experiencing highly-elevated levels of memory and desire. Afterwards, when asked to relate their experiences, they used such descriptors as 'trance' or 'hypnosis.' How did your own experiment go?"

"My experiment was conducted using Labyrinth on an unsuspecting group of organic subjects and one enhanced subject," Josef continued on without explaining where or how his experiment had been conducted. "Interestingly, the enhanced subject did not experience any notable results as she had been previously treated with Labyrinth to grow the memory sectors in her brain. However, in the organics, Labyrinth worked perfectly—most of my subjects became convinced that they had experienced some level of trance which led to time travel. Many of them believe that they were able to look into their own futures. After the first experiment I received hundreds of unofficial requests from organics who wanted to recall the past or see the future; this has led to many opportunities for unofficial experiments. With the exception of one or two who experienced some negative psychotic episodes, the drug works uniformly in most of the test subjects. But the environment must be carefully controlled."

"And the crystals? Did the prisms provide a suitable focal point to anchor the subjects' attention?"

"Suitable for such a small test group. Of course, we had to control the lighting, the noise—basically every stimuli in the room. The prisms worked because the subjects could hold them and touch them. As they did so, they became individually convinced that their new sensory experiences were emanating from the crystals so their minds accepted what was happening and did not try to resist. In a small gathering, the prisms were ideal, but for use in a larger setting they are impractical. Also I have perceived that the level of mind control is very limited—other than enhancing memories and suggesting possible future outcomes, Labyrinth did not produce much response from its 'victims'."

"Yes, Herr Doctor, but as I told you before, this was just the first generation. The second generation—Level Two—is capable of producing more profound reactions," Heinz answered proudly. "Level One must be ingested. To be able to deliver the drug to a subject without his knowledge required that he ingest food or liquid containing it. One reason the original formula took so long to develop is that we had to find a pharmaceutical that would mix with alcohol so that it would be undetectable in the blood stream of the individual consuming it. Additionally, the drug had to have a chemical structure that would not negatively interact with the alcohol, thereby causing the death of the subjects and calling attention to the experiment. Still, the very fact that the drug had to be ingested caused it to act more slowly and wear off more quickly. It made it harder to control."

"Level Two does not require ingestion—it is absorbed directly through the skin into the blood stream. Just one drop applied to a surface is enough to cause immediate results."

"How long does it remain potent on the surface of its delivery method?" Josef was staring into the glass bottle. He had noticed the heavy glass on the small vial when he picked it up—now he understood why such a thick bottle was needed.

Heinz noted his interest, "We have not only used double-reinforced glass, but we have painted the bottle with a thin coat of lead. This will keep Labyrinth from permeating its container. In answer to your question, the length of time that the drug remains potent when applied to a surface depends on the medium of delivery. On a hard, non-porous surface, such as metal, one application might affect only the first person who touches the object. Trace amounts might have a slight effect on the next person to handle the object, but most of the drug will have passed to the first user. In a porous substance, such as paper or cloth, the uses could be almost infinite until the item is washed with water or chemicals."

"What if Labyrinth could be applied to a medium at the time of manufacture? For example, if it were applied to treated paper—how long would the drug continue to affect someone touching it? How long would it remain potent?"

"Indefinitely. Labyrinth does not break down—ever. If the medium were treated at the time of manufacture so that the drug became an intrinsic part of the paper or cloth in question, it would forever affect anyone touching that substance."

"Perfect," Josef responded. "And the other properties? The widespread success of this drug cannot depend on a controlled environment. Have you corrected these design flaws?"

"Level Two does not require a controlled environment. Unlike Level One, Level Two does not enhance memory—it suppresses memories and emotions as well as inhibitions."

"The same drug?" Josef looked skeptical.

"Indeed, Herr Doctor. Remember that we initially created Labyrinth to grow the memory sectors of the clones so that they could retain the memories of their sires. It was only after we began to experiment with the effects of this memory drug that we saw its other properties—how susceptible it made subjects to all suggestion. A worthwhile tool for mind control on a major scale, however, should not produce intense memory—it should produce forgetfulness."

"And this drug can do that?"

"It can. The human mind is like a labyrinth—as we travel more and more deeply into it, we unlock new doors which hold the key to who we are. Level One worked on the surface of memory—helping subjects recollect details from the past with which they had some strong emotional response. Level Two will blur and fade those emotional responses—it not only fades the memory itself but the emotions and feelings of the subject. As it works it erodes the cortexes of the brain that store the human capacity to love, to hate, to desire, to envy, to trust and to protect. In other words, Level Two kills the emotions that contribute to what we call 'humanity'. As these emotions are faded, the memories and values connected to them also fade and disappear. As the capacity to love disappears, so do family ties, memories of a happy childhood, longings for a spouse, and so on. Patriotism, religious fervor, values and teachings of youth can all be diluted until they no longer have any genuine effect on the subject."

"Fascinating. Good work, Heinz," Josef was still staring at the vial he held, but he sounded genuinely impressed. Heinz felt very proud.

"And Level Three?" Josef queried. "When will it be ready?"

"We are still experimenting with the formula. Level Three will require a variety of extensive tests, on both organic and enhanced subjects. To ensure that it is working properly, we require a ratio of at least three to one organics versus enhanced. Because the enhanced subjects have already been treated with other versions of Labyrinth, without a wide variety of organic test subjects it is impossible to fully determine the true extent to which the new drug is working."

"You will have your subjects when you are ready for them," Josef replied coolly, "And you can conduct as many experiments as you require for as long as you need. I have already secured an unlimited supply. You are quite certain that when Level Three is complete you can replace organic memories entirely?"

"Quite certain," responded Heinz, "We will be able to use the drug to completely subvert the memories of an organic. We can convince the president of the largest bank in America that he has lived his entire life as a pig farmer in Nairobi—or vice versa."

"How long?"

"A year to a year a half if I can conduct unlimited experiments. Any organics will do in the initial stages of testing, but as I progress I will require organics from all walks of life—from transients to business executives and street prostitutes to faithful church-goers. I need to test the effects on people of varied socio-economic, political and religious backgrounds so that I can be certain the drug is effective in 'erasing' everyone."

"Whatever you need, you will have. Just let me know how many and from what background, and I will have them delivered to the laboratory. You can even specify hair and eye color if you like." Josef was self-satisfied and smug, as usual. Heinz was excited, but even he shuddered inwardly at the realization that everything Josef said was true; he actually could deliver men and women from all walks of life to be unwilling human guinea pigs for Heinz's experiments. That was part of what made working for Helmick an exciting experience, and it was also what made it an unnerving one.

"One final caution, Herr Doctor, Level Two still requires a 'talisman' if you will—some object on which the organic can fix his attention. It is not necessary to control the outward environment the way we did with Level One, but a visual stimulus is required, and, of course, we must have a delivery medium that a wide variety of people will want to touch to bring them into contact with it."

Josef smiled broadly and looked directly at Heinz. "The delivery system is already in place, as is the visual stimulus. You get Level Three ready; I have everything else well in hand."

Without another word, Josef rose and strode from the jet. Heinz, who had remained standing during the meeting, returned to his seat and fastened himself in as the jet began to roll down the runway.

CHAPTER 21

Fred had called Joshua Sinclair on the secure line that GenTECH had provided for all voice communications, and Joshua had immediately put him on speaker so that Jarrod could hear Fred's end of the conversation.

"I have it from a very reliable source that five or six times a year a jet lands at a private Dubai airstrip, and Josef Helmick boards the plane. He remains on board for a period of time between thirty minutes and several hours and then disembarks and drives away. No one else ever leaves the jet, and it never takes off with Helmick on board.

"No flight plans are filed in Dubai, but I was able to find flight plans filed in Switzerland that appear to line up with the Dubai visits. They are filed under the name Lutz Von Hess, which I believe is one of Josef's many aliases—I have been able to verify that he uses at least a dozen.

"I have an informant at the airstrip who will notify me immediately the next time the jet lands. If we get lucky, I might be able to catch Helmick in the act."

"What act would that be?" Jarrod inquired.

"The act of holding some sort of secret meeting on the plane. It would probably guarantee him at least thirty seconds in jail," Fred said with a laugh. "I'm just trying to verify that he's holding these meetings, because, if he is, they're probably tied to his cloning operation in Switzerland."

"I found out something else that I think will be of interest to you," Fred continued. "Rashid, the concierge, told me that a few weeks ago the Club of Rome held their annual meeting in a private dining room of the Burj Khalifa, and Josef Helmick was inducted as their new secretary-general. He swears that he oversaw the food service personally and was constantly in the dining room until all non-members were required to leave before the speeches began. Interestingly, Rashid tells me that Josef's date that night was a beautiful young American whom he called 'Amanda.'

"I went onto the Club of Rome's website and discovered that they did hold their annual meeting last month and that they inducted their new secretary-general, Lutz Von Hess. There is no mention of Josef Helmick anywhere on the website, but I am convinced that Josef Helmick, a.k.a. Lutz Von Hess, is the new secretary-general for the Club of Rome.

"By the way," Fred added, "did the DNA on the blood sample I sent you from the girl who was found in the dumpster behind the Burj Khalifa come back?"

“Yes, we got it Tuesday morning,” Joshua responded. “She was an exact match for Amanda Sutton. We know for sure that she was a clone. The problem, of course, is that we can’t prove that Helmick was the one who cloned her.”

“We may not be able to prove it,” Fred interjected, “but we know it’s true. When the kitchen boy here told me about the body in the dumpster, I could hardly believe it. The officer on duty, apparently, made a call and then told Paolo to never call the police again because of anything he found in the dumpsters. If the kid hadn’t stolen the ring the victim was wearing, we wouldn’t have had any DNA. He was afraid if he tried to fence it he would get caught. Muslim law would have required that his hand be cut off, and he didn’t want to risk that. When I began asking questions, he saw his opportunity to sell it to me risk-free. He thought the ring was real, but it was just costume jewelry. I didn’t tell him that, though. I paid him a couple of thousand for it explaining that fenced jewelry always sells at a discount. Send me a picture of Amanda Sutton—I want to show it around to the staff and see if they can identify her as Josef’s date.”

“Fred,” Jarrod interrupted. “I think it’s time for you to come home.”

“What?” Fred was stunned. “Is there a problem?”

“No problem; we’re more than satisfied. We never dreamed that you would be able to find out so much in such a short time. You’ve surpassed all our expectations. But this is getting dangerous. Someone very powerful is protecting Helmick, and it's just a matter of time until they come after you."

"Someone a whole lot more powerful is protecting me," Fred responded, "and it's just a matter of time until He calls Helmick to give an accounting to Him. I'm not afraid, and unless you don't want me working for you anymore, I'm staying and seeing this through to the end."

Jarrod and Joshua looked at each other, and then Joshua nodded. "Okay," Jarrod said into the speaker, "but whatever else you do, be careful."

CHAPTER 22

Josef's driver pulled up to the Dubai Marina where a small speed boat awaited. Josef boarded the boat, and it sped through the waterway toward Nikolai Sokol's waiting yacht where lunch had been prepared by Francesco Corteloni, the world's most renowned chef.

Josef had known Nikolai since childhood. Karl had introduced them during Josef's first trip to Europe when he was thirteen. The senior Helmick was cloning racehorses for Sokol Farms at the time, and also, as Josef recalled, young boys for Sokol's personal enjoyment. Josef had been surprised at how genuinely alike Karl and Nikolai were; they both had the same contempt for existing society, the same passion for a New World Order, and the same callous disregard for humanity. In spite of these similarities, or perhaps because of them, the two men were never friends. Where Karl loved science and believed that it held the key to righting all the wrongs of an imperfect world, Nikolai loved money. Karl sneered privately to Josef that money was the only mistress that Nikolai could ever give himself to completely, and in a sense that was true. Unlike most men, he did not merely long to possess or use money; Nikolai was obsessed with gaining control over all money—everywhere. He was said to understand monetary policy and currency better than any other living person, and he had used his knowledge of the workings of money to make himself one of the five wealthiest men in the world.

Sokol's past was even more mysterious than Karl Helmick's. Little was known about him that could be verified. His official biography stated that he was born in Czechoslovakia in 1951 and was a youth of seventeen when the Soviet Army invaded the country in 1968 to quash a reform movement that was just beginning to sweep the nation. The invasion was Nikolai's moment of opportunity; he was an unimpressive youth from an unimpressive family—his own father was said to have been part of the reform movement. The younger Sokol, however, was ambitious, and as a young man in a community longing for freedom, he immediately distinguished himself to his country's new occupiers as an eager informant. Six months after the occupation, Sokol's father was hanged and his mother and five siblings, including a little sister of three, were sent to a Soviet re-education camp where all of them died. In his later years, Sokol's many opponents accused him of betraying his own family and sending them to their deaths—an allegation he never denied. When questioned during a television interview about his activities in Czechoslovakia during the Soviet occupation, he responded only that he learned at an early age that survival is the only true morality.

What was certain was that in 1971, when he was twenty years old, the Soviet-controlled government gave him a special pass to go to Moscow for a year, and in 1972 he was allowed to emigrate to London to study finance and economics. From that moment, every door was open to Nikolai. After graduation, he went to work for an investment firm where he met prominent men from all over the world. He was inducted into the Club of Rome on his thirtieth birthday, and shortly afterward he moved to New York City where he started a hedge fund that invested heavily in U.S. real estate. As his wealth and prominence increased, he became a king maker of sorts—betting against international currencies and making himself ever richer in the process. He invested heavily in politics, land, gold, and ideas—his think tanks produced the men and women who set policy for presidents, monarchs, industrialists and bankers worldwide.

Nikolai was the first person to reach out to Josef after the explosion at Doppelganger. Josef was never certain how Nikolai knew where to find him; he was in Brazil partying in a club after having visited the estate of Arturo de Silva when a beautiful blonde girl of about eighteen approached him and asked him to dance.

At Doppelganger Josef had been denied all female companionship, and for the past few months he had made up for his former austere life by indulging himself with the most beautiful women he could find—acting out all of his fantasies. After several weeks Josef had believed that he had found the one thing that had been missing from his life. He had convinced himself that all he needed to do was find a constant supply of beautiful young women, and he would be entertained forever.

The moment Josef reached out and took this girl's hand, however, everything changed. She was intoxicating. Her voice, her perfume, the softness of her skin seemed to fill his senses. They danced, and then he took her to his hotel suite to spend the night. Josef felt as if he were moving inside the perfect dream, and he could not allow it to end—ever. As the night wore on he realized that the only possible conclusion to such a perfect union was for him to kill her, very slowly and very painfully.

It was Josef's first Pleasure Kill. He had watched many of the boys at Doppelganger die, and when he was older he had been the chief executioner of those who proved to be defective. But that was different. It was business. Defective clones were eliminated and disposed of in the crematorium. The kills were quick and clean. A Pleasure Kill was different; it must be made to last as long as possible. The pain must be intense. Josef knew this instinctively, but it was his first Pleasure Kill, and he was clumsy. The girl died after only two hours. Yet, it was a beginning. He knew that he could clone her and experiment with her until he had perfected his craft. Then he would dispose of her DNA and find another suitable subject. Immediately, he collected the necessary samples.

As Josef was leaving his hotel room the next morning, he had opened her purse and found a note handwritten on a piece of exquisite cream-colored stationery with the initials "NS" in an intricate scroll at the top. The note read simply, "Allow me to express my condolences to you for your loss, Josef. Maya is the first of many gifts that I can provide for you; have lunch with me on my yacht this noon."

At twenty-one years of age, Josef was himself a billionaire, and under other circumstances he would have sent back a note responding that there was nothing that Sokol could give him that he could not obtain for himself. But he had slaughtered Sokol's gift, and he weighed his options. If Sokol came after him, there would be nowhere to hide. He would meet Sokol on his yacht and call his bluff. If Sokol reacted badly, he would deal with that situation to the best of his ability.

When Josef had boarded the yacht, Sokol was waiting for him on deck. He extended his hand and asked, "Did you enjoy Maya?"

Without hesitation, Josef had responded, "I enjoyed her very much. She's dead. Is that a problem?"

Sokol's face betrayed no emotion. He shrugged slightly and replied, "For her, yes; not for me. I anticipated that something like that might happen so I chose the girl carefully. She will not be missed."

"Who was she?" Josef inquired.

Sokol looked directly into Josef's eyes and replied, "She was my granddaughter."

Josef had always been glad he had accepted the invitation; Sokol had influence, connections and power, and he had opened up a world to him that he would have never been able to access on his own. After twenty years, two or three times a year Josef still received a handwritten note on the same distinctive stationery reading simply, "Have lunch with me on my yacht this noon."

Sokol had just celebrated his ninetieth birthday and rarely appeared in public. Josef had offered many times to "rejuvenate" him, but Sokol always refused, saying that he preferred to finish his life as he had lived it. Josef suspected that the real reason for the refusal was that Sokol feared Josef might be planning to replace him with an enhanced version of himself who would answer only to him. That was actually true, but what Sokol did not know was that in spite of all his precautions, Josef had systematically collected all of the genetic material he needed in order to make a perfect copy, and now with the improvements to Labyrinth he could make this copy obey him completely. His frequent lunches with Sokol provided a unique opportunity for Josef to dispose of the organic Nikolai and replace him with the enhanced one. Only one thing prevented him from doing so—Nikolai was in the process of executing a plan to usher in the New World Order, and Josef did not yet have all of the pieces of that plan. Nikolai was careful to tell Josef only what he needed to know at the moment, and even with all of his spies, including his many paid informants in various government-surveillance agencies worldwide, Josef had never been able to discover exactly what Nikolai was planning to do or how. He needed the old man's blueprint as well as his connections in order to make Sokol's vision a reality. Therefore, Josef waited patiently, having lunch with the old man whenever summoned, closely watching him through a network of spies, and biding his time until enough pieces were in place so that he no longer needed his mentor. When that time came, he would personally end Nikolai's existence.

Josef was all smiles when he boarded the yacht. Nikolai was seated at a table on the deck enjoying a glass of champagne. His excessive weight, combined with his advanced age, made it difficult for him to move, so as Josef approached, the old man remained seated and merely waved a greeting.

"Welcome. You have been busy, Herr Doctor. I heard about the magic show you performed for the Club. The entire group has talked of little else. It seems you made quite an impression."

"I always make an impression," Josef smiled smugly, "but the demonstration was less magic and more science. You should have been there to see for yourself—they stared into those crystals as if they had actually journeyed through a time warp. You would have been thoroughly amused."

"Ah, but I did see it. Like God, I see everything, while I remain unseen, behind the veil, as it were. I watched the entire evening as it happened. I was very impressed. So you are now confident of your drug? You are sure of what it can do?"

"Quite sure. My chemist has just finished perfecting the second level and is now working on the third. Using Labyrinth, we can remake the human race after our own image. People will remember what we tell them to remember, venerate what we order them to worship and perform the tasks we give them to perform, all without question. I must tell you, though, that my chemist was very concerned that we find a delivery medium that everyone will want to touch in order to absorb the drug. I assured him that this was not a problem."

Nikolai chuckled, "No, it is not a problem at all. Our delivery system is the one thing that everyone in the world, great and small, rich and poor, most desires to possess." His tone grew more serious, "Everything must be ready on time, Josef. I cannot overemphasize the importance of this. In eighteen months, the International Monetary Fund and the World Bank will hold a joint meeting in Switzerland to announce the world's new reserve currency—the Dunamas. A group of us from around the world have pledged a portion of our real estate holdings and gold and platinum reserves to back the new currency—so far we have just a little over two hundred fifty billion Euros. Of course, this has been tried before—on more than one occasion. The developed nations of the world always resist an independent reserve currency because such a monetary system prevents any one nation from dominating the others economically. This time is going to be different." Nikolai pointed to a sealed envelope.

Josef picked it up and opened the pouch. Nikolai continued, "In this envelope you will find the exact specifications for the new currency. The image of Gaia will be on each bill with the Altar as a backdrop. Various denominations of currency are noted in your instructions. Labyrinth must be laced into the currency at the time of printing so that it permeates each bill." Josef glanced at the instructions and then turned back to Sokol.

"At the IMF meeting in eighteen months," Nikolai continued, "the presidents, prime ministers, monarchs and premiers of each developed and developing nation will be invited to attend. They will each be made a gift of ten bills in denominations which will be roughly equivalent to one thousand Euros. As they hold those bills, they will absorb Labyrinth into their blood streams, and they will agree that this time, a world reserve currency neutral of any country is very much in the best interests of each nation and of the world at large. Our goal is that they will each pledge their nation's national land and precious metal reserves to back this currency. As they do so, Dunamas will rapidly overtake every other currency as the soundest monetary system in the last hundred years.

"After we have finished with the heads of state, we will next meet with the presidents of the world's largest banks, investment houses and stock markets. Each will be made a gift of Dunamas, and as each leader of the world's financial systems handles the money, he or she will be made to understand that only by converting to this currency can the world's prosperity be insured."

"Brilliant. Truly brilliant, Nikolai," Josef's admiration was sincere. "Money truly is the one substance everyone in the world longs to hold and touch."

"Yes, but not everyone handles currency. That is the reason for the second envelope," Nikolai pointed to a smaller pouch. "In that envelope are the specifications for a new type of debit and credit card for Dunamas. These cards will utilize your own laboratory's invention of specially-compressed and sealed paper incorporating the qualities of plastic without the environmental downsides. These cards will be infused with Labyrinth so that as they are distributed throughout the globe, each person absorbs Labyrinth into his skin. Dunamas will be the vehicle to usher in the global utopia."

"*Dunamas*—the Greek word from which we get the English word 'dynamite.' I must compliment your sense of humor, Nikolai. You are using the world's money to dynamite the present world into extinction."

"*Dunamas* is the Greek word for force, Josef. As you said yourself in your speech at the Club, the goals of sustainability can only be achieved through force on a level never before experienced. Our Dunamas combines force with greed—one of man's most primal instincts. Force combined with desire cannot fail—there is one man in a million who can resist it."

"And after we are finished, there won't be any. As Labyrinth helps us achieve our goals, we will no longer need paper currency or cards. In a world of only five hundred million people we can most easily tattoo children with a barcode at birth and assign them an account with debits and credits based on their pre-determined station in life and the tasks they are selected to perform. We have never been able to do that because of overwhelming opposition from all different sectors of society, but as Labyrinth breaks down organized opposition to globalism, and we are able to thin the world's population to manageable levels, this work of controlling the wealth will become much easier."

Josef continued, "There is one other thing, Nikolai. Since you watched the proceedings at the Club, you know that I used a talisman of sorts—a crystal prism—on which to focus the attention of the participants. For Labyrinth to work properly, even in its second and third generations, it requires a focal point on which the brain can center its attention. We have found this to be true in all of our controlled experiments. Since Gaia and the Altar are the imagery you have selected for the New World Order, I must return to Germany to secure the Altar's transfer so that we can reconstruct the original temple to Athena and Zeus, thus re-establishing it as a place of worship rather than a museum exhibit. This component is essential to our success. Do you have the funds we discussed for this purpose?"

Sokol nodded, “I have already set aside one billion Euros to match the one billion you yourself have pledged to deposit in the German treasury as soon as the Altar is allowed to leave the country. I must caution you again, Josef, money alone will not procure the Altar for you. In order to persuade the German government to allow it to leave the country, you must have the aid of one who is as emotionally invested in this project as you are financially.”

Josef was indignant that Sokol refused to trust his powers of persuasion where this artifact was concerned. He could not protest, however, because he still needed Sokol. Trying to look interested, he asked, “And you have found such a man?”

“Demetri Kairos—the Turkish Minister of Cultural Affairs—will assist you. I have already made the arrangements. My jet will fly him to Berlin to meet you, where he will negotiate on the behalf of the Turkish government to have the Pergamon Altar removed to its original home in Turkey.”

“Kairos—a Greek is the Turkish Minister of Cultural Affairs? How did that happen?”

“Kairos,” Nikolai explained, “is Persian and Greek. His father claimed to be a direct descendant of Alexander the Great and the only rightful heir to the Greek throne. Of course, since the Greeks no longer have a monarchy, it was a moot point, but he liked to tell the story of how Alexander the Great threw off the Spartan ways in Persia to explore the delights of the lovely Persian women. He claimed that from one of these unions, millennia before, his parentage sprang. He also claimed to be the true and rightful ruler over Persia—but since the Iranians also have no king, that, too, was a moot point."

"An anonymous man to come from such a glorious lineage. How is it that I have never heard of him?"

"You have...Kairos is not his real name. Demetri changed it after his father died. But I think you will recognize the family name, Karras."

Now Josef was interested. He did, indeed, recognize the name of Greece's most prominent shipping magnate and the reputed head of an organized crime syndicate spanning several continents. "Aristotle Karras? Yes, that name I know. I remember when he died."

"Indeed. I knew him well—almost as well as I knew your father. I met Ari when he was a young man possessing a great deal of ambition but little else. My hedge fund financed his first shipping line—a start-up meant to compete with the powerful families whose lines ruled the Mediterranean. We financed three ocean liners for a young man of twenty-five with no cash."

"A risky venture—even for you," Josef was listening carefully.

"Not at all. Young Ari did not have cash, but he had a connection to a heroin distributor in Mumbai who was looking for a safe way to transport product into Europe. I used my connections to help Karras with customs and government agencies worldwide. He, in turn, paid back his initial debt within two years, and he paid me a premium every year after until his death."

"What happened to him? Did a competitor finally find him?"

"No. He was on his yacht with only his brother—who was his business partner—and Demetri, who was about fifteen at the time. Both of the older men had been drinking heavily, and they began to argue. A scuffle ensued, and both fell into the sea and drowned. Demetri said that he was not able to pull them out of the water because of the darkness combined with their inebriated conditions. A year later his mother mysteriously fell ill and died.

"After his mother's death, Demetri sold the shipping line. I helped him find a buyer, and I also helped him convert the cash into real estate. He and his cousin Iona were the only heirs; she is his stunning counterpart and a devoted worshipper of Gaia. They married when he was twenty and she was fifteen—I attended the ceremony; it was very beautiful and intensely pagan. At the time of his marriage, Demetri legally changed his name to Kairos, as the alias afforded the couple the privacy and anonymity that they could have never achieved under his father's appellation. Now they live off their vast incomes from their investments, and he devotes his time to securing artifacts from the ancient world and returning them to their original homes. I helped him secure his post as the Turkish Minister of Cultural Affairs, as I have aided in every important decision he has ever made. He and Iona are extremely grateful to me and willing to assist fully in anything I desire. The recovery of the Pergamon Altar is of special importance to him, and he will use every resource at his disposal to aid in bringing it back to Turkey. He will be invaluable to you in completing this mission."

Demetri Karras, or Kairos, or whatever he called himself—already Josef hated him. Apparently, Sokol had already completed the arrangements; therefore, Josef would just have to remain quiet, tolerate Kairos and wait. He knew better than to openly oppose Nikolai Sokol.

Sokol was watching him carefully and could see the contempt on his face. Relishing his ability to manipulate one of the world's most powerful men as though he were merely a puppet, he raised his glass in a toast. "To the success of our mission, Josef."

Josef raised his own glass and returned the toast, "To the mission. We are about to make eight and a half billion people disappear!"

CHAPTER 23

Heinz Felhaber was leaving his laboratory in the armored car that transported him from one section of Helmick Enterprises to another. Nightfall came early in the Swiss Alps, so although it was only 5:00 P. M., it was already quite dark. Normally he would have been going home to enjoy a meal expertly prepared by world-renowned chef Francesco Corteloni. Actually, the meals were prepared by an enhanced version of Corteloni—Josef had obtained DNA from Corteloni and his sous-chef while they were catering a private party for Nikolai Sokol. These copies prepared all of the menus and the food for the higher-level employees of Helmick Enterprises. Heinz enjoyed their creations, but secretly he had always wished that he could sample an original meal prepared and served by the organic Corteloni so that he could judge any differences for himself.

Tonight, however, he was eating a sandwich in the car as he traveled alone up the dark, winding road. The driver did not speak to him, nor he to the driver. This was one of the peculiarities of working for Helmick—the staff was not allowed to communicate with one another unless it was absolutely necessary for the performance of duties. Josef despised the ordinary elements of friendship, conversation and normal human interaction that marked most of civilization, and he had worked to create an environment as devoid of these properties as he could manage. The enhanced members of the Helmick team appeared to miss nothing in being deprived of these ordinary human interactions. Heinz, however, being organic, still remembered life with small talk, idle jokes and meaningless but pleasant interactions that delight the human heart, and he was often lonely.

Heinz was on his way to the castle where Josef did all of his entertaining on the estate. The ancient stone structure was massive and impressive. Technically, it was supposed to be a museum of medieval artifacts, and in one sense it was. In the bowels of the castle was an expertly-fitted torture chamber filled with every type of implement of cruelty and suffering imaginable. The ground and upper levels were adorned with priceless artwork, rugs and furnishings. The castle could sleep fifty guests; over the years it had seen its share of week-long parties. Most often Josef used the castle as a lure for prominent men and women whose DNA he wanted to obtain without their knowledge. Many were the unsuspecting subjects of some type of experiment, but they left the property never knowing that they had been used as guinea pigs. Occasionally, though, Helmick invited a group there for a very special private party, and during those events, he always suggested to his guests that they "take the party downstairs". Those unfortunates never left—when the agony he inflicted on them finally ended, their remains were destroyed in a crematorium he had constructed at the rear of the property.

Heinz knew all of this; he had even been present when the torture chamber was in use. The screams that reverberated through the rooms bounced off the stone walls, and the cries of torment seemed to grow and swell until they filled the entire structure. He hated coming here; since the day he had discovered the existence of the chamber, he had always believed that one day, when Josef no longer found his services necessary, he, too, would meet a hideous death in that subterranean dungeon.

Fortunately, that day was not today. Josef was still safely in Dubai, and Heinz had received a message from him that the organics to be used in the Labyrinth experiments would be arriving this evening. There were five in all. Heinz's mission was to administer Labyrinth to each and then to "rewrite" their memories, beginning with their memories of what would take place this weekend. When they left the estate, they were to have no memories of Heinz or the castle—he would set a memory for each of them that would fit with the new persona he was about to create.

The truth was that Heinz really had no idea how Level Three of Labyrinth would perform on organics. It worked in the tests on the enhanced subjects, of course, but the enhanced subjects had already been treated with Labyrinth several times in order to stimulate memory action and brain growth. As Josef exterminated and remade them to correct any physical imperfections, their natural brain functions became weaker and weaker, until, not unlike copies made on a copy machine that become increasingly fuzzier with each new generation, their memories and their overall mental functions became so clouded that they would probably have believed anything they were told about themselves.

"'Enhanced!'" Heinz sniffed to himself, "What a laugh!" Josef's clones were enhanced physically to the point of stunning beauty, but their intellectual capacity was so diminished that they could barely remember to inhale and exhale without being instructed to do so. It seemed to Heinz that if Josef really wanted to gain control over the world's population, he would be ahead to have the chemist construct a virulent biological weapon that would annihilate ninety percent of humans, and then he would be free to repopulate the world with his enhanced copies. The end result would not be unlike the infamous "Zombie Apocalypse" so feared and desired fifty years before—only with beautiful people rather than hideous ones. Heinz knew better than to make that suggestion to Josef and risk the beating he would receive, just as he knew better than to tell him that his clones did not even possess the cunning and survival skills of many animals. Instead, he remained quiet and continued modifying Labyrinth until he could practice on organic specimens who had never before been exposed to any of its properties. At their last meeting Josef had promised him an unlimited supply; now he was receiving five. When he arrived at the castle, he would be given a brief description of his subjects, including what they were to remember and what they were to forget. He did not know where Helmick had procured these particular subjects, nor did he care. Like everyone employed by Helmick, he worked on a "need to know" basis, and none of these details was anything he needed to know. Josef had found them; Josef had arranged for their transport to the castle, and Josef would arrange for their transport back.

Ψ

Two weeks earlier, as Kevin Leeds was entering his office after completing a lecture for his freshman class at Harvard, his PCD rang. A familiar mechanical voice spoke, "You have been selected to assist the Guardians in an experiment for the greater good of mankind. Further instructions await you in your office." The incoming number was blocked, but he recognized the mechanical voice. He had received these calls before, and the message was always the same. When he opened the door to his office, he saw a plain manila envelope lying on the edge of his desk. Inside was a note that said simply, "What would you like to make someone forget? What would you like to make that person remember? Input the name of the person into a word-processing document in the university-issued communication device along with the answers to these two questions, and save the document as 'amnesia'. We will take care of the rest."

Professor Leeds thought carefully for a few minutes. He loved mind games. Supplying subjects for experimentation was one of his favorite duties as a Guardian of Mankind. He was always fascinated to see how easily the most closely-held values of ordinary people could be manipulated.

Taking a smart chip from his desk, he quickly backed up all of the important documents on his office PCD, including the sixty-five page start that he had on his new book entitled, "Population Engineering for the Benefit of Mankind." When he was finished, he opened the word-processing software, entered the name "Kelly Carpenter" followed by a description of what he wished Kelly to forget and a description of what he wished Kelly to remember, and then he shut down the PCD.

The next morning when he arrived at work, he turned on the PCD only to discover that it had been infected with a virus that had destroyed everything on the hard drive. He smiled as he shut it down and called Michael in the Harvard IT department who wondered aloud to the other techies how Professor Leeds contracted so many malicious viruses when no one else in the department was affected.

Ψ

Kelly Carpenter was a freshman at Harvard. This semester was her first time away from home, and she was having a hard time adjusting. Until his retirement her father had worked in the Texas oil fields and, though Jack had never made a lot of money, he had provided well for his family and had lived frugally so that he could provide a stellar education for his daughter. Jack had always had big plans for Kelly; he wanted her to have a better life than he and her mother. Jack wanted Kelly to be an attorney, and sending her to Harvard was his dream. She had studied hard in high school and had made excellent scores on her SATs. The fact that she was a private-pay student was an important factor in her admission—few students could qualify under the rigorous terms now set by student loan agencies, and Harvard still admitted a handful of students who were not from elite families so that they could claim to have a diverse student body.

At home in Texas, Kelly had been very involved with her Baptist church group. When she was sixteen, she had gone on a youth mission trip with YWAM to India, and while there she had worked on dramas for street ministry. With her golden blonde hair and sparkling blue eyes, Kelly attracted attention wherever she went. She was not a classically beautiful girl, but she was very pretty in a wholesome, corn-fed sort of way. She possessed a naturally outgoing personality that made her popular in her high school, popular with her friends at church and popular with the mission trip leaders at YWAM.

Harvard was a different story. Most of the students came from wealthy Northeastern families, and they were contemptuous of Kelly. She still wore her purity ring; her dorm roommate ridiculed her for even having one. There were cute guys on campus, but when they found out how straitlaced she was, they would not even talk to her. Initially, she was invited to a couple of parties, but when she did not participate in the drinking and drug use, she was not invited back.

Then there was Professor Leeds. His freshman class, "Bioethics, Population Control, and the Future of the Human Race," was a required course at Harvard. Leeds scoured each freshman class for students like Kelly—fresh-faced Bible-belters who had come to Harvard through the hard work and frugality of an ambitious parent. He made it his special mission to destroy the faith of each one so that when they returned home, their parents would hardly recognize them. This semester Kelly was his special project, and it seemed to her that he spent every class tormenting her. He frequently asked her questions; then he ridiculed her responses in front of the other students and made her feel like the most ignorant person who had ever dared to walk the corridors of the great old school.

Outwardly, Kelly stood up to him and defended her faith. She suffered through the C's he gave her—her other grades were A's. She handled the mocking and the ridicule and the ostracism with the same cheery disposition with which she had always met life. Inwardly, however, she was lonely and miserable, and she wished desperately that she could fit in and be more like the other students.

When an envelope arrived in the mail saying that Professor Leeds had recommended her for an all-expense paid, one-week stay at a castle in Switzerland where she would take part in a specially-selected bioethics student conference, Kelly was astounded—and flattered. Leeds appeared to hate her; why would he choose her for this opportunity over the students he clearly favored? Maybe he was, as he claimed in class daily, just a tough professor trying to get the very best out of his students—maybe he did not truly dislike her after all. She asked him about the recommendation when she passed him in the hall, and he told her that of all his students she was the best suited for this experience because it would allow her to gain a new perspective on bioethics and the future of the human race. As an added bonus, simply by attending, Kelly would receive extra credit which would bring her class grade point average up to an A-. A few days later Kelly was sitting at her gate at JFK waiting for the flight that would carry her to her new adventure.

Ψ

On the same day that Kevin Leeds received his telephone call, His Majesty Luis Carlos of Spain also received a call on his PCD followed by a plain manila envelope with the same cryptic instructions. Luis Carlos did not even have to consider his choice. While he was in Dubai at Josef's installation as secretary-general of the

Club of Rome, Ines had announced her engagement to Eduardo Quiñones. She had privately assured Luis that the engagement was only to promote the movie she and Eduardo were making together. The lavish wedding would be no more than a publicity stunt to command the attention of the world's tabloids. She and Eduardo were one of the world's most beautiful couples, and the tabloid stories of their passionate off-screen romance, which was now culminating in a fairytale wedding, was the stuff that blockbuster ticket sales were made of. Luis Carlos' vanity was almost enough to convince him that she was telling him the truth and that she did not care for Eduardo, but, inwardly, he was seething with jealousy. Eduardo and Ines would be photographed everywhere, from the tasteful church wedding to the racy honeymoon video that they already planned to post to the Internet. The thought of her cavorting openly with the handsome, often shirtless novella star was almost more than the aging monarch could bear.

Taking his PCD which he reserved specifically for communications with the Guardians, he input "Ines Jimenez" into the word processor. He wanted Ines to forget that she had ever met or known Eduardo Quiñones, and he wanted Eduardo Quiñones to forget that he had ever known her.

A few days later, Ines received a letter from a courier sealed with Luis Carlos' personal crest. Inside was an invitation for her and Eduardo to visit a Swiss castle for a weekend as a pre-wedding getaway. The timing was not good since they were planning their wedding and all of the publicity surrounding it, but when Ines called Luis Carlos to thank him for his generosity and ask if she could postpone, he told her that this was his early wedding gift to her. He had commissioned the castle especially to provide her and Quiñones a place to de-stress before their big day, and he could not change the dates. He hoped that she would accept his gift.

Luis Carlos had been her patron and primary means of support for years; Ines could not refuse him. Besides, she was touched by his gift and imagined that it meant that he was finally accepting her marriage—he had been behaving like a petulant child ever since her engagement had been announced. When she explained to Eduardo that the invitation was really a summons, her fiancé readily accepted. It was, after all, an all-expense paid vacation—it would be romantic and fun, and Switzerland would provide a great backdrop for more impromptu photos that they could leak to the Internet.

Ψ

The final invitations to Helmick's Swiss hideaway went to Vasana and Ishan. When Hemraj Ambani received the message and the accompanying package, he lost no time recommending them both. Vasana was now actively working to force him out of his father's company, and Ishan was supporting her fully in the coup. Since his vision in the crystal, Ambani had thought repeatedly about having them both killed—a successful assassination would solve many problems. The primary impediment to this plan was that Vasana and Ishan were both in London surrounded by bodyguards. He could not afford to have a failed attempt at an assassination because both his sister and his brother-in-law would immediately suspect that he was responsible, and they would redouble their efforts to eliminate his interest in the empire.

A few days later Vasana received a hand-delivered sealed invitation at her hotel room in London. The handwritten note, inscribed clearly in her brother's penmanship, was an invitation to meet him in Switzerland to discuss the terms of Hemraj's "surrender". Vasana was ecstatic—for all of her schemes, she and Ishan still did not have enough votes to depose him as chairman of the board, and they knew it. Still, she had worn him down with her persistence—she had never dreamed that it would be so easy. She and Ishan were practically dancing as they boarded their private jet to Switzerland.

Ψ

At 8:00 Friday evening Kelly arrived at the castle where Heinz was waiting to greet her. In his left hand he held her description and the answers that Kevin Leeds had provided—what he wished her to remember and what he wished her to forget. He also had a copy of the cover story that had lured her to Switzerland. "Good evening, I am Heinz, your host for the conference this weekend. I am here to make your stay comfortable. You are the first of the students to arrive. We have prepared a special meal for you to welcome you to Switzerland. Allow me to show you to your room."

As the remaining guests arrived, Heinz tailored his greetings to match the specific stories that they had been told. When Vasana and Ishan arrived, he informed them that Hemraj's jet had been temporarily grounded for a mechanical malfunction and that his arrival had been delayed until the following morning. However, Hemraj had taken pains to have an exquisite meal prepared for them along with an exceptional vintage of wine.

Eduardo and Ines were the last to arrive. Heinz showed them to their rooms and informed them that His Majesty had ordered a bottle of Dom Pérignon White Gold to celebrate their upcoming wedding and that he would soon be delivering it to their rooms along with the feast that the king had requested in their honor.

Two hours later, the guests were served a sumptuous meal prepared by the enhanced Corteloni, and with it, their first tastes of Labyrinth.

Ψ

By the end of the week, Heinz had completed all of his tests. The subjects were physically unharmed and unaware that they had been part of a science experiment. Through heavy dosing with Labyrinth and the use of visual and auditory stimuli, Heinz had attempted to erase the undesirable memories and replace them with memories that he had implanted. The experiment appeared to have succeeded; he had given each subject a polygraph as part of the "final exam", and each had answered questions about his new identity with no detection of any trace of deception.

On the final day Heinz read over the criteria for each subject:

"*Kelly Carpenter*: I want her to forget everything that is important to her parents and ties her to them. I want her to remember everything that is important to her in her new life."

"*Vasana and Ishan Pai*: I want them to forget everything about their previous lives. I want them to remember that they are work slaves from the lowest caste. They are less than dogs and are eternally grateful to Hemraj Ambani, who is like a god to them. They owe him their lives because he has allowed them to work as his servants, even though they do not deserve the honor of serving him."

"*Ines Jimenez and Eduardo Quiñones*: I want Ines to forget that she was ever an actress or that she ever met Eduardo Quiñones. I want Eduardo Quiñones to forget that he ever loved Ines Jimenez. I want his memory of her to be so vague that if he were ever to meet her again, he would not recognize her. I want Ines to remember a life of total seclusion and her great love for the only man who was ever deserving of her. I want her to remember the passion and joy that only he could bring to her life. I want Eduardo Quiñones to remember that Ines Jimenez was killed in a plane crash shortly after they finished their last film together."

The question for Heinz was whether the effects would last. On enhanced subjects similar experiments had produced permanent results, but since enhanced subjects often did not have a lifespan of more than eight or nine months, "permanent" was a very short time. Organic subjects were entirely different, and Heinz was not so sure that, over time, they did not have the capacity to reach deep into their own psyches and rediscover their true identities. To know the answer to that, he would have to rely on feedback from those who had submitted their names for the experiment in the first place.

Ψ

Kelly Carpenter had returned to Harvard. Heinz had kept her family history exactly as it had been presented to him with one important difference—he had replaced Kelly's memories of her work in church and her mission trip to India with memories of working for environmental causes and left-leaning atheist organizations. In her new memories her mission trip to India became an international conference for PETA, and her volunteer work had been for Planned Parenthood. She no longer wore her purity ring; Heinz had taken it from her when she was in Switzerland and had manipulated her memory so that she believed that she had abandoned purity at fifteen. She remembered that her parents were Baptists, but she no longer had any memories of having shared their faith.

She had not called her parents in more than a week. When she had first returned from Switzerland and they had argued with her about her new belief system, she had hung up on them. She was confused about why they both insisted that she had once embraced Christianity. She had never even pretended to share their faith, and she could not deal with their refusal to admit that. For the time being, it was easier not to have any contact with them.

Her conservative clothes had given way to shorter skirts and sexier, lower-cut tops. She was flirtatious, and her speech was peppered with profanity and suggestive comments. Professor Leeds noted the changes in her immediately, and he completely approved. Kelly was now his favorite student.

Now, Kelly constantly ridiculed Missy Mayfield, the only other student in the class from a Christian background. Missy was so irritating that Kelly could hardly bear to be in the same room with her. She hated everything about Missy, and she wanted to make her suffer for clinging to a faith that deprived its adherents of every pleasure life had to offer and for trying to force her beliefs on others. She had the odd feeling that a long time ago she had known Missy, or someone like her. It was not quite a memory; it was more of a fleeting glimpse of something from her past that she could never quite bring to the surface. She would sometimes feel it moving to the front of her brain, but before she could lock into it, it was gone.

Since returning from Switzerland, Kelly had been bothered by strange dreams. She dreamed of a trip to India where she was standing before a Hindu temple with a group of students who were involved in street theater, and she was performing stories from the Bible. She dreamed that she was attending prayer and Bible study in her parents' home. She dreamed that she was serving Thanksgiving dinner at a homeless shelter and handing out tracts to those who had come there to eat. She was determined that these dreams were not going to interfere with her life at Harvard, but they were frequent and worrisome, and she wondered how she could have such clear dreams about things she had never experienced.

Several weeks later Kelly was on her way to her dorm when she saw Missy walking toward her. When Missy was directly in front of her, she stopped and said, "Kelly, today I was praying for you, and the Lord told me to tell you that Jesus loves you."

As soon as Kelly heard those words she knew that they were true. She knew, no she remembered, that Jesus loved her. She felt as if she were emerging from a deep fog, and all of those memories that had been floating just out of her reach began to come back. She remembered her childhood in the small East Texas towns where her father had worked. She remembered the country church they had attended when she was ten years old. She remembered Jill, the pastor's wife who had been in charge of the children's ministry and the love for Jesus that she had instilled in Kelly. She remembered what she had wanted most in life.

She had wanted to go to Bible College and earn her degree in children's ministry, and then she wanted to marry a pastor and work in the church with him. Jill had influenced her more than anyone except her own parents, and Kelly had wanted to spend her life helping children know Jesus the way Jill had helped her.

The leaves were turning, and the campus was alive with gorgeous color. Kelly walked to the nearest bench, sat down, and began to cry. Through her tears she looked at the beauty of God's creation and thanked Him for reminding her of what she had most wanted from life.

That evening she called home, and Jack answered his PCD. "Daddy, it's Kelly. I love you, and I want to come home. I don't want to stay at Harvard. I want to go to Bible College and work in children's ministry. Is that okay?"

The call lasted for two hours. It was the happiest conversation of Jack Carpenter's life.

Ψ

The week after their trip to Switzerland, Vasana and Ishan awoke on Hemraj's estate—in the servant's quarters. Vasana pulled on a ragged one-piece dress that she imagined she had worn for many years and went to the kitchen to begin preparing breakfast for the family. She remembered Hemraj as her master—remembered that she had been born into the Ambani household as a servant with few more rights than a slave. When she was twelve, her mother had arranged for her to marry Ishan Patel—the gardener's son who was now the gardener himself.

Hemraj was in a state of ecstasy when he saw the transformation. He had long fantasized about killing Ishan and Vasana but this—this was a thousand times better. They were now his groveling slaves. He could beat them, starve them, and work them late into the night. They remembered him only as the heir to the property and their master, and they were very grateful that he allowed them, undeserving as they were, to serve him. This was the most intoxicating feeling he had ever experienced.

During the long days, Vasana labored in the kitchen and at the laundry and performed arduous household tasks, and at night she returned to the servants' quarters to sleep on the floor next to her husband and the rest of the household staff. All through the night, she was tormented by dreams of luxury in which she was no longer the servant but the mistress of such an estate. In these nighttime fantasies she wore designer clothing instead of rags. Her skin, now dry and unwashed and lice-infested, was perfumed and soft and radiant. She was respected and admired wherever she turned, but each morning, as the first light came over the horizon, she awoke to the awful reality of her new life.

As Vasana's dreams became increasingly more vivid, they consumed her. During the day as she performed her tasks, she fantasized that she was a princess who had been kidnapped and sold to Hemraj. After a few weeks, she began to confuse her fantasies with reality. Deep depression set in as her glittering dreams of former grandeur clashed with her newfound grinding poverty and slavish labor. One day she did not rise at first light with the other servants. When she did not respond to their calls, they left her where she lay. Later that morning, when it was fully light, the manager of the household staff went to the servants' quarters and found her lying in a pool of her own blood. She had been stabbed in the stomach and had bled to death where she lay—the wound appeared self-inflicted. Considering her tenuous mental state, no one was surprised that she had apparently taken her own life. Ishan had disappeared without a trace.

Ψ

One week after the trip to Switzerland, Ines Jimenez awakened alone in her apartment in Barcelona. In her absence, Luis Carlos had removed every trace of Eduardo—his personal effects and pictures had all been disposed of, so when Ines awakened, there was nothing to remind her of her former lover. Carlitos, who had been in the care of an enhanced nanny who knew nothing about either Ines or Eduardo, was returned later that day.

The following morning the king's private secretary released a statement to the press announcing that Ines Jimenez had been killed in a plane crash in the Swiss Alps. A few days later, Luis Carlos transported Ines and Carlitos to a beach-front home he kept in the quiet coastal town of

Alicante where she was to live in virtual seclusion except for his frequent visits.

Initially, Luis Carlos was overjoyed. Since the day he had met Ines, he had dreamed of arranging their lives so that he could keep her entirely to himself. Secretly, he hated her career because it afforded her increasingly greater opportunities for independence which must eventually take her away from him. And, of course, he hated Eduardo. Now, her career was gone; Eduardo was gone; her opportunities for a life without him were gone. He had achieved exactly what he had always wanted.

Yet, something was very wrong. It was as though, when Ines forgot Eduardo, she also forgot Luis Carlos. Gone were the smoldering looks and seductive whispers which had so delighted him. Gone was the passion and heat; she was now cool and distant. In the past she had appeared eager to please him when he visited; her happiness seemed bound to his pleasure. Now, she did not appear to care for him at all. She seemed depressed and uninterested and aloof. It was as if Heinz's experiment had doused all of the fire that had burned in Ines—the fire that Luis Carlos had always hoped to control and dominate but had never wanted to extinguish.

Ines remembered only that she had always lived in luxury and seclusion and that her sole purpose in life was to be constantly available to Luis Carlos; she had no memory of Eduardo Quiñones. Even so, she felt a longing that she could not explain. It was as if she had fallen in love with an apparition. She felt a deep yearning for someone whom she had never met. She could not see his face, but she felt his presence. She was certain that if she could only reach out and touch him, the loneliness and sadness that dominated her every waking hour would vanish. With each passing day, she became more convinced that somewhere there was a man whom she could love completely—a man who would bring the passion and joy to her life that she so desperately longed to find.

One Friday, Ines was alone in Alicante. Luis Carlos had gone to Madrid for a family event, and Carlitos had left earlier in the week for boarding school. Ines was bored and lonely, and she decided to go to one of the five-star restaurants in the resort suburb of San Juan. Sitting in the night air of the restaurant's courtyard listening to the rhythms of Spanish guitar, she felt more alive than she had for months. As she sat drinking sangria and enjoying the music, a waiter brought her a bottle of champagne and told her that it was a gift from a fellow patron. When she turned to see who had sent it, she saw a man approaching her table. He was young and handsome, but it was not his appearance that made Ines' heart leap. In that first moment when she saw him moving toward her, she felt that she had found the one for whom she had searched for such a long time. Before he had traversed the room, she knew how his voice would sound, how he would smell, how her hand would feel in his.

"Excuse me, Señorita. Are you alone this evening?" he asked politely.

"Unfortunately, yes," she smiled at him seductively.

"We share the same misfortune. Allow me to introduce myself. I am Eduardo Quiñones. I came to Alicante this weekend to be alone, but this evening when I walked into the restaurant and saw you, I knew that I had come to Alicante to find you. Have dinner with me, please, and you will make me a very happy man."

Ines placed her own delicate hand into the hand that Eduardo extended to her, and he led her back to his table. They were inseparable for the remainder of the week. When Luis Carlos telephoned to say he wanted to visit, she told him that she was sick with flu and could not see him. She put him off this way for weeks, until one day he saw the announcement in a tabloid at a newsstand: Eduardo Quiñones and a mystery woman "with an uncanny resemblance to Ines Jimenez" had been married quietly at a seaside resort in Spain and left for their honeymoon in Italy. When Luis Carlos saw the photograph of Eduardo and Ines in Italy, tears of rage filled the old man's eyes, but he knew it was too late. Before Switzerland he had shared Ines with the movie industry, her fans, and Eduardo; after the experiment, he no longer possessed any part of her.

Ψ

Heinz was preparing his report for Josef, and he knew that he must choose his words carefully. Based on the feedback from those who had chosen the subjects for the experiment, the exercise had been a colossal failure. He could not, however, tell Josef that Level Three Labyrinth had not met expectations; to do so would certainly ensure him an immediate trip to the castle's dungeon.

After giving the matter considerable thought, Heinz began to enter his report into his PCD: "The initial findings on the five subjects chosen for the Level Three Labyrinth experiments are very promising. We have been successful in eradicating unwanted memories and replacing them with memories that serve our purposes. This function is of utmost importance in realizing our goal of controlling the actions and desires of organics.

"It must be remembered, however, that, unlike enhanced subjects, organics are imperfect. They possess physical, mental, and emotional flaws that go uncorrected and, in time, may bear heavily on their behavior as well as their desires.

"At the time that our subjects departed Switzerland, they had accepted the memories we had implanted as being accurate recollections of their past lives. Within three to five weeks, however, the subjects began rejecting their new memories. Although they were unable to recall the memories that we had eradicated, they began to search for their past lives in a number of ways. Among these were nighttime dreams and waking fantasies that reflected their past. The subjects seemed to be incapable of letting go of their former selves—even though they did not know that their former selves had existed.

"I have concluded that organics become who they are through a series of choices that begin in childhood and continue until death. Even if their memories are altered, the organics tend to revert back to those choices. This process is quite common among organics and has been recognized in every cultural group since recorded history. It has been called by many names—the human spirit, the soul, the will to believe—but, whatever name it is given, it produces the same result. Organics believe what they choose to believe and, under normal circumstances, nothing can be done to change that.

"As an organic myself, I can attest to this inherent flaw. When I was a child, I determined that there is no god, and I chose to pursue science to discover the answers to life's mysteries. I believed that every answer to every question could be found in a test tube, and I believe that to this day.

"My brother, who was only two years younger than I, chose a different path. He was mesmerized by the church and was determined to give his life to it. My parents were not religious, but they were not atheists, either. They went to church on the high holy days, and the rest of the time they lived as they chose. But my brother had such a passion for the church that he spent every moment that he could working with the priests, and when he was old enough, he became a priest himself.

"He and I had many arguments about religion—his passion for it and my rejection of it—but neither convinced the other to his way of thinking. We had made our choices about what we were willing to believe long before we were capable of constructing a reasonable argument in defense of those beliefs. As we have aged, each of us has become more fully rooted in the belief system that he chose so many years ago.

"My recommendation is that we begin immediately working to further develop a process to make these changes to the memory banks permanent. I have performed several surgeries in which I have removed a few specific brain cells containing the memories from one subject and transplanted them into another. Because these cells become a permanent part of the brain, the memories cannot be rejected. Using Level Three Labyrinth to enhance the process should ensure that we achieve the desired permanent results."

When Heinz had finished his report, he took a deep breath and hit the send button. He hoped that he had been creative enough to convince Josef.

CHAPTER 24

Hadad's hands trembled as he called his cousin, Saman. He had finally managed to uncover information that Josef Helmick would be willing to pay a great deal to acquire, and he must move quickly.

Hadad had not talked to Saman for months, but he was the mechanic who serviced Josef Helmick's cars. At least that is what Saman told everyone; in truth, he kept them washed and cleaned, checked the oil and filled them with gas. Josef would never have entrusted Saman with a more important role in maintaining his fleet. Josef did not even know Saman's name and would not have recognized him if they had passed one another on the street. Nevertheless, Saman boasted at all family gatherings that he alone kept Helmick's cars in perfect running order, and he hinted that Helmick was very indebted to him.

Hadad knew that his cousin was a liar, but he wanted to get a message to Helmick, and he thought that if he paid him, Saman would be a willing courier.

After an extended time exchanging meaningless chatter, Hadad finally came to the purpose of his call. "I have important information for your employer. I must talk to him; if you can arrange it, I will pay you handsomely."

Saman was caught off-guard. "Herr Helmick will not speak to you. Give me the message, and I will deliver it to him."

"Oh, that I could," Hadad replied smoothly. "I would entrust you with my life, but my words are for Herr Helmick's ears only. Tell him that I have information about the American. I am certain that he will talk to me."

"How much will you pay?" Saman asked. "A conversation with Herr Helmick is worth much."

"One hundred dollars American."

Saman felt a pang of disappointment, "Five hundred."

"Two hundred," Hadad countered.

"Four hundred," Saman pressed.

"Two hundred. Take it, or I find someone else."

"Done. I will help you because you are like a brother to me," Saman lied. "The money is not important. This is about family. I will give him the message."

Saman stood just outside the garage door thinking how he would deliver the message to Herr Helmick when Josef came tearing up the street and stopped his Lamborghini a few feet from Saman. "Have Ludwig look at my car. The brakes need work. And get someone out here now to take me home."

Saman could not believe his luck. "Yes, Herr Helmick, I will drive you myself," and he scurried off to get a suitable car.

When Josef was settled in the back seat and Saman had pulled onto the street, he spoke, "Herr Helmick, it is my good fortune to find myself in your presence today. Praise be to Allah who has brought us together! I have a message for you from Hadad."

"Who is Hadad?"

"I am surprised, Herr Helmick, that you do not know the name, that you have not had previous dealings with him. Hadad is a buyer and seller of real estate, but his main business is information. No one knows more about what goes on in Dubai than Hadad."

"Never heard of him," Josef replied. "What is the message?"

Saman handed a business card over his shoulder. "Hadad says to call him at this number. He has information about the American who is asking about you."

"Pull over," Josef ordered, "and get out of the car."

Saman immediately brought the car to a stop on the shoulder of the road and stepped out. Josef, too stepped out of the car and faced a frightened Saman. The gun was in Josef's hand before the car stopped, and, now he brought it up and shot Saman directly in the heart. Stepping over his body, Josef slid into the driver's seat and sped away.

Twenty minutes later, Josef was in his apartment at the Burj Khalifa. He heard Hadad's PCD ringing on the other end of the line and then, "Hello?"

"You have information for me?" Josef asked without identifying himself.

"Herr Helmick?" Hadad inquired.

"Do you have information for me or not?"

"Yes, Herr Helmick. I am at your service. I have eyes and ears everywhere, and I have learned much about the American who is here asking about you."

"What could you possibly know that would interest me?"

"I think we must meet in person. Such sensitive information must be carefully guarded."

"What is your address?" Josef asked coldly.

"401 Kabul Square. Can I expect you this afterno…." The line went dead, and for the first time in a long time Hadad felt genuine fear.

As Hadad waited for Josef, he began to think that he had made a serious error in contacting him. He had not doubted that Herr Helmick would be willing to pay a great deal to know about the American who was so interested in Helmick's affairs, but now he was not sure. He strained to hear the sound of someone at the door, but, at the same time, he wished that he would not come. Something told him that Herr Helmick would not be willing to play his game and pay his price.

Just when Hadad had convinced himself that Herr Helmick was not coming, he heard the door open and the sounds of men's voices in the reception area. His receptionist was speaking, but he could not understand what she said.

Within seconds Josef entered Hadad's private office and sat in the chair across from him. "Now tell me, what information do you have?"

Hadad smiled nervously and licked his dry lips before he began, "One of the sous-chefs at the Burj Khalifa overheard Paolo Castro, the kitchen boy, talking to the American about a ring he had taken from the body he had found in the dumpster a few weeks earlier. The American bought the ring from Castro for an excessive price and shipped it to New York. The shipping label read, 'Jarrod and Joshua Sinclair, GenTECH Enterprises, 113 Sinclair Plaza, New York, New York.'"

Three minutes later Josef rose and left a clearly shaken Hadad sitting at his desk wondering what to do next. As he opened the outer door and stepped into the street, Josef gave a quick signal to the men who had accompanied him. Before he sped away, Josef heard the sound of round after round of ammunition being fired, as the receptionist, the fat clerk who had just returned from running an errand, and Hadad, slumped into lifeless bloodied heaps.

CHAPTER 25

Hadad had known of only two names, besides his own, of contacts he could confirm Fred had made in Dubai. The first of these was Paolo, who was now hanging from his own belt in the tiny closet he called an apartment. The second was Walid's grandfather, Afshin.

The last rays of light were fading from the filthy alley as Josef entered Afshin's crumbling dwelling. The stench of rotting food and human waste permeated the air. The death of Walid must have left the old man with no one to care for his personal needs, and so he sat rotting away in this dark little cave of a room.

"Come closer, German," the old man hissed as Josef stepped through the door. "I have been expecting you." His gnarled hands beckoned for Josef to approach. Who could have warned the old man that he was coming? Immediately Josef was on guard—was someone else here? He drew his Luger and waited for his eyes to adjust to the fading light. The room was quite empty except for the hideous old man.

"Why do you disturb me? What do you seek here?" The hoarse, raspy sound emitting from Afshin's throat barely seemed human.

With the Luger still in his hand, Josef approached. "Your grandson, Walid, was acting as a guide for an American here in Dubai. You are going to tell me everything you know about the work the American was doing and what he wanted."

"First you pay!" droplets of the old man's saliva sprayed Josef as he emphasized the final word while extending his palm.

Josef rested the barrel of the Luger against Afshin's temple. "Do you feel that? You have two minutes to tell me everything I want to know, or you will never speak another word. Whatever relatives you have left will spend the next few days scraping your brains off these walls."

To Josef's amazement, Afshin laughed. "You have no power to kill me, German. But I invite you to try, if you dare."

Josef had killed dozens of men and always they begged for their lives. Afshin's response unnerved him. He pressed the Luger into the old man's temple. If he shot him, he would have no other source for finding out about the American. He stood in the hazy light pondering what to do; the stench was making his stomach churn. With his free hand he drew a few coins from his pocket and tossed them onto dirt floor with a thud. "A choice, old fool, because I am in a generous mood. You will tell me what I want to know. If I like what you say I will pay you with gold. If I do not, I will pay you with lead. Agreed?"

Afshin cackled again."Agreed! My grandson was weak. He worked for the American and embraced the American's God. His death was inevitable; if he had not died in the market I would have killed him myself while he slept. No one who serves that God can live here."

Josef shoved the barrel of the gun more forcefully into Afshin's temple. "I have no interest in your grandson, and I don't believe in any God. Who was the American and why did he hire Walid? What did he want? Who is he working for?"

Afshin raised his withered hand and pushed the barrel of the gun away from his own temple. Josef's impulse was to stop him, but he did not. "Walid told me very little—only that the American was visiting the man Hadad and that he was investigating a series of murders, both here and in other places. He never told me who the American worked for."

"I am wasting my time here," snapped Josef disgustedly.

"Patience. I merely said that Walid told me little; I never said that I did not know the answers to your questions. But you must pay...and more than a few coins on the floor. I will tell you what you want to know...more than you want to know—for the right price."

"So far you have told me nothing. What is the right price to you old man? How much?"

"A small house in the city of Pamukkale, near the cavern where Pluto's breath pours forth from the earth."

Josef hesitated for a moment before answering. "If I like what you tell me, you will have your price. If not, you have bought your own death."

"Take your gun away," the old man ordered. "Put it back in your jacket."

Josef withdrew the gun but continued to hold it in his hand. Afshin seemed satisfied. "Walid called the American 'Fred'. He is a detective. He works for two who hate you, who serve Fred's God. They sent him to our country to bring you to justice. You will not be able to stop Fred—he is old and weak, but you cannot stop him from completing his task."

"Who?—give me a name?" Josef demanded.

"I do not know the name. Fred received many communications from them. They are brothers—more than brothers—and they are Americans like Fred. They will destroy you."

The blind man could not see the anger flashing in Josef's eyes. The Sinclairs—it could not be anyone else. He knew that they consulted for GenCEN; that is why Fred had sent them Amanda's ring. They were the ones who had sent Fred to Dubai. Afshin was wrong—they would not destroy him. He would order a hit on Fred from his vacation home in Switzerland, where he was going immediately after leaving Berlin. His flight to Berlin was leaving in two hours and he could not delay it, but as soon as he finished his errand for Sokol, finding Fred would be his top priority. Then, he would lure the Sinclair brothers and their families to Switzerland where he would dispose of them in his dungeon. No one would ever know what had happened to them.

The Luger was still in his hand, and he straightened his arm to fire the kill shot.

Perhaps the old man sensed what was about to happen, for he now spoke again. "There is more…."

Josef lowered the gun, "Out with it."

"You were not born of a woman, like ordinary men. You say you believe in no god, yet you believe you yourself are god. I know what you seek—the Altar of Zeus. You seek to use the Altar to control all men and declare yourself to be god. You believe that you can possess it, but you cannot. No one possesses the Altar; the Altar possesses them. The Altar will humiliate you; you will crawl on your knees and grovel before it, and then it will destroy you. You have no idea of the power it holds and no respect for it. The Altar will break you. Now show me what you have in your pocket." The withered claw reached towards Josef, and he instinctively backed away.

"I have nothing in my pocket," Josef tried to steady his voice. He was still holding the Luger, but all possibility of shooting Afshin had somehow vanished. No one anywhere knew that he was a clone. That knowledge had died with Karl Helmick, and Josef had never shared his origins with any person. How did Afshin know? He could not know; it was impossible. In 2041 most people did not believe that successful human cloning had ever been achieved—a man as ignorant as Afshin living in blindness in a filthy, stinking hole could not begin to understand the most rudimentary concepts of cloning. So why would he say that Josef did not come from a woman? Someone was feeding the old man information to toy with him. But who?

As Josef struggled to gather his thoughts, he heard the old man's voice. "You carry a crystal in your pocket that you use to tell the fortunes of the weak and foolish. Give it to me."

Almost against his will, Josef felt his own hand reach into his pocket and retrieve the crystal prism which rested in a black velvet bag. Josef observed that his own hand was shaking slightly as he handed the small velvet pouch to Afshin. It was as though he was watching an image of himself from far away—as if he no longer had control over his own actions.

The claw seized the velvet cloth and felt for the opening. Finding it, Afshin carefully deposited the crystal into his other palm, and closing his hands over it he rubbed both hands over the talisman as he muttered some words in a language Josef could not identify. The ceremony probably lasted less than a minute, but to Josef it seemed as if time stood still.

When the withered, broken hand finally lifted from the crystal Josef observed that it was glowing with a strange orange light. No, that was not possible. The room was too dark; there was no light for the prisms to reflect. Josef struggled to regain control of the situation. The old man was playing mind games with him. Perhaps, in the specks of dust that filled the air there was some sort of incense—some primitive hallucinogen.

"When you find the courage to face it, it will show you your future," the old man's smile was filled with mockery as he offered the still-glowing crystal to Josef. The prism was inexplicably warm as Josef returned it to its black velvet purse. His own hands were still shaking as he deposited it into his pocket.

"Now leave me, German," Afshin's breath was like the stench of a grave. How had Afshin gotten so close to him that he could feel his breath? In those sightless eyes, Josef imagined that he could see something looking back at him—a penetrating darkness that peered deep into his own mind and mocked and taunted him. It was the most horrifying sight he had ever experienced.

Turning, he staggered out the doorway into the alley. His legs were so weak they could hardly support him. After a few steps he vomited uncontrollably onto the packed earth. For the first time since becoming an adult, Josef was terrified.

CHAPTER 26

Fred was eating breakfast with the Sinclairs in their suite in Dubai. They had chosen a British-owned retreat that catered to businessmen and heads of state who wanted to keep a low profile, and it had built its reputation on ensuring its residents privacy in one of the world's most opulent settings.

Seated at the table with Fred and the Sinclairs was Harold Baker, their IT specialist. According to Jarrod, Harold was "the best in the business" and could open any electronic file, regardless of the sophistication of the encryption used to protect it.

"You may talk freely," Harold said looking at Fred. "I swept the entire suite for bugs less than an hour ago. It's clean."

Fred smiled, "I'm certainly glad to know that, because I don't doubt for a moment that Helmick has informants everywhere who would like to record everything that's going on here and sell it to him. This morning as I was leaving the Burj Khalifa, Rashid, the concierge, told me that Josef left a few days ago for Berlin to meet with Chancellor Helmut Schmidt and Demetri Kairos, who is the Turkish Minister of Cultural Affairs, to negotiate a transfer of the Pergamon Altar from Berlin to Bergama. Kairos is a name you probably don't recognize, but I am sure you are familiar with his notorious father—Ari Karras."

"The one who owned the Greek shipping lines? Is Kairos his son—the gangster turned pagan art collector? There are lots of rumors that he killed both his parents, but he's still on everybody's A list." Jarrod looked puzzled, "Why would he be giving you information?"

"Not giving, selling. I recruited Rashid as an informant the day I arrived. Today he tried to act very mysterious and negotiated for a while, but we settled on three hundred dollars."

"Where's Bergama?" Joshua inquired.

"It's the modern name for Pergamon."

"Why do you think that's of any special significance?" Jarrod asked. "Josef is not religious. He would have no use for the Altar. He's always been all about science. I can't see him suddenly developing an interest in mythology."

"Don't be so sure of that," Fred responded. "The Altar has been used throughout history to control the masses. You're aware that Hitler used it as the model for his podium in Nuremberg where he consolidated his power and laid the foundation for the Third Reich?"

"Yes, our mother was a history major, and she talked a lot about Hitler and the Third Reich."

Fred took a sip of coffee and continued, "The Altar is more than a collection of marble friezes. Last year my pastor did a series of Wednesday night teachings on the seven churches in the book of Revelation, and he spent several sessions on the church at Pergamos. In chapter two Jesus says that the church at Pergamos is in the city where Satan's throne is located, at the very center of satanic worship. Jesus, himself, referred to the Altar as Satan's throne on earth. That's pretty powerful.

"A lot of people believe that when the ruins of the Altar were discovered in 1878 and moved to Germany, an evil was unleashed there that has been at work ever since. Both world wars saw Jewish persecutions—although World War II was much worse. I'm convinced that when the Altar came to Germany forces were set in motion to annihilate the Jewish people. Then, when Hitler came to power, Satan had his perfect vessel to bring about their destruction. We all know that Hitler's hatred for the Jews was more than ordinary prejudice; it was an obsession.

"The word Holocaust means 'a wholly burnt sacrifice.' The Nazis built their crematoriums to implement their 'final solution' but I believe that, for Hitler, the cremations were far more than an efficient means to dispose of the bodies—they were altars for his burnt offerings—his sacrifices to Satan."

"Whoa!" Harold exclaimed. "You're weirdin' me out, man."

"I'm not trying to weird anyone out," Fred replied, "but I want everyone here to understand what we're dealing with."

Fred looked at Joshua, who had remained quiet during most of the meal. "Do you think this is the beginning of the end?" he asked. "Could Josef be ushering in the Anti-Christ—or maybe even be the Anti-Christ?"

"Only if we allow him to," Joshua answered. "In every generation Satan has tried to bring the Anti-Christ to power. But the Bible says that he cannot come until the one who is holding him back steps out of the way. That one is God's Holy Spirit. I am convinced that we can hold back the Anti-Christ as long as God's people are willing to stand against him.

"There could be only one true Christ—Jesus Christ, the Messiah, the only begotten Son of God. He came at a specific time in history to fulfill the scriptures and overcome Death and Hell.

"With the Anti-Christ it's different. Anyone who is given over to Satan will do. He is an imitator and a fraud, and God has given His people His Holy Spirit to hold him back. History has seen many Anti-Christ types—Nero, Antiochus Epiphanes, Robespierre, Hitler, Stalin and dozens more. They have all had one thing in common—each wanted to annihilate God's people and set himself up as the ruler of a one-world government. That is why we are always one generation away from continuing to hold him back; each generation offers a new candidate.

"Chapter 12 of Revelation says that we overcome Satan by the blood of the Lamb and by the word of our testimony. Jesus has already shed His blood on the cross, and millions of Christians all over the world are standing against Satan and his forces. As long as we are faithful to boldly share our testimonies, we will hold back his coming. One day God's people will be too few and too weak to care enough to stand against the forces of Satan, and when that day comes, the Anti-Christ will take power. But today is not that day!"

"For right now, Fred, how would you like to have full access to Josef Helmick's apartment while he's away?" Jarrod interjected.

"You're kidding!"

"Nope, I'm as serious as a heart attack." Jarrod reached inside his jacket pocket and pulled out an official GenCEN ID and handed it to Fred. "After you found the location of Helmick's Swiss property we were able to have a satellite pointed at it, and a few weeks ago we got a photograph that we are ninety-five percent certain is Heinz Felhaber. That, along with the DNA match to Amanda Sutton on the ring you sent us, and confirmation from the hotel staff that she was Helmick's date after she died, was enough to get a GenCEN search warrant for his apartment here and his estate in Switzerland. Show this to the concierge at the Burj Khalifa and he will let you in. I am sending a team of GenCEN agents with you, just to guard against any possibility that someone might decide to shoot you.

"I've been holding onto this ID for several months—waiting for the right moment to use it. I'll send a coded text to GenCEN right now so that they can get their agents in place."

"How long will that take?" Fred inquired. "Nobody has any idea how long Josef will be away."

"They can be at the Burj Khalifa in five minutes," Jarrod replied. "I made certain the agents were in place before Josh and I arrived yesterday. They've been waiting for the green light. A team will be here to pick you up before you finish that cup of coffee. The sixteen other agents will be waiting for you at the hotel."

CHAPTER 27

Josef stood at the center of Berlin's Museum Isle. Nikolai Sokol had informed him that he would meet Demetri Kairos at this location, and they would view the Pergamon Altar together. The following morning, they would have their meeting with Germany's chancellor to request that the Altar be restored to its original home on an acropolis in the ancient city of Pergamon, renamed Bergama in modern times. Josef was impatient and looked at his watch. He despised tardiness as a sign of both disrespect and inefficiency and this Greek, or Turk—or whatever Demetri was—had kept him waiting for thirty minutes.

After a full forty-five minutes had passed since the specified meeting time, Josef saw a man striding toward him. "Josef Helmick, I am honored to make your acquaintance." Josef stared at him coldly, but Demetri extended his hand in a friendly fashion. "Nikolai sent me your photo and dossier so that I could recognize you among the thousands of tourists milling about today. I hope you will forgive my tardiness. I had breakfast with Nikolai on his yacht, and he simply would not let me leave. He said that you would understand."

Josef kept his composure, but inwardly he was seething. Nikolai knew how he hated to be kept waiting; he had done this on purpose, knowing perfectly well that he would have no choice but to wait. Josef looked forward to the day when he could punish this vulgar, greedy Czech as he deserved, but he reminded himself that this was not that day. Josef needed Nikolai to accomplish his purposes, and, apparently, that also meant that he needed Demetri. He smiled his most charming smile and returned the handshake. As he did so, he studied Demetri carefully.

He was about thirty-five years of age and approximately the same height as Josef, just under six feet tall. Even in his charcoal suit, which was just one shade lighter than black, Demetri appeared lean and hard. His dark hair, which was the color of a charcoal briquette, matched his suit exactly. His hair was thick and naturally wavy and just slightly too long but very flattering. He had a flawless porcelain complexion that shone as if he had never had a blemish or a breakout of any type. His chiseled masculine features were situated perfectly on his face, as if he had been sculpted from fine Greek marble. Josef was stunned by his flawless perfection—it was unusual to see such beauty anywhere, and particularly in an organic. But it was Demetri's eyes that immediately captured Helmick's attention.

His large almond-shaped eyes turned down slightly at the corners, which made him appear a little melancholy, and they were framed by thick black lashes. The eyes were gray—not gray-green or gray-blue or any of the other faded variations of eyes that Josef had seen so often in his studies of organics. These were the color of storm clouds reflected in the sea; they were the color of liquid silver reflecting light; they were the color of the silver lining beneath a cloud. They were rare and remarkable, and they immediately captured Helmick's attention.

When Josef was a child, he had collected butterflies and kept them in his room pinned inside picture frames. When he became a man, he discovered a more interesting collection—eyes. Whenever he saw a person with a remarkable eye color, he cloned that individual and then harvested the eyes for his private display. Heinz had created a chemical solution that would preserve the eyes and prevent deterioration, and through this process Josef had been able to keep some of his early trophies for more than a decade. He had collected all shades of irises—blue and violet and green and even yellow. He had collected sets of eyes from specimens with heterochromia, and he displayed these sets with their different-colored irises together. He had collected so many rare specimens for his wall of eyes that he was beginning to think that there was nothing new left to add to his collection. Now, however, looking at Demetri, he knew that his eyes would be an ideal addition to the wall. During this visit, he must secure the DNA needed to clone him.

If Demetri were aware of the intense interest with which Josef was examining him, he did not show it. "I am delighted to be able to meet you here so that we can tour the museum together. Nikolai indicated that you had not seen it before. You have spent much time in Berlin, though?"

"Much time," Josef responded in as friendly a fashion as he could manage. Now that he had discovered his own personal interest in Demetri, he exhibited as much charm as possible. "I have been in Berlin countless times since I was a boy; I used to come here with my father, but we did not spend our time in museums. I have never had any use for relics that are put on display to entertain gawking tourists."

"My father and I also visited Berlin frequently. We came to this island every visit. We spent the entire day at the five museums. Most of that time was spent at the Pergamon Altar and the antiquities museum, where my father recounted the mythology of the Greeks and Trojans and gods and mortals. Now I bring my own son, and together we walk through the exhibits and recount the stories of our heroic past."

"How old is your son?" Josef inquired.

"He is eight. He begged me to allow him to accompany me on this trip, but I told him that I had to work and would have no time for him. He can recount the old stories better than I—his mother has schooled him so thoroughly in Greek mythology that he knows these tales more intimately than our great poet Homer. He would have enjoyed meeting you, and I think you would have enjoyed meeting him as well. But this day, I am your guide to the Altar and it's ancient past. Allow me." Pointing toward the entrance to the Pergamon Altar museum, he motioned for Josef to step ahead of him, and he followed. A guard standing duty at a locked door opened it for them, and they stepped into a massive structure housing one of the most impressive artifacts of the ancient world. Josef and Demetri were the only two people in the room, which was noteworthy considering that the island was filled with tourists, and the Pergamon Altar was the chief attraction. Josef noted the absence of tourists but said nothing to Demetri.

"I paid for a special viewing today—a command performance as it were—for just the two of us," Demetri informed him. "Museum Island attracts over one million visitors each year, and most of them come to see this. A proper viewing is almost impossible. I paid the curator to lock the building down so that we can view the structure as it was meant to be viewed—reverently, without interruption."

The structure was massive and imposing—over thirty-five meters wide and thirty-three meters deep—carved from ancient Greek marble with a slight gray vein. The stairway alone was over twenty meters wide.

"What you are seeing here is the reconstruction of the western side of the Altar. In antiquity the eastern side would have been the critical one because sacrifices were made facing east, but when the archaeologists began their excavation in 1878 at the acropolis of Pergamon in Turkey and removed the friezes to Germany, they either failed to understand or failed to appreciate the significance of the eastern side, and so they reconstructed only the western portion and used the friezes they had excavated on the base they constructed for it."

"It is a temple to Zeus," Josef sounded bored, "The Germans who moved it were celebrating the discovery of an ancient archaeological find. The western piece with the staircase was the most impressive; naturally, they focused their efforts on that." As he spoke these words, Helmick made his way up the marble staircase and admired the German reconstruction of the marble columns which supported the flat marble canopy atop the structure. It was a very impressive work of engineering.

"It is not a temple," Demetri corrected him. "It is an Altar, and it represents virtually all of the ancient Greek gods. The marble friezes," he pointed to the friezes in high relief adorning the Altar, "tell the story of the Gigantomachy."

In his entire life, no one had ever dared to correct Josef. This was going to be a long trip. "If, as you say, it is an Altar to all deities, where was the temple? The structure originally sat alone on a hilltop. And if it is an Altar for all deities, why is it commonly referred to as the Altar of Zeus?" Josef snapped.

Demetri ignored his harsh tone. "On another hilltop above it sat a temple to Athena. This altar is believed to have been an accompaniment to that. The Pergamon Altar was commissioned by King Eumenes II of Turkey. Probably, the work was done by various artists from ancient Athens and Rhodes. Since Zeus ruled over all the gods and was father to most of them, to say that it is an Altar to him is to recognize his lordship over the lesser deities."

Demetri motioned for Josef to return down the staircase so that he could point out some of the stories represented in the friezes at the base. "You see here the story of the Gigantomachy—an ancient race of giants who were born from Gaia the earth, the primordial goddess, who is also the grandmother of Zeus and ancestress of all the gods. Gaia became angry with her grandchildren living on Mount Olympus and encouraged the giants to rebel against them. In order to triumph over the giants, the gods had to enlist the help of a mortal, and they called on Hercules. It was the son of Hercules, Telephus, who in Greek mythology came to Pergamon and founded the city, so the Altar is as much a tribute to his life as to any of the gods."

Josef did not like art; he had never liked art. The only history and past relics with which Karl had been concerned had to do with the Third Reich. Karl had considered art, music and literature to be "feminine" pursuits for the weak-minded and soft-bodied, and Josef agreed. For more than one hundred years this display had been one of the premier sites in Berlin, and now, as he stared at it, he could not imagine why anyone, even someone living in the city, would bother to darken the door of this place.

Josef had expected the experience to be more mystical than it was proving to be. Retrieving the Altar and returning it to Bergama had been Nikolai's idea. Josef had cooperated only because of the Altar's connection to the Third Reich. In 1934, the young Fuhrer had wanted a commanding visual for the National Socialist Party rallies in Nuremberg, and he had commissioned a young architect named Albert Speer to replicate the structure as an imposing backdrop for the Fuhrer's speeches. Using the Pergamon Altar as inspiration, Speer had designed the *Zeppelintribune* at the Nuremberg Parade Grounds, and his creation quickly became one of the most famous visuals of World War II. Some of Hitler's most powerful speeches were delivered from his pulpit strategically positioned at the center front of the massive edifice. Since most of the rallies were held at night; Speer had designed the *Zeppelintribune* with 150 lights which shone to the heavens, illuminating the structure as a "cathedral of light". The goal was to create visuals that were intimidating to the opposition and awe-inspiring for the many true believers, so that the German people could accept and embrace their new Supreme Ruler—the new god who stood before them as a man but demanded all-consuming worship and sacrifice. From that stage, he summoned the Hitler Youth into service; from that pulpit, he introduced the Nuremberg laws of 1935 which stripped Jews of their German citizenship and rights as participants in German society. From that pulpit, he received the accolades of the people as he saluted and called out "Sieg Heil"—"Hail to Victory,"—while the German people cheered wildly. From that pulpit, he transformed Europe into a slave labor camp and successfully annihilated nine million people with little internal resistance.

On his first trip to Germany, Josef had gone with Karl to the Nuremberg Parade grounds, and Karl had described to him what he had felt as he had stood there listening to Hitler's speeches. At only ten years of age, Karl had committed his life, his abilities, his accomplishments and his efforts to the Third Reich—a complete renunciation of himself and subjugation of his will that he had never regretted. Karl had told Josef that one day Josef would be the new ruler of the world—one day, all the world would stand before him in adulation just as they had stood before the Fuhrer. Over and over he had watched *Triumph of the Will*, Hitler's official propaganda movie showcasing his own triumph over all opposition in Germany. Even as a child, when Josef watched this film and the many other videos of Hitler's Reich, he would mentally superimpose himself over the Fuhrer's image and fantasize how it would feel to have the nations submitted to him in obeisance. When he visited Nuremberg and saw the ruins of the *Zeppelintribune*, he felt a connection to it, as if it were not history but the future calling to him from the ashes. He had assumed that he would experience something similar today.

This, however…this ancient marble cathedral to mythological beings wrestling each other for control in an epic battle—far from finding this structure inspiring, Josef merely found it gaudy and boring. The experience was so…Mediterranean. Josef hated Mediterranean people; he found them vulgar and distasteful. As he examined the friezes and the priceless marble artwork, he felt a deep hatred for it. True, he needed a visual to ignite the mass hypnosis that he planned to induce with Labyrinth, and this one was world-famous, but he would not use this monstrosity as a permanent podium. One generation—that was all he needed. One generation of believers who would accept the New World Order and forget themselves and their own beliefs and values and superstitions. If he needed this decaying old structure to secure Nikolai's full assistance and to ensure the world's loyalty, then so be it. Unlike his aging accomplice, Josef would never age—he had the gift of immortality which had been passed on to him by his father. He would use this monument to superstition for one generation and then grind it into powder and drop it into the ocean. After that he would erect a forty-foot statue of himself—that would be the only visual he would need.

"Breathtaking, is it not?" Demetri had been prattling on pointing out the various scenes from Greek mythology depicted in the friezes. The sound of his voice had been white noise for Josef's thoughts; now he realized that the Greek must imagine that he was lost in private reverie. He elected not to disappoint his guide.

“Exactly what I was just thinking. I wonder…I do not see a place for sacrifices. Where did the faithful sacrifice their gifts?”

“The fire altar probably evolved over the centuries. Scholars believe that this structure was endowed between 170 B.C. and 159 B.C. Libations of all types, including wine, fruit and cakes would probably have been offered to the gods. Homer tells us that the ancients burned the legs and thighs of their animal sacrifices before the gods, and the remainder of the creature was enjoyed as a feast at the temple.”

“Animals only?” Josef raised an eyebrow. “I understood that mythological blood lust extended far beyond animals.”

“Officially, the tales of frequent human sacrifice are just stories meant to excite the imagination, but the worshippers of Gaia, the earth goddess, will tell you that human sacrifice has always been the only kind the gods truly value. This Altar saw many such sacrifices; it was eventually reduced to ruins only because the sacrifices stopped. Come.” He motioned for Josef to follow him up the stairs.

“The fire altar would probably have been positioned somewhere here,” he continued when they reached the top of the stairs. “It would have taken many forms over the centuries. In the first century A.D., it was in the form of a bronze bull. An Athenian metal worker, Perillos, designed it for the tyrant Phalaris. The bull was hollow and sealed on the outside except for a metal door. When the victim was sealed inside, a fire was lighted under the statue which cooked the sacrifice to perfection—it was said that the gleaming bones were sold as jewelry. The scent of burning flesh became a spicy incense to the gods and rulers. Perillos also constructed the Altar so that the screams of the victim were distorted through a series of lines and stops to emerge as the soft bellowing of a bull.

"Since the victim's tongue was normally severed before he was imprisoned inside the bull, he was incapable of calling out words, so only the screams and cries had to be muted. Unfortunately for Perillos, who expected a reward for his creation, Phalaris thanked him by shutting him up in his invention and very nearly roasting him alive."

"Ingenious," now Josef was interested. Greek art and sculpture bored him, but all methods of torture fascinated him, and unlike Demetri, he had actually seen a brazen bull in action—in the dungeon of his own castle.

"Indeed. Later Phalaris also perished in the bull. By the first century A.D. human sacrifices were almost completely confined to criminals and political prisoners. These sacrifices met the gods' desire for blood while serving as a harsh reminder to the citizenry of the brutal cost of disobedience to their leaders. How long the bull served Zeus we cannot be sure, but it was still in use in the first century, when the Biblical book of Revelation alludes to the sacrifice of the leader of the church in Pergamon to Zeus. As an enemy of the state and the gods, he would have been sentenced to die in the bull. For at least two centuries A.D. the bull continued to consume those who stood in opposition to Zeus. But at length, the monotheistic religions, especially Christianity, destroyed the worship of the ancient gods and put men at odds with the earth."

"Christianity has been the bane of every society that has ever embraced it. Its adherents deserve to be roasted alive. On that we can agree," Josef smiled.

Demetri looked at his watch. "Our time here is ended. Be my guest for dinner. I took the liberty of making reservations for us at the Adlon Kempinski; they have prepared for us a table overlooking the Brandenburg Gate." Dinner at one of Berlin's oldest and finest restaurants was always a welcome experience, and Josef wanted to spend more time with Demetri; he was pleased, therefore, to accept the invitation. Together the men walked to the street and entered the armored car awaiting them.

CHAPTER 28

Three hours later Demetri and Josef were at the Adlon Kempinski seated at a table overlooking the Brandenburg Gate. The opulent old landmark had been rebuilt on its original site after World War II and had earned every inch of its reputation for exceptional food, service and atmosphere. Once a favorite dining spot for wealthy international tourists, the hotel had consistently upgraded its clientele as well as its menu so that now only the elite of the world's elite could even get a reservation. Tonight, Josef and Demetri dined on the restaurant's signature dish—red mullet with sea urchin sauce—as they enjoyed their extraordinary view.

Demetri ordered an expensive bottle of wine but then surprised Josef by drinking only water.

"You don't drink wine?" Josef mocked. "And may I ask why not?"

"I never drink when I am working. As the minister of cultural affairs for a Muslim nation, if I were to be seen enjoying a libation in public, I would offend those who employ me. I do my drinking at home."

"And where is home for you? Turkey or Greece?" Josef inquired.

"Home for me is 'the Labyrinth.'" Josef started visibly as Demetri uttered this final word, and he quickly looked at him to see if the Greek were toying with him. Demetri appeared to be looking out the window at their spectacular view, but in reality he was using the glass as a mirror to gauge Josef's reaction.

Labyrinth was a closely-held secret. Only Josef, Heinz and Nikolai Sokol knew of its existence, and only Josef and Heinz had access to it. If Sokol had told Demetri about the drug, this was a serious infraction of their relationship. Even with a man as powerful as Sokol, Josef could not overlook such a betrayal. He wanted to demand that Demetri explain what he knew, but his odd host continued gazing out the window.

"I love Berlin; it is such a beautiful city. Do you not find it so?" Demetri appeared to be changing the subject as he turned back to Josef.

"What is The Labyrinth?" Josef responded carefully, trying not to betray his surprise.

"It is my own personal island in the Mediterranean. My family has made their home there for decades."

Josef relaxed a little. "Amazing. I don't recall ever seeing it on a map."

"Nor will you," Demetri answered. "Labyrinth is not on a map. It rose up out of the sea when my father was just a boy. He and his father were on a fishing boat after an earthquake. Suddenly, the waters began to move, nearly capsizing their boat. They thought it was a tidal wave or the beginnings of a tsunami, but as they watched, the island rose out of the sea. My grandfather did not think much of it. After he and my father bailed the water out of the boat and set themselves back on course, he seldom mentioned the island. My father, however, was convinced that the island was a gift to him personally—a sign from the heavens. When he had finished working with his father each day, he would often jump out of the boat and swim to the island. When he grew older and he could manage the boat himself, he visited the island several times a week.

"It seemed to my father that the Labyrinth, which he named for the island in Greek mythology where the Minotaur was imprisoned, grew every time he visited it. Soon he began to believe that it concealed a treasure that would make him rich beyond his wildest dreams. Eventually, he proved to be right."

"He found a treasure…on an island…born from a storm?" Josef stared at Demetri.

"Of a sort. One day when he was exploring the island, he heard a group land in a small boat. They were heroin dealers who had stopped to stash their shipment because they had learned that Interpol was waiting for them when they landed in Italy. My father thought about taking the drugs for himself, but he knew that this would be suicide. Instead, he left the stash untouched and waited—and watched. Over time, he discovered that the heroin dealers stopped there often.

"Another day he was alone when a yacht drew up. My father was a beautiful young man, and he was sunbathing on his private beach. The proprietor of the yacht sent a servant in a skiff to ask my father to join him on board for a drink. The owner of the yacht was Nikolai Sokol; they became fast friends. My father was correct; though he was a young man with no formal education and limited skills from generations of poverty, the Labyrinth had brought him into contact with the means to make more money than he had ever imagined. He determined that it would always remain our family home."

"Your father was Ari Karras—an infamous man and yet admired by millions worldwide. You live on his island, but you no longer use his name. Why?"

"As you said, my father was infamous. He had both powerful friends and powerful enemies; I was the last person to see him alive, and that made me something of a target. As I was an only child, when my mother died the following year, there was no reason to continue to use the family name. My exquisite cousin, who is now my exquisite wife, agreed with me that we owe the Karras name nothing—it is a name belonging to the desperately poor in the fishing villages and to those who escape poverty by any means necessary. The name no longer suited our station, so we changed it."

"To the Greek word for 'time'?" Josef pressed.

"To the Greek word for 'opportunity'," Demetri explained. "*Chronos* is the word for time; *kairos* means 'an opportune moment'. Kairos was the youngest son of Zeus and the god of opportunity. I, too, value opportunity. I covet opportune moments as some men covet money, or women, or fame, or honor. Opportune moments are the stuff from which life's greatest treasures are born."

"So you are a god, then? No wonder you admire the friezes at the Pergamon Altar. They are family portraits," Josef was openly mocking him, but Demetri did not seem to notice.

"To read Homer is to discover that there is little difference between gods and mortals, except that the gods live longer. I am not bound to specific religions—they are tools for helping men process what the human consciousness can never fully understand. I am, however, very interested in the philosophies that attempt to define divinity. The names and attributes of the deities change with the seasons, but the philosophies drive mankind. I have studied them all so that I can travel among my many worlds. When I have business in Greece, I attend Mass with my Orthodox colleagues. In Turkey, I pray at the mosque every Friday. If men still sacrificed to Zeus and Athena, I would bring a libation of wine regularly. I am as comfortable in one place of worship as another."

"Your wife, though, is a worshiper of Gaia, is she not? Nikolai tells me she very beautiful, by the way—that she bears a close resemblance to you. Does she have the same remarkable gray eyes?"

"Iona is a portrait of beauty—I have never seen her equal anywhere. And yes, the eye color is very dominant in our family; my father and uncle had eyes this hue. Iona and I share this trait, and we have passed it on to our son. Iona says that it is a sign that we are descendants of the goddess Athena—her gray eyes were a distinguishing characteristic often mentioned by Homer. She tells our son that Athena asked Poseidon to send the Labyrinth to our family to rescue us from poverty and give us our current station in life where we can we serve Gaia.

"So, yes, Iona is a devotee of the ancient immortals, but her devotion, especially to Gaia, is shared by many true adherents of the world environmental movement. Iona brings Gaia a daily offering when she is on the Labyrinth; when she is not, her offering is the time she devotes to environmental causes, population control and sustainable initiatives worldwide. She says that Gaia finds more pleasure in these time offerings than in any gift of fruit or wine. I think she is probably right."

Josef smirked, "You cannot really believe in these ancient cults?"

"I believe in many things," Demetri met his incredulous stare coolly, "You have spent many years with the Club of Rome; you know many of its members intimately, I am told." Josef tried not to change expressions, but inwardly he winced. It was true that he had engaged in sexual acts with many of the Guardians, but these liaisons were carefully-protected secrets which had been primarily for the purposes of obtaining blackmail material on the most powerful men in the world should he ever need to use it. Nikolai had given Demetri much too much information—this would have to be dealt with.

"Do you really believe that the men in that room have any allegiance to Gaia?" Josef responded cynically. "Nikolai is a great admirer of your wife, I know, but Gaia is a symbol of hope for unwashed hippies and tree huggers; her adherents will never number more than a tiny group of misfits. The men in the Club of Rome may pay lip service to Gaia in an invocation, but what they really worship is themselves. They venerate power, money, control—not some ancient superstition. The Guardians know what I know—all religion is mythology, and all mythology is primitive man's attempt to explain and control the elements. Cults, churches, mosque—all are equally useless except for the power they allow the leaders to wield over the masses."

"If you really believe that, then why go to the expense and difficulty to bring the Altar back from Germany? Why not just leave it in the museum where it sits?" Demetri probed. "This ancient Altar is not just a collection of images from old Greek myths. It is the true story of mankind. All beings—gods, giants and mortals—are the children of our mother Earth. Just as the gods of

Olympus together with the mortal Hercules battled the giants—the forces of nature—we also strive to control the earth because we, like they, forget that we owe her our very existence. In antiquity this connection to Nature was respected and revered. With the advent of Christianity, the reverence for the earth faded. In mythology Gaia, the Earth, was not created—rather, she emerged from Chaos, the empty void, and when she mated with the heavens she gave birth to the gods. Though the gods could control the elements they could never completely subdue Gaia. Then Christianity began to overtake the ancient religions. Christianity took the Judaic concept of male Creator who had formed the earth and the heavens and all living things and then finally created man in His own image to rule over His creation, and added to it the idea that this God cares so much for men that he would send his Son to die for them. These teachings changed everything. Rather than a pulsating, powerful, passionate goddess, the Earth was reduced to a created object which had been brought into being for the service of man. Men and women were more important than anything else on this planet. By teaching that their God would die for them, Christianity firmly set the individual at the center of the universe, and as it did so it brought subjugation of the earth and the advancement of men as her masters. Soon the respect for Gaia was gone. Some of the respect was returned with the advent of Darwinism as men once again learned that the Earth is our true mother—the primordial element and the source of life. Today we have many on this planet who respect Mother Nature but only a small fraction of those understand that they owe allegiance to Gaia. There are still far too many who have pledged allegiance to Father God—the natural enemy of Gaia. And two thousand years later, they still worship a God who died for them instead of a goddess for whom they must die.

"That is why you need the Altar, Josef. It is not merely a collection of ancient art dug out of a mountaintop in Turkey. It is the key to unlocking the human psyche and transforming the human race. The Altar can reconfigure the value system of billions of people."

"What makes the Altar valuable is what it represents to the world," Josef contradicted. "You mentioned my speech at the Club of Rome. When I challenged the attendees that I could do in eight years what they have failed to do in nearly fifty, I was not just making an entertaining dinner presentation. I can succeed where they have failed because I can change the conditions that have caused their failures. The greatest single obstacle to the advancement of the global environmental movement and the New World Order is not individual property rights, or individual wealth, or nationalism. The preeminent threat to global environmentalism is Christianity. Because of Christianity people insist that national sovereignties matter and they have individual inalienable rights. Christianity gives people hope in something greater than themselves; it teaches them, as you have indicated, that there is a God who loves them and will help them, and that belief inspires them to fight all attempts at enslavement. It is because of the Christian belief in the Second Coming that no amount of marketing about global warming and the ultimate waste and destruction of the world has had any major impact on behaviors. Adherents to Christianity don't care if the world is depleting all of its resources; they are staring up at the sky waiting for their God. And they are so certain of His care that they will risk their lives to protect not only their own liberty but that of others.

"As long as Christianity exists, the world's people will never fully embrace the environmental movement; they will never voluntarily reduce the world's population; they will never fully subjugate themselves to the New World Order. Christianity destroyed ancient Rome; it had weakened Germany so much that Hitler could never mold the Germans into the force for change that he needed them to be. To bring massive change in behaviors you need to give mankind a new symbol—a new visual. For two thousand years that symbol of hope has been a cross; now it will be the Pergamon Altar. The Altar symbolizes the defeat of Christianity; the death of the faithful roasted alive in a bronze bull with their glistening bones afterwards used as ornaments. It is a symbol of the subjugation of all religions to the New World Order. By bringing back the Altar and making it a symbol of a new religion—a religion that centers on respect for the earth, we can control the behaviors and values of the world's population. We can inspire those who love the earth, and we can intimidate the skeptics into silence and submission. By showcasing the Altar's bloody history and its victory over the ancient Christians who opposed it, we can inspire fear in our opponents. It will be a symbol to the whole world that a new time has come."

"In other words, you plan to use it as a theatrical prop?" Demetri's remark angered Josef, and the Greek watched the disgust spread across his guest's face before he spoke again, "Do not be offended. I heard about the mind games you played at your induction as secretary-general of the Club of Rome. Most of the guests were very impressed, some were truly frightened, and others were concerned about turning over so much power to a man they believe can read minds. But you and I both know that your crystal prisms cannot reveal the future. So now, what? You want a bigger, more impressive visual?"

"Sokol must have told you this. He is wrong, Demetri; the crystals are not props. I was able to show the Guardians of Mankind the past, the present, and the future—in one moment."

"I would like to see a demonstration," Demetri was clearly baiting him. "Do you have a crystal with you now?"

Josef thought for a moment. He still had the crystal Afshin had cursed. It rested in its black velvet bag where it had lain since his encounter with the strange old man. He had it in his luggage, but after the dire warning Afshin had given him about the crystal showing him his own future when he was ready to face it, he had not opened the velvet bag to examine it. At any rate, his trick would not work unless he could dose Demetri with Labyrinth, and Josef did not have any with him.

"I left it my other coat, so, unfortunately, I will not be able to oblige you. But I can assure you that the experience that the Guardians had was completely authentic."

"Did you know that crystals have souls?" Demetri leaned back in his chair and studied Josef. "I know that as a man of science you don't believe in human souls. Sokol has told me all about you—you believe only in science and its power to correct the 'mistakes' of nature. But Nature makes no mistakes—even the harsh events of the universe—the tornadoes, the tsunamis, the earthquakes—those are her way of communicating with us to tell us that we cannot continue to ignore her. We are all connected to her life-force—men, plants, animals, and minerals. On the surface a crystal is like a beautiful woman—sparkling with nuances of color and personality, yet seemingly cold and aloof. But if you examine the crystal under a microscope you will see in the mineral composition its soul—exploding with light and fire and passion. This is the reason that those who respect the ancients reverence crystals—in the soul of a crystal it is possible to see the reflection of your own soul. If you want true insight into yourself and the universe, take a long look into one of your own crystals and see what you find there."

This conversation was oddly reminiscent of Josef's encounter with Afshin. Demetri was now talking in confidential, hushed tones—as though he was trying to frighten Josef, but Josef was not frightened; he was incredulous.

"You are correct; I do not believe in souls—for men, plants, animals or crystals," Josef answered curtly. "I believe in science and the power of the mind. I believe in authority and symbols of authority. I believe in a New World Order where those with intelligence and cunning make the decisions for the masses too stupid to properly order the world. If I could create such a world without a symbol of superstition, I would do so. I do not need additional insight—I understand everything about myself, the universe and nature that I will ever need to know. Consequently, I know that in order to control humankind we must substitute the prevailing superstition with a new one that meets our needs. Religion, of whatever sort, is the opiate of the masses. Find the right opiate, and they will drug themselves into insensibility."

"If this is really what you believe, then you are in grave danger. I warn you, Josef, for your own sake, you are about to embark on a quest you do not understand. You cannot master the Altar—the Altar has only one master, and he will not submit to you. You do not choose the Altar; the Altar must choose you."

"Do you really believe that the spirit of Zeus inhabits the Altar and waits for a time to be set free again to rule the earth? Why would an ancient Greek god conceal himself in an old piece of marble?" Josef smiled cynically.

"Zeus is one name, but he is known all over the world and called by many names. The Romans called him Jupiter, the Scandinavians called him Thor; the Egyptians called him Ammon. The Hebrews called him Abaddon. Every culture knows him by the name they choose for him. His name is not important; he is the Force that controls the minds and desires of all men and women on this earth. He is at work everywhere, every day, in every corner of the world. It is his voice that whispers to a commander of an army outpost that the men in his regiment should rape the women in a village to humiliate and subjugate the people, and then it is his voice that whispers to the enraged husbands that they should kill the regiment in revenge.

"He is the one who suggested that the assassin murder the Archduke Ferdinand and thereby start World War I; he inspired Hitler to invade Poland. He is present at the beginning of every war; he walks along every battlefield gloating over the dead and dying. He stands in the interrogation room and whispers to the torturer how to extract the most pain in order to procure the desired information from his hapless victim. He sits at every peace negotiation and breathes the lies into the ears of the world leaders that become the basis for peace treaties that are never honored.

"He is close at hand watching every child who is ever beaten or violated. He entices a lonely wife to abandon her vows and give herself to her neighbor; he tells her husband about her crime and demands that he kill her to restore his honor.

"He teaches one man how to make himself rich through cheating, theft, extortion and crime, and then he shows another man the first one's treasure and suggests a plan for how to kill the owner of this abundance and thereby procure it for himself.

"He whispers every act of betrayal, murder, cruelty, and lust into the minds of mankind. He allows the man who loves to gamble a few wins just to make certain that he will remain fixed in his habit, and then he sits back and watches him lose all he owns. He shows men how to make themselves rich through narcotics, and then he offers those narcotics to those he knows cannot resist. He sees every heart, every thought, every longing; he knows every weakness and dark desire of every person who ever has or ever will live, and so he knows what will tempt and seduce each one. And because of this, his power is immense and stretches far and wide—across every continent, people group, race, creed and language.

"He is not imprisoned in the Altar, Josef. He has been with you your whole life—from your infancy. But on certain occasions in history, when he has watched mankind a long time and knows the conditions are right, he suggests to men to move his Altar, which is the center of his power here on earth, so that he can reign openly."

"No ancient spirit suggested that I move the Altar, I can assure you," Josef smirked. "And nothing whispers in my ear."

"You are wrong. The Altar alone chooses where it will live; it seeks to be near the Force. The Altar chose to be constructed in Turkey at Pergamon. By demanding the blood of the faithful, the Altar stood against Christianity in Turkey until finally the Force had driven it out. For over a thousand years the Ottoman Empire dominated Europe with Turkey as its base of operations. European Christian children were marched away as slaves to the Ottomans as their parents looked on helplessly—a tribute to the Ottomans and a testimony to the power of the Force. The Force and the Altar made the Ottomans the rulers of much of Europe. But as Europe became stronger, the Altar sought a new base of operations—a place from which it could continue to exert influence for the Force. In the late 1800s, it revealed itself to your German archaeologists for the express purpose of being removed to Germany. From there, the Force ruled over two world wars, the rise of Fascism and Communism, and the reemergence of Islam and terrorism. Now the Force is moving again, and the Altar must move with him—to help him consolidate his power. When he has become ruler over the entire world, he will elevate Gaia to her rightful place in the hearts of men. He is choosing a new home—that is why you are here; the Altar has sent for you."

Josef stared at Demetri. He would enjoy murdering this Greek. He had not planned to kill him, but now, after hearing this mystical gibberish about the Force, murder seemed to Josef to be the only logical response. He could teach Demetri a little about real force before he finally extinguished his life. Not here, though. In a few days Josef would be heading back to his Swiss estate and his castle with its dungeon deep in the bowels of the mountains filled with centuries of ancient instruments of torture used by medieval masters to punish those who opposed them. Every barbaric instrument of pain and cruelty ever conceived was represented in this room in one fashion or another, but unlike their original owners, Josef had the added benefit of expanded knowledge of the human form and biology and unlimited access to drugs which allowed him to bring his victims to the brink of death while depriving them of that final escape. He had lost count of the number of men and women who had begged for death in that room. One man who had particularly angered him had lived for three months in a state of intense suffering, and he died when he did only because he managed to free himself of his bonds and take his own life while Josef was away on business.

He had not yet decided how long he would keep Demetri alive, but at this moment his fantasies were fixed on the image of a mangled, bleeding form, almost unrecognizable as his handsome arrogant dinner companion, barely able to whisper his entreaties for death. Josef would invite the entire family—families were so interesting to kill together; one could learn so much about the family dynamic. Would Iona and Demetri beg for the life of their son and the lives of each other, or would each attempt to trade the other two in exchange for their own lives? As they witnessed one another's beauty being destroyed through torture, would they try to help each other? Perhaps he would allow Demetri's last sight to be that of his wife and child's perfectly gleaming bones being made into jewelry—just before Josef removed his eyes and shut him up in the brazen bull to roast. The eyes of all three would be permanent souvenirs in his collection to remind him of the agony of their screams and the scent of their roasting flesh.

As the vision faded, Josef realized that Demetri had been watching him carefully. His expression was oddly familiar, and for a moment Josef imagined that Demetri could actually view his fantasy; yet he did not appear shocked or afraid or angry. He was smiling—not a happy or a pleasant smile or even a conciliatory smile. His smile was strangely mocking. In Kairos' deep gray eyes was a familiar, taunting expression. Where had Josef recently seen that same gaze looking back at him? Suddenly he remembered—he had seen the same taunting mockery in the sightless eyes of Afshin the beggar.

The fantasy was now gone, and Josef was consumed by the same horrifying coldness he had experienced when he left Afshin's hovel. Somehow Demetri had gained control of the situation. As Josef struggled to remain calm, Demetri watched, savoring every emotion and every slight change of expression.

Keeping his voice perfectly controlled, Josef lifted his glass, "If the Altar has brought us here at the command of the Force, then we should drink to our host. To the Force."

Demetri lifted his glass, and the men finished their dinner quietly.

CHAPTER 29

At precisely 10:00 the following morning Josef's car pulled up outside the *Bundeskanzleramt*—the headquarters of the German Chancellery in Berlin. Overnight a storm had moved in, and a cold rain was pouring as Josef stepped out of the car and under the umbrella his driver held for him.

On the previous evening Josef had informed Kairos that he had many business issues to attend to this morning, and he would meet him at the Chancellery for their appointment. Considering Kairos' extreme tardiness the day before, Josef surmised that he probably would not arrive until the meeting was almost over and Josef had made all of the arrangements without him. Josef would be sure to let Nikolai know that after the old man insisted that he bring Demetri, he had not even attended the negotiations, and his presence in Berlin had been completely unnecessary.

The *Bundeskanzleramt* had been constructed at the beginning of the twenty-first century in a post-modern style of concrete and glass. The Chancellery building celebrated Germany's reunification and the reestablishment of Berlin as the seat of government. The building also celebrated the triumph of modernism, efficiency, and simplicity over the excesses and abuses of the past. Eight times larger than the White House, the *Bundeskanzleramt* had been built without any of the artistic touches that graced the old buildings of Europe. It was new, clean, modern and austere.

For decades this massive but no-frills building had been headquarters to an equally austere, unpretentious government. Germany had embraced its new fiscally-conservative, uncharismatic leaders with enthusiasm and trusted these leaders to navigate it through worldwide recession, difficulties with the Euro, and frequent bickering among the nations of the European Union. Indeed, they had done such a good job that for the past ten years Germany had enjoyed a rapidly-growing economy and burgeoning individual wealth.

This prosperity had brought increased German prominence and national pride, and it had led the people to look for more photogenic leadership. They had found it in their newly-elected chancellor Helmut Schmidt and his wife Adel. Helmut and Adel were young—early forties and very glamorous. They represented Germany's new People's Party. Helmut was an engineer's son who had worked his way up in the party through luck and skill. His wife Adel was a television actress in Germany—she had never reached star status, but she did have a following. Schmidt had narrowly won the election and was in the process of putting together a coalition government with which to lead the nation, so every move he made now mattered for the future of his chancellorship. Josef knew all of this, and he was prepared to make an offer that the chancellor could not refuse.

The security guards standing watch at the entrance had been told to expect Josef, and they promptly escorted him to the elevators which took him to the chancellor's floor. A staff person was waiting there to escort him into the offices. As he neared, he heard the sounds of laughter and a conversation that was well underway. He entered the room to find, to his intense disappointment, that the Turkish Minister of Cultural Affairs was already comfortably seated across from Schmidt's desk. Demetri set down his cup of coffee and rose to greet him.

Noting Josef's surprised reaction at seeing them already engaged in conversation, Demetri explained, "I came around a little early—not as part of the official visit but because we are old friends. Our wives both sit on the board of the International Council for Women and Girls as well as a number of environmental organizations. We have all known each other for years, so Helmut and I have been here catching up."

"*Guten tag*, Herr Helmick," Helmut greeted Josef as they were introduced. "I am honored to meet you."

"The honor is mine, Herr Schmidt," Josef lied and took his seat across the desk from Helmut.

They made small talk about Demetri's and Josef's uneventful travel to Berlin, about the exceptional quality of the food and lodgings at the Adlon Kempinski, and about the dreariness of the rain which continued to pour with no sign of a break.

"Yesterday the weather was clear; I hope you were able to take advantage of it and see some of the beautiful history of our city."

"Indeed," Josef responded. "In fact, we spent the afternoon on Museum Island touring the exhibits. The Pergamon Altar was of particular interest to us."

Helmut smiled and nodded. He had known this was coming and had been waiting for it. "Yes, I know that is why you and Demetri have come—to ask me to return the Pergamon Altar to Turkey. You must understand why this is impossible. Turkey has requested the return of the Altar on two other occasions—in 1998 and in 2001. Both times the Staatliche Museen Berlin refused. The artifacts that comprise the Pergamon Altar were not stolen from Turkey—they were excavated and legally removed by an agreement with the Ottoman Empire which ruled over Turkey in the late 1800s. We broke no law and violated no agreement. Our government has taken every precaution to protect and restore it. We even negotiated with the Soviet Union to restore the pieces they had removed during wartime. Germany invested millions in the restoration of the Altar in the 1990s to repair marble damaged by rust from metal clamps and fasteners. Our nation has been a remarkably good steward of this treasure; we simply cannot part with it."

Josef was prepared with his answer, "I appreciate the expense that you have incurred while the Altar has remained in your custody, and I also understand that many years of costs must be reimbursed, with interest, before any transfer from Berlin to Turkey can occur. It is in that spirit that Nikolai Sokol and I have each committed one billion Euros to the German treasury to compensate the nation for the Altar. Even with nearly two hundred years of interest, you must agree that this is an excellent return on your investment, Helmut."

Helmut continued smiling but still shook his head, "Your offer is most generous, but you must understand that the Altar's presence in Germany is not merely a matter of money. Since the Altar first arrived on German shores, it has been a source of national pride to the German people. Museum Island is one of the top tourist attractions in Berlin; more than one million visitors a year journey from numerous countries to view the treasures on display; the Pergamon Altar is the chief attraction. For me to return the Altar to Turkey now would be to rip the heart out of Germany and throw it into the Mediterranean. The people would never forgive me."

Now Demetri spoke, "Helmut, this time it is different. The official request that I bring to you from the Turkish government is not based on any claims of malfeasance on the part of Germany. We do not claim that the Altar was taken fraudulently or illegally. In fact, we acknowledge in our request that Germany has acted within its legal and moral boundaries to keep the Altar and that you have honored it as it deserves. We merely ask that it be restored to its original home atop the acropolis at Bergama—the site where it was constructed.

"Officially, that is my request. Unofficially, I am here today as your close friend. Our wives both serve tirelessly for the good of the environment. This morning Iona and Adel are in Rio de Janeiro at the annual Earth Summit where they will pledge their time, talents, and resources to a sustainable environmental future. Tonight they will attend the Earth banquet where they will once again renew their devotion to Gaia. We cannot achieve a sustainable global future unless we first give Gaia all that is hers. We cannot elevate her to her proper place without the Altar. If Adel and Iona were here today, they would tell us that the concerns of the Earth surpass all individual concerns of national boundaries and national pride, of history and protocol. The Altar does not belong to Turkey any more than it belongs to Germany. The Altar belongs to the Earth and through the Earth to all of the peoples of the world. It is on the Altar's behalf that I implore you today to return it to the place of its origin so that its Force can be unleashed."

Helmut sat quietly for a moment, staring down at his desk. Both men watched him carefully; neither spoke. Finally, Helmut spoke to Josef, "If I agree, you will pay the money to the treasury that you have indicated?"

"The funds are prepared and awaiting wire transfer as soon as we have received a signed agreement from you," Josef confirmed

"And the Altar itself? Who will take responsibility for its disassembly and removal to Turkey?"

"Nikolai Sokol has agreed, as an added incentive above and beyond what he is paying into the treasury, to assume responsibility for all costs of dismantling and removing the Altar. His own transportation company will pack and ship the artifacts to the coast; the curator of the Pergamon Museum and the director of the Staatliche Museen Berlin are encouraged to be on hand as this takes place, and Sokol will reimburse the cost of their time to the German government. Land transportation has already been arranged and cleared through President Andre Moreau of France, and His Majesty Luis Carlos of Spain has arranged for uninterrupted land transport through his country and use of the Strait of Gibraltar. From there, it will be taken by sea to its destination. There will be no stops for customs inspections, no handling by low-level security agents, no prying eyes to disturb it. It will arrive safely and ready to be reassembled. Nikolai Sokol guarantees all of this personally—to you and to the people of Germany."

Helmut looked at them thoughtfully, "We could make the announcement at the United Nations General Assembly meeting, I suppose. Germany is among the most environmentally-conscious of all nations. We could announce that we are returning the Altar to the Earth."

"Yes," Demetri agreed. "Your chancellorship would be immediately celebrated by all those who understand the significance of such an action. You would have the support of powerful men and women from every corner of the globe."

"There is one more thing," Helmut looked at Josef. "It may be as Demetri says; I may have the admiration of powerful men and women from all corners of the globe. But for me to give away one of our nation's most valued treasures, I require more than money and more than admiration. I require a place at the table where those men congregate. In addition to all you have promised, my release of the Altar requires my membership in the Club of Rome. Make me one of your Guardians of Mankind, and the Altar is yours under the terms you have previously specified."

"Agreed," answered Josef.

Ψ

Demetri was taking an evening flight to Turkey; Josef was going to Switzerland. They parted in the lobby of the hotel.

"It was a genuine pleasure to meet you, Josef," Demetri shook his hand. "Nikolai speaks of you often and fondly."

"So I have noted," Josef responded. "I hope to meet you again soon. I have business in Gstaad for a few days, but then my time will be free. Please join me there, with Iona and your son, as soon as she returns from Brazil. I have a private castle in the mountains—we can go there for a small celebration of our victory this week—just the four of us. I have an impressive collection of artifacts that should be of great interest to you and your family and a basement filled with amusements—something for each of you."

Demetri barely changed expressions, but the corners of his mouth curled into an almost imperceptible smile. With that he turned and walked out of the lobby and stepped into the waiting car.

CHAPTER 30

Nikolai Sokol was drinking coffee on his terrace overlooking his estate in Saint-Tropez. On one side was a magnificent view of a seemingly endless expanse of ocean and blue sky dotted with only a few fluffy white clouds. On the other side was his personal rose garden and beyond that his private vineyard. At that moment the warm breeze mingled the aroma of the grapes with the scent of the roses into an intoxicating perfume that filled the air and delighted his senses. Ordinary men never experience life, he mused. Day after day spent in work and drudgery to scrape out some sort of living is a miserable existence at best. Billions of humans occupying their years on the planet engaged in such struggles cannot possibly have lives worth saving. They cannot be said to be engaged in the pursuit of happiness—they have no idea what pleasure even is. Fortunately, control of the world with its money, its governments, its resources and its opportunities, was given long ago to the Guardians of Mankind. Yet, even the Guardians had proven to be small-minded and weak; even they could not be fully trusted with ordering the affairs of men. Even the Guardians needed a Guardian to rule over and judge them—that person was Nikolai Sokol.

He was contemplating this when the call came in on his private personal communication device. The caller was the concierge at the Burj Khalifa. "Mr. Sokol, you instructed me to inform you of all activities concerning Josef Helmick. Armed officers from GenCEN are presently in the hotel with a search warrant for Helmick's apartment; they are up there now tearing it apart. These international authorities appear to have the full cooperation of both the local police captain of Dubai and the federal police force of the UAE. They are locking down the building now. Local and state police are stationed outside the property to check the identities of every person entering or leaving the building. They are also shutting down all communications in and out of the building. I wanted to call you while I had the chance."

"Good work, Rashid. Who else have you told?"

"Only you. You are my only call."

"Tell no one that we spoke. Are you calling from a line in the hotel or a PCD?"

"PCD. The switchboard has been shut down. This is a very organized operation—they came in at mid-morning. I hid my device and did not turn it in when I was told so that, at an opportune time, I could find a hidden place from which I could call you. I am in a storage closet on the basement level of the building."

"Good. Are there any liquids in the closet with you?"

"There are," Rashid confirmed, adding that there were various cleaning agents and bleach.

"Place the PCD in a bucket and cover it with bleach. No one must be able to trace this call. Stay in the closet. I will send someone to get you. Under no circumstances are you to call anyone else or tell anyone that you and I have spoken. Do you understand?"

"Perfectly," answered Rashid. "I will await my rescue."

Nikolai pressed the screen on his PCD and the call immediately connected. The old man spoke quickly but clearly. "There is no time to be lost. GenCEN has issued a search warrant for Josef Helmick's apartment at the Burj Khalifa. Interpol and the FBI will follow immediately with arrest warrants for him and his entire team. We must move up our time line and set our operation into action now. Under no circumstances can he be arrested; use your own network but only your very best operatives selected from Special Forces. Helmick, everyone who works for him and those with whom he has had extensive personal contact must all be eliminated—including those Guardians who took part in his private experiments. I am sending you a list. There must be no loose ends. Start with Rashid—the concierge at the Burj Khalifa—he is hiding in a storage closet in the basement where he just destroyed the PCD he used to contact me."

"I will take care of it immediately. What about the Altar?"

"The Altar is ready. My transport company has already dismantled it; your submarine can pick it up tonight."

"I am honored by your favor, Nikolai. My network is at your disposal; my men are in position. I will activate them now."

"See that you do. I will pay you a visit you in a few days." Nikolai disconnected the call and picked up his cup of coffee.

Within five minutes a young member of the Dubai police force entered the basement of the Burj Khalifa and walked directly to the storage closet where Rashid had imprisoned himself. No one heard the gun shot that put a bullet between the concierge's eyes and left him lying dead in the closet. Taking out a plastic bag, the officer bagged the bleach-soaked PCD, pocketed it, and locked the door behind him, leaving the body to be discovered by a member of the staff three days later.

Ψ

Ishan Pai was sitting in a dark SUV across the street from the headquarters of Ambani Global in Mumbai. A few weeks after his trip to Switzerland, he had regained his memory. He was not sure why or how—but one morning well before sunrise he awoke knowing who he was, who

Vasana was, and where they both were. He could remember both his old life and his present one. His wife was sleeping fitfully next to him—he could hear her incoherent mutterings from the dreams that tormented her every night. He rose quietly from his sleeping mat and went to the gardener's shed to retrieve the knife he had used the previous day. When he returned, he pushed the blade completely through Vasana's stomach until it exited through her back. She woke for only a moment—her eyes looked at him with ghastly recognition. He wondered if in that moment her memories also returned. It did not matter; she bled to death without the exhausted servants lying next to her ever awakening.

Ishan Pai had wealth of his own that Hemraj had never been able to control. When he left the Ambani estate, he went first to a small family vacation home in the mountains. There was a floor safe there with money he could use to leave the country; from there he traveled to another family home in the Cayman Islands where he plotted his revenge.

Ishan waited for Hemraj's car to pull up to the entrance. Ambani was in high spirits—he was about to announce that shares of Ambani Global had more than doubled since the death of his sister and brother-in-law a few months earlier that had ended the internal squabbling for control of the company.

The driver opened the door, and when Ambani was out of the car, the driver turned and shot him five times in the chest and stomach. He then jumped back into the car and sped down the street just as he had been instructed to do when Ishan had hired him. As employees of Ambani Global ran into the street to see what had happened, and passersby crowded around the crumpled body of Hemraj Ambani, a man stepped forward and offered to assist. "Let me through; I have medical training," Ishan Pai lied. The ruse worked; Hemraj looked up in horror to see Ishan standing over him. Ishan's face was the last thing he ever saw.

Two blocks away, Ambani's vehicle screeched to a halt as a sniper fired multiple rounds through the windshield, killing its only occupant—Ambani's driver/assassin.

Ψ

Luis Carlos was having his breakfast alone on the terrace off his bedroom at his palace outside Madrid. Patricia had gone to the South of France without him and taken the girls. She often left him alone now. She had always been understanding of him and his frequent dalliances, but lately she, too, seemed to have grown weary of him. He was a man living in isolation—without family, without his son Carlitos, without Ines. He thought he would like to kill them all.

The houseboy serving him was the newest addition to the palace staff. The boy, Pablo, was very attentive and served the king's breakfast and then waited silently for the monarch to begin eating.

After a few bites, Luis Carlos began to feel ill. The day was not hot, but he was sweating profusely, and he felt a tightness in his chest he had never before experienced. It was as though someone had wrapped an iron band around him and was squeezing it until he could not breathe.

"Boy," he summoned Pablo, "I am ill. I need help. I need a physician, immediately." The boy moved obediently toward the wide double wooden doors that connected the suite to the rest of the palace, but, instead of going for help, he closed and locked the doors and then barricaded them from the inside with a piece of furniture.

"Boy, what are you doing?" gasped the king. "I told you, I am ill. Call for my physician. I need a hospital. I am having a heart attack." Pablo did not respond but stood watching with his arms folded as Luis Carlos' pain and terror increased. Within half an hour the old man was lying motionless on the floor where he had fallen with his eyes still open. Pablo left the doors locked but removed the piece of furniture with which he had barricaded them, and then, jumping over the balcony into the soft black dirt of the garden below, he fled the estate on foot and hitchhiked into the city. It was early afternoon before one of the maids discovered the grotesque scene in the bedroom.

Ψ

It was noon on the campus of Harvard. Kevin Leeds had just finished his morning lecture and was heading out of the building toward the cafeteria when he heard a rifle crack. He stopped and listened. For the past twenty years Harvard had employed trained armed guards on campus to deter shooters. Sure enough, through the windows he could see the armed security running toward one end of the campus. More shots—followed by loud screams and panic. “It’s a sniper! There are two of them!” Students and faculty began running for cover as fast as they could as the armed, masked men continued firing. Their strategically-placed accomplice, who had positioned himself on the roof of the building overlooking the Bioethics Research Plaza, monitored the open radio frequency through which the campus security communicated. From his vantage point he easily eliminated each armed target who appeared. The men on the ground shot random students with amazing precision as they made their way to the entrance of the Bioethics Building.

Leeds saw them coming and scrambled down the hall. It never occurred to him that he might actually be the target; Leeds imagined that this was an act of terrorism or a political statement. He had locked the lecture hall door before exiting; now he fumbled desperately with his keys to reopen it. Just before they entered the main corridor, he managed to throw open the door. Frantically, he locked it behind him and hid behind the podium while he waited for the terror to pass.

He could hear muffled voices at the door; they almost certainly had seen him flee into the hall. Their faces were masked so he could not identify them, and there were many running, screaming targets on the campus; they had no reason to pursue him. In the corridor he could hear more screams and more shots being fired. He cowered behind the podium and listened.

To his horror, light was filling the room. The door was opening—the door he had locked from the inside. It was not being broken down; it opened gently as if the intruder had a key. The lights came on, and he could hear footsteps. Leeds was shaking so hard that he felt as though he might break into tiny pieces. He held his breath. Surely they weren't looking for him. Surely this was a random act. He could still hear shots—still hear cries of pain and terror. Why had they entered this room? The room was empty—except for him. The footsteps stopped directly in front of the podium where he had drawn his lanky form into the smallest ball possible. When the podium was kicked aside, he let out a barely perceptible whimper. The last sound Professor Leeds heard was the rifle crack that drove the bullet into his brain.

The masked men exited the building and signaled to their compatriot on the roof that they had completed their mission. With expert speed and precision, he fired two kill shots that ended both their lives. Then he removed his mask, re-entered the building from the roof and took his place among the other armed security guards.

Ψ

Two days after Ambani's execution-style murder, Ishan Pai's private jet landed in London. With Hemraj and Vasana both dead, he was the majority stockholder of Ambani Global. The law firm that represented him had released a cover story that Ishan and Vasana had been in an auto accident in the Swiss Alps, and Vasana had died. Ishan had actually escaped the burning car but had developed amnesia and so did not remember his true identity. Due to another fiery auto accident which had taken place the same night on a nearby stretch of road, the Swiss authorities had confused the corpses and mistakenly listed both Vasana and Ishan as dead.

Ishan would attend Hemraj's funeral. If Ramita stayed out of his way, she would be allowed to live though he would exile her to a secluded estate at the opposite end of the country. He would not have extended even this courtesy except that she had been on a world cruise during the time that he and Vasana had been enslaved on her estate, and Ishan had determined that she did not have any knowledge of what had taken place there. Were it not for that, she would have perished along with her husband.

Hemraj was dead; the shrill, nagging Vasana was dead; Ishan was rid of the entire family. His father and older brother had died several years before of natural causes. For the first time in his life he was his own man—liberated of familial and matrimonial constraints. He had always wondered how it might feel to be free. Now he knew—it felt wonderful.

A car with a driver was waiting for him on the tarmac. He was being driven to the splendid Claridges Hotel where he would spend the night. In the morning, he would travel to the London office of Ambani Global where he would preside over his first meeting as the new chairman of the board. To keep stock prices high, Ishan needed to convince the world that he was capable of continuing on with the company just as Hemraj had, but this was a challenge he was ready to accept.

The driver stopped at the entrance to Claridges. As Ishan stepped into the magnificent lobby, replete with its majestic columns, intricate woodwork, gleaming black and white marble floors, and sparkling chandeliers, he paused to drink in the splendor. This was his first stay at Claridges since his ordeal, and he was seeing the world through new eyes. A stunning young woman of no more than twenty-two with turquoise blue eyes and long blonde hair cascading around her shoulders watched him from a chair in the lobby. Slowly she rose and walked toward him. Her black silk dress accentuated her perfectly proportioned figure; her five inch black pumps showed off her long toned legs to their best advantage.

"Mr. Pai. I am Maya, a gift to you from Nikolai Sokol. I think you are expecting me."

"I certainly am, and I must say, you are even more exquisite than I imagined. I would like to buy you a drink in the hotel bar."

"I would be honored to have a drink with you," Maya smiled coyly, and then whispered, "but in your room."

By the time he had finished his drink, Ishan was weak and sweating profusely. Maya took his personal communication device and sat on the edge of the bed watching him gasp for breath and beg for help until finally he had breathed his last. Then she walked out of the room and downstairs through the hotel lobby. The car and driver that had brought Ishan to Claridges was waiting for her at the entrance, and she and the driver sped out of London hours before Ishan's body was discovered.

CHAPTER 31

Fred had been sitting in Josef's private office in his apartment in the Burj Khalifa since mid-morning. It was now a little past 10:00 P.M., and he had not even made a dent in the huge volume of information stored on carefully-labeled smart chips and orders neatly written on the lined yellow pads recovered from the apartment's various wall safes. In one of the safes, Fred had found personal effects of his victims—among them a carved pipe and an intricate bracelet—personal reminders of the lives he had taken. He knew that all serial killers keep souvenirs of their victims so that they can pull them out and touch them, and smell them, and relive the experience. He had believed that Josef would keep souvenirs of his victims so that he could relive his part in the gross experiment in which he had been involved for the past fifteen years. He was, however, completely unprepared for the magnitude of human trafficking that he had uncovered.

It was all there. Detailed accounts of the thousands of copies he had provided for the privileged classes from every corner of the world. Fred was especially fascinated by the account of a European financier who had no heirs and was unwilling to leave his wealth to distant relatives. He had married four times but had no children. Then, at the age of seventy-four, he had married a twenty-two-year-old law student whom he had met when he attended an event for the university where she was studying.

The girl, Angelica, had been smitten by him. She had admired his intelligence and wit and had stood spellbound while he told her stories of his youth. As he had looked into her gray eyes he had seen something that he had never found in any other woman. He had felt as if he were a schoolboy, and suddenly he had blurted out, "If I were forty years younger, I would invite you to dinner."

She had replied, "If you were forty years younger, you would not fascinate me as you do."

Godfrey Marshall was hooked. Six weeks later they were married, and three months after that Angelica had announced that she was pregnant.

Godfrey had been ecstatic. Tests revealed that the child she carried was a boy. What more could a man want—a beautiful devoted wife and a son. Godfrey had finally gotten everything he had ever desired.

Then, when she was in her second trimester, Angelica had been speeding down the country road that led to his summer house when she had lost control of her small car and crashed into a tree. At the hospital both she and the child were pronounced dead on arrival.

Godfrey was inconsolable, but on the day the cremation was to have taken place, he received an anonymous message delivered by a courier: “Your wife and child can live again. Reply through courier.” Godfrey was astonished because he had kept the deaths out of the media. No one at the hospital would have dared leak the news. Anyone at his organization would have known the penalty for divulging the information.

Godfrey had taken the message and scrawled a one-word reply at the bottom—“yes!” and then he had signed it and returned it to the courier.

A few days later Godfrey met Josef Helmick in Gstaad where, without Godfrey’s knowledge, Josef collected a DNA sample from him. Godfrey agreed to Josef’s terms—five times his normal fee to clone Angelica and their unborn child.

At the end of three months, Josef presented Godfrey with an Angelica copy whose pregnancy had advanced to the precise point where it would have been if she had lived. Complete with the original Angelica’s memory bank, the copy was, in every respect, exactly as she had been prior to the accident. In spite of the unsettling aspects of the account, it appeared to be a rather touching love story.

Josef, however, was not one to miss an opportunity. He had immediately recognized the existence of all the right conditions for future blackmail if he chose to exercise that option, and so he did a little investigating that turned up some fascinating information. First, with a simple DNA test he verified that the child was not Godfrey's; then, he discovered that the beautiful law student with her mane of red hair and penetrating gray eyes did not exist. Angelica was, in fact, Carey Williams, a dancer at a club in London who had met Godfrey's young assistant Bill O'Grady a year earlier and had been sharing an apartment with him until Bill could find the perfect opportunity to arrange an "accidental" meeting between Godfrey and her. Bill knew the old man's taste in women, and he had handpicked Carey to seduce him.

Bill had been careful during that year to make certain that Carey did not become pregnant, but as soon as she and Godfrey were married, he had made impregnating Carey his first priority. When the child was born, he and Carey would be set. She would funnel money to him from the various accounts—Godfrey would deny her nothing—and he would be in a perfect position to marry her and take over when the old man died. Godfrey would never suspect a thing. He was in love, and, even if he were to become suspicious, his vanity would prevent him from admitting, even to himself, that his darling Angelica could ever be unfaithful.

Bill did not have long to wait. A little more than a year after Godfrey junior's birth, the old man died of a massive heart attack. There was no foul play; everything was as it appeared to be. And so Godfrey's wife and his fortune passed to another man and another man's child. And, with Bill O'Grady as the new chairman of the board,

Josef received a sizable check from the organization each month for "consulting fees."

Fred rubbed his eyes and walked to the window. It was dark and still. He knew that during the daylight hours, if one were to climb to the top of the tower, he could see a section of the earth's curve, but now all he could see was vast darkness dotted with the lights that defined the city. Beyond the city lay only blackness and sand.

Ψ

The next morning Fred was up early and was once again examining the information on the smart chips. The account of Peter Kessler and his son Dieter was there. The copies of the starlets who were sold as sex slaves to Prince Abdul were carefully accounted for. It was overwhelming and sickening. After a couple of hours Fred felt queasy.

The magnitude of Josef's operation was almost beyond comprehension. Some of the copies had been used for the sadistic pleasure of his clients, but most were attempts to restore loved ones. Husbands, wives, children, parents—these made up the greater part of Josef's business. It was a testimony to how far a man will go to give those he loves eternal life and to gain eternal life for himself.

Fred opened his attaché case and scooped the smart chips into it. He had all the evidence that Josef had left. If one of these smart chips contained an account of what had happened to Alexander and Kathleen Sinclair, it might take many hours to find it. If that information were not on those drives, then it did not exist.

Harold Baker had been working all night compiling information, but he stopped to say goodbye to Fred. "He had an amazing operation here. Nothing was connected to any on-line electronic device at any time. All orders were placed on old-fashioned, lined yellow note pads. Even the data stored on the chips was accessed through an old laptop that had never been connected to the Internet. In the modern surveillance age, there was no way to get surveillance on his operation—absolutely nothing to hack. The only way he could be stopped was through old-fashioned detective work. If you had not come here and spent months collecting evidence, he would have never been stopped. Looks to me like Josef was actually right about one thing—sometimes the old ways really are best."

Fred shook his hand, and said "Thanks for all your hard work, Harold. I'll see you in New York."

Fred climbed into the limousine waiting for him at the curb and closed the partition between the driver and him. Leaning his head back against the seat he sighed deeply. "Dear God," he said, "why are people willing to do anything to ensure eternal life except the one thing that will give it to them? They'll spend any amount of money, they'll perform the most heinous acts, they'll sell their own souls trying to get it. The only thing they won't do is accept you as their Savior and take the free gift of eternal life that you provided for them two thousand years ago on the cross.

You are as close to them as their own heartbeats; yet, they refuse to come to you. Dear Jesus, please send revival to these people. Let those who have sat in darkness all these years find you. Please send your Holy Spirit to sweep across this land like a raging fire and stir their hearts and help them understand that you are the only way to eternal life."

CHAPTER 32

Jarrod and Joshua had divided the smart chips between them, and each searched the labels of the ones in his pile for a clue that one of them might contain information about their parents. Eventually they would examine each smart chip to glean all pertinent information about Josef's clients, the clones he created for them, and the purposes for which they were used. For now, however, they were looking for answers to how their parents had died. The labels contained number sequences which were meaningless to anyone not privy to the cataloging system, but Joshua suspected that the first three numerals on each label indicated into which group the information contained on that particular smart chip fell—one sequence for clones of family members, one for domestic workers, one for sex slaves, etc. Thus, he began separating his pile into smaller piles according to the first three numerals on the label. As he sorted the chips, he turned one over that contained only the date 09/05/2021.

"I found it!" he shouted, and his heart was pounding as he held it up for his brother to see. Both men were on their feet, and within seconds they covered the distance between the communication device and the table where they had been sitting. September 5, 2021 had been their twenty-first birthday, and it was the day their parents had died at Doppelganger. For more than twenty years they had searched for answers; now, they could hardly believe that their search had ended.

When the text came up on the screen, they discovered that Josef had written a detailed account of that day:

"In the days leading up to my twenty-first birthday Karl Helmick, the man whom I had always known as my father, promised me that on that day he would present me with the most wonderful gift I had ever imagined. As fate would have it, he kept his word—although not in the way he had intended.

"Early that morning he sent me on a fool's errand at the far end of the property. I knew at once that he was only sending me away so that my gift could be delivered and he could 'surprise' me later in the day at my party. However, I pretended not to know and did not return to the compound until noon.

"Upon my return, I knew at once that Karl was disposing of a human body in the crematorium. When one is frequently subjected to the odor of burning flesh, he is soon able to differentiate between the scent of burning cattle and that of burning men. At first I thought that it was one of the boys who had proven to be defective, but I soon learned the truth. Karl had invited Alexander Sinclair to come to Doppelganger so that he could enlist his help in a scheme that Karl had devised to clone himself and, thus, gain eternal life. When Sinclair, who was a fool by anyone's standards, refused, Karl killed him and had his body removed to the crematorium.

"Karl then sent his driver to Santa Fe to bring Sinclair's wife to Doppelganger so that he could dispose of her as well. Karl assured me that she, too, was dead but whether she had already been placed into the crematorium, I do not know. It made no difference; within an hour all of Doppelganger would become a crematorium.

"Karl called me into his office and began to reminisce about his youth and his love for Josef Mengele, an SS doctor who had served at Auschwitz. He rambled on for some time, though I did not hear most of what he said, but then he told me something that changed my life. He said that I was Josef Mengele—a perfect clone who had been formed from the great doctor's DNA. I was astounded and very pleased. For the first time in my life I felt free—free from the control that Karl had always exerted over me, free from his expectations, free from him. I knew at once that this was my opportunity to make my freedom permanent.

"As I thought about the implications of Karl's living forever in the form of a succession of his own clones, I became enraged. He intended to keep me under his boot. He intended to control my every movement for all eternity.

I would not allow that to happen! Quickly I stepped behind his chair, and with one swift motion I snapped his neck. His bones were old and brittle, and they gave way under my hands like a small bundle of dry twigs.

"I then activated the system that Karl had built into every building at Doppelganger so that in case of an emergency he could set off a chain reaction that would demolish every structure on the premises and ignite an inferno that would destroy all traces of our activities there.

"From a small hill overlooking Doppelganger I watched as the buildings collapsed and burst into flame. I had never felt such power as I felt at that moment. I knew then that no one would ever again presume to control me. I would live as I chose, I would do as I pleased, and no one would be able to stand against me!"

That was all that Josef had written. The brothers sat silently staring at the screen as if they expected more. But there was no more. Those few short paragraphs told the story they had been seeking since their twenty-first birthdays, but it was not the story they had expected to find. They had always been so sure that Josef had killed their parents; it seemed inconceivable that Karl was their murderer. They had always despised Josef, but because their father had trusted Karl, they had trusted him too. Only their mother had seen Karl Helmick for what he was—an evil old man without conscience who would sacrifice anyone to achieve his goals. Their mother had also been right about Karl's cloning activities; he had been cloning humans. She had suspected that all the children at Doppelganger were clones; she was even convinced that Josef Helmick was a clone of Josef Mengele. Their father had always told her that she was wrong, but, in the end, it had been he whom Karl had deceived.

Jarrod spoke first, “Mom was right.”

“Yeah,” Joshua replied, “she was right about pretty much everything.”

“She was always right,” Jarrod responded. “She would come out with some things that we thought were pretty off the wall, but she always turned out to be right. How could Dad have been so sure that Karl wasn’t cloning humans?”

“I don’t know. I guess because he liked Karl so much he refused to see the truth.”

The brothers again fell silent. They had believed that when they finally had proof of what had happened that final day at Doppelganger they would feel a sense of triumph. They had imagined that they would have closure concerning their parents’ deaths, but they found no victory in Josef’s account. It changed nothing. Their parents were dead, and nothing could bring them back. The man who had killed them was also dead. It was true that Josef’s account proved that he had detonated the explosives that had killed everyone else at Doppelganger, but his was not the hand that had taken their parents’ lives. They had spent all of their adult lives chasing a ghost.

CHAPTER 33

The next morning Jarrod was already seated in the living room of their hotel suite in Dubai when Joshua opened the door of his bedroom. "Were you able to sleep?" Joshua asked.

"Off and on. How about you?"

"I was awake most of the night. GenCEN has already called in Interpol and the FBI; we have to turn over all of this evidence immediately, or we can be charged with withholding information pertaining to a genetic crime."

"Yes, I know. I want you to turn over all of the chips to them. They will arrive within hours after you tell them what we have. In the meantime, make a copy of the chip telling about Mom and Dad's death. I want us to keep it so that we won't ever start questioning what we saw yesterday."

"Are you going somewhere?" Jarrod inquired.

Joshua was silent for a few moments before he answered. "I have hated Josef my entire life. I know that you could take him or leave him, but not me. From the first day I laid eyes on him I wanted to smash his face in. That's why I couldn't sleep last night. I kept feeling that God was leading me to find Josef and witness to him before GenCEN arrives to make the arrest."

Jarrod stared at his brother in disbelief. "Are you kidding me? Do you think Josef is going to sit politely while you tell him about salvation through Grace and then make a last-minute decision to accept Jesus?"

"No, I don't. I expect him to laugh in my face, but I'm not responsible for what Josef does; I'm responsible for what I do. I wrestled with this all night, and I know that I have to be obedient. Pray for me that when I see him again I'll be able to do what I was sent to do, because if I don't have the Holy Spirit sustaining me, I'll kill him with my bare hands."

"Josh! Josh! Josh!" Jarrod exclaimed, "All of the crazy genes must have passed through the placenta to your side. Why do you always have to do something like this? You're crazy, but if we live long enough, you'll drive me crazy too!"

"Will you do this for me?" Joshua asked his brother. "I need for you to give me an eight-hour head start. I've already called our pilots, and our jet will be ready for take-off when I arrive at the airport."

"Of course. You knew I would before you asked."

Ψ

On the security monitor stationed on the desk in his study Josef saw the black SUV pull up at the gate of his Gstaad vacation home. He knew instantly that it was a special armored edition, and he watched with interest to see who would emerge. He was not afraid; he had been immune from police scrutiny at any level for so many years that it was inconceivable to him that anyone would attempt to intrude into his affairs. Still, as he watched the door open, he felt a slight thrill, as if a single drop of ice water were running down his spine. He could not see the face of the man who opened the door of the driver's side and climbed out, but as soon as he saw the thick copper-colored hair and determined that the driver was well over six feet tall, he knew at once that it was one of the Sinclairs. It had been twenty-five years since he had seen either of the Sinclairs, but, instantly, the hate and rage that he had felt for them at their last meeting was back in full force. Josef waited to see the other brother emerge, but whichever one this was, he was alone.

Josef now felt that he had the advantage. He walked to the front door and threw it open before Joshua had a chance to ring the bell.

Josef stood staring at the man on his doorstep without saying a word.

"Josef, I'm Joshua Sinclair. I don't know whether you remember me, but our fathers were friends, and we met when we were boys."

Josef struggled to keep his composure. Joshua and Jarrod Sinclair were the two living people whom he hated more than anyone in the world. Through his contacts, Josef had kept abreast of their every move. He knew about GenTECH and their consulting work for law enforcement. He knew when each of them had married and the names and numbers of their children. He knew everything about them that it was possible for him to know.

Josef had longed for the moment when he would be able to exact his revenge on them for that day at Doppelganger when they had mocked him and treated him roughly. They had failed to recognize him as the future master of Doppelganger and had refused to acknowledge him as their superior.

Perhaps, during all of these years the Sinclair twins had not thought about him at all. That was the one eventuality for which Josef was entirely unprepared. "I think you are mistaken," Josef replied. "I am certain that we have never met."

"Well, we have," Joshua countered, "and I need to talk to you. May I come in?"

Josef stepped aside and allowed Joshua to enter and then led him to the study.

Joshua walked to a large brown leather Chesterfield chair and sat down without waiting to be invited. Josef took a seat opposite him. Joshua took a deep breath and began, "Yesterday your Dubai apartment's security was breached, and your records were confiscated. The chips have been decrypted and turned over to GenCEN. Last night Heinz Felhaber was arrested at his Swiss estate—or I should say your Swiss estate—and he is singing like a canary. Agents from GenCEN and Interpol are currently on their way here to arrest you. You will be taken into custody within hours."

Josef's mouth had opened slightly, and he stared at Joshua in horror and disbelief. "And I suppose you have come here to help me make my get-away? Even someone as unsophisticated as you cannot expect me to believe such obvious lies."

"It's the truth. And, no, I have not come to help you escape. I have come because, whatever the eventual outcome of the investigations, you are going to spend many years in prison. Even if you are eventually executed, and I believe that you will be, you are probably looking at fifteen to twenty years of appeals. I hope that you will use those years to get your spiritual life in order."

Josef was now seething with anger. "You are insane! Do you really think that you can walk in here and tell me that I need to get religion and that I will fall on my knees and ask you to lead me to Jesus?"

"Actually, that's exactly what my brother said when I told him I was coming here—almost verbatim."

"You should have listened to him. Now get out of my house!"

"I'm not leaving until I say what I came here to say," Joshua continued. "I want you to know that Jesus loves you. He hates the things you've done, but He loves you, and He'll forgive you if you will truly repent and ask for His forgiveness.

"He has seen everything that has ever happened to you. You didn't have a mother or a father; your life must have been very lonely, but He was always there, Josef. Jesus has been waiting for you to come to Him since the day you took your first breath. You possess intelligence and wealth and prestige, but you have chosen to waste those gifts. I have come here to tell you to seek Him with all your heart. You can never undo what you have already done, and you will pay for your crimes, but you can find the peace that has always eluded you."

"Do you suppose that you are the first person to try to persuade me to become a Christian?" Josef asked with a voice as cold as steel.

"When I was ten years old your father came to Doppelganger do some work with Karl. One day he came upon me while I was walking on the grounds unescorted, and he told me about Jesus and about His love for me. I was disgusted and infuriated, but I never let him know. I pretended to listen, and when he had finished, I smiled at him. He never suspected that all the while he was talking I was imagining the different ways I could kill him and dispose of his body. He was such a fool!

"My education at Doppelganger included the study of all the world's major religions. Karl said that I must understand the superstitions that drive men—even men who appear to possess intelligent scientific minds—if I were to fulfill my destiny. I know a great deal about Christianity; I dare say I could take you in a debate."

"I'm not here to talk about religion," Joshua countered. "I'm here to tell you what it means to have a personal relationship with Jesus Christ. To know His love is the greatest joy that anyone can experience. When you know Jesus, you are never alone; you are never without hope. He brings peace in the midst of despair and gives purpose to every life."

"I have heard this before," Josef replied. "A few years ago I was walking through the streets of Dubai when I saw a young woman preaching to a group of women and children. She was quite ugly—repulsive, really—but she was young, probably no more than fifteen. I stood at the edge of the crowd and waited for her to finish. When the other women had left, I approached her and told her that I wanted to know more about Jesus. She was so happy. I asked her if she would come to my apartment to talk to my wife and me about Jesus, and she eagerly agreed. When I had her inside, I told her that my wife was ill and asked if she would agree to go to her room to talk to her. She never suspected a thing until the door of my soundproof chamber slammed shut.

"She had eyes like a cow—large and brown and stupid. I have never enjoyed killing anyone as much as I enjoyed killing her. I kept her alive for two days stripping every inch of skin from her body while she begged Jesus to save her. Before she died she told me that her name was Rashin, and she said that she forgave me. It has been four years, and I still feel immense pleasure when I think about it. I suppose you are correct after all. Your Jesus has brought me a great deal of joy."

Joshua reached inside his coat pocket and pulled out a small New Testament and laid it on the table near his chair. Then he rose and walked from the room. When he was inside his car, he shut his eyes and bowed his head. "Dear, Jesus, I pray that Josef will read your word and that he will be saved." As he drove away, Joshua realized that for the first time in twenty years he was finally free from the anger and hatred for Josef that had always held him captive.

CHAPTER 34

Josef had been sitting alone in his study with his head in his hands for the two hours since Joshua had left. It was over—everything was gone. His relationship with Nikolai and the Guardians had ensured him immunity from prosecution, but if GenCEN had arrested Felhaber and exposed their operations, that protection would evaporate like the morning mist. They would not wait for the authorities to act—they would kill him themselves. He was overwhelmed by feelings he had never before experienced—utter shock and disbelief. For the first time in his adult life he was no longer the master; he was a victim of forces more powerful than he.

What should he do? Where should he turn? He had never had any faith—any belief in anything spiritual. For all his protestations to the contrary, the crystal prisms were only a magician's trick he used to control others. Where did a man who relied on neither God nor the devil, Heaven nor Hell, turn for help in his darkest moment? Josef, after all, possessed the secret to immortality, so he had never needed to concern himself with thoughts of the afterlife—something he would never experience.

He thought again of the prism that Afshin had handled. Since that day, Josef had never looked into it. It remained shrouded in the black velvet purse where it rested safely in the bottom drawer of his exquisitely carved, oversized desk. The old man had told Josef that the prism would show him his future when he was ready to face it. Never had he needed to know what lay ahead of him more than now. Yes, that was the answer. He would look into the facets of the prism and see his own future, and then he would know how to seize control of his own destiny and reclaim everything that had been lost.

Going to the bar, he opened a bottle of wine tainted with Labyrinth. Until now he had never used the drug, but he knew that the time had come to allow it to do its work. Labyrinth would open his mind and allow him to see with perfect clarity. Through the facets of the prism he would access his own eternity.

The wine was a little murky in the glass, but Josef paid no heed. He drank deeply until he had drained the flute completely, and then he opened the velvet bag and positioned the prism in his palm. The crystals began to shimmer and glow, and he felt it grow warm in his hand. His hazel eyes focused on the facets, and within seconds he was transported from the library.

He was seven years old again, standing on the grounds of Doppelganger on a rainy evening. He could feel the rain splashing against his shoes as it hit the paved walkway and bounced upward. The thunder gave a loud crack, and lightning slashed the sky with a jagged white light. He and Peter were walking to the infirmary; Peter was holding the umbrella.

This was the night Eric had died. Karl had sent for him to be taken from his dormitory to the infirmary so that he could watch. Eric had already been strapped into a chair when Josef arrived, but the little boy was not fully aware of what was about to happen to him until he saw Josef standing in the doorway. Then his face took on a look of complete horror as Josef watched Peter inject Eric with the same lethal cocktail that Karl administered to faulty animals. The boy struggled desperately for air as his breathing constricted and finally shut down. The entire process had taken no more than a quarter of an hour. Eric was the first person Josef had ever watched die. Josef could see every contortion of Eric's countenance—he could hear every gasp for breath. He remembered the ghastly look on the boy's face when life finally left him.

After it was over, Peter had walked Josef to the crematorium to watch the workers load in the body. Karl had ordered this, too—if Josef were to be master of Doppelganger, he had to know how to dispose of the weak and unworthy. Josef could still hear the sound the furnace made when it started and smell the stench of burning flesh.

He continued to stare at the crystal—today was his thirteenth birthday. He was on the motorcycle Karl had given him. The pride that he had felt at being given such a gift while the other boys watched morphed into shame remembering how he had overturned it in front of them….Now the Sinclairs were visiting Doppelganger; he could feel Joshua lifting him up off his feet by his own collar and hear their taunts. The humiliation was as potent as it had been the day the encounter had taken place….Now he was alone with Karl, living as the favorite son in the private home of a depraved old man who masqueraded as a philanthropist. He could smell Karl; he could feel his touch. He was reliving the intense hatred and disgust he had experienced every time the old man came near him.

Now he was twenty-one. He could again smell the stench from the crematorium. This was the day that Karl murdered Alexander and Kathleen Sinclair. He was sitting in Karl's office. He could see how old and feeble his "father" now was—his pale blue eyes were rimmed with red, and his hands trembled as he asked Josef for his help in attaining immortality….Now he had the whip around Karl's neck—Josef could hear him sputtering and gasping for breath as he tugged impotently against the whip around his throat. Josef was reliving the murderous anger he had felt for Karl for as long as he could remember, and now he could feel the old doctor's neck snap like a twig in his hands….He was standing on the hill overlooking Doppelganger detonating the explosives. He was more excited at that moment than he had ever been in his life. As he watched the buildings implode into flames, he imagined that he could hear the children and their attendants screaming for help.

The prism turned in his hands of its own volition. Now he could see his life since he had left Doppelganger. He was holding Maya, the first woman he had murdered. Her body was so close to his that he could feel her heart cease to beat. He wanted to feel her die—to look into her terrified eyes as her life left them. He had relived these murders in his mind every day, but never with the clarity that he was experiencing now. Every smell, every sound, every sensation were just as they had been the day they had happened....He was sitting at the top of the Burj Khalifa meeting with Prince Abdul and Anis as he took down his first order for clones of starlets....He was looking at his first Marilyn clone, thinking how perfect she was and how much he would enjoy the identical one he had made for himself.... He was receiving payment to clone Peter Kessler's son. He was receiving tens of millions of Euros. He felt power surge through him—he was the most important man in the world. No one could do what he could—kings and presidents and prime ministers groveled before him and paid whatever price he demanded for what he offered—immortality for family or for themselves, a second chance with a loved one, an opportunity to live out their darkest fantasies with no consequences.

He was standing at the podium at the Club of Rome the night he had become secretary-general. He was observing the trance he had cast over the attendees—the uncomfortable looks all across the room when they realized that he could guess their visions and that he had bared their innermost secrets....A badly-burned Amanda Sutton was writhing in torment as the acid he had poured on her consumed her flesh. She was begging him—first for her life and later for her death....He was at the United Nations addressing the world about environmentalism....He was standing in the Pergamon Museum with Demetri....He was negotiating with Helmut Schmidt for the release of the Altar. As he had grown to middle age, he had often wondered if he were capable of accessing any of Josef Mengele's memories; now he knew that even with Labyrinth he could not, but the day he left Helmut Schmidt's office after having secured the Altar, he experienced a connection even more palpable. The Altar connected him to a Force that had commanded history as it destroyed one nation and elevated another to power. From the pagans who sacrificed Christians on it in ancient times, to Adolf Hitler who replicated it before he began his ascent to power as the leader of the Third Reich, the Altar was a timeless reminder of the power that the Force bestowed on those who controlled it. Josef was now among the mighty who commanded it.

He was inviting Demetri and his family to Switzerland....He was in Afshin's hovel in Dubai. The old man's filthy, gnarled hands gripped the prism; Josef could still hear him hiss, "Look into the prism, and see your own future when you find the courage to face it."

The whisper had barely left Afshin's lips when Josef felt the prism turn again in his hand, and he felt his own gaze being drawn into the soul of the crystal. Instantly, he was engulfed in darkness—not the darkness of a moonless, starless night or even the darkness of a sealed room or cavern. Rather, it was the deepest, most foreboding blackness that he had ever experienced. Not a single pinprick of light penetrated anywhere; even the tiniest speck of light would have shone like a strobe in this endless night.

Josef was falling, and though he reached out for something to break his fall, he could not catch onto anything. Nor could he see into what he was falling—he could not see anything or measure the distance he had fallen or how much further he had to fall.

The heat was intense and stifling—he could feel his breathing constricting because of the scorching air that tortured his lungs. The stench was terrible—all around him was the smell of decay and putrefaction and burning flesh. These odors were familiar to him from his youth at Doppelganger, but they were magnified to an intensity he had never before experienced.

He was surrounded by misery. He could hear the sounds of torment, pain, sadness, loneliness, grief, disappointment and every sort of suffering reverberating through the chamber. But even more than hearing these audibly, he could feel them. It was as though all of the pain and sadness and loneliness and grief and pride and anger and hatred and suffering and torment that had ever existed since time began had been captured and confined in this space, and he was experiencing all of it inside himself at one time. He was completely alone, empty and cut off from everything and everyone. It was the most desolate, terrifying sensation he had ever experienced. And as he continued his downward descent he knew instinctively that he would never be able to escape from this place. He was imprisoned in this hopeless misery for all of eternity.

His mind was struggling to reject this vision. Even as he continued to fall he could sense that his physical self was attempting to free him of this ghastly portent of the future—his hand was trying to drop the prism. Finally, his fingers released the crystal, and he was once again sitting in his library. His heart was pounding; his hair and clothing were drenched in perspiration. When he looked up, he saw Karl standing in front of him.

This was not the old, feeble Karl just minutes away from the death; this was a younger man. This was the Karl he remembered from his childhood, the one who had moved him into his house when he was just thirteen. The apparition stood in his gray suit and smiled slightly—the cruelest, most sinister smile imaginable—and beckoned with his index finger for Josef to draw near. It was a gesture with which Josef was familiar and which made him tremble inwardly when he was a boy—that smile and that gesture always meant that something terrible was about to follow.

Josef staggered to his feet. His legs felt like lead; he could barely stand, but he forced himself up onto his feet. Taking the keycard to his motorcycle, he stumbled from the library and outside to the bike. When he looked up at the window he could still see the specter watching him and smiling.

He started the bike and pealed out of the driveway as though he were being chased. His only thought now was to get away from that library, from the prism and its hideous vision and from Karl. He could hear his victims now, but rather than their final moments of torment he imagined that they were taunting him, laughing at him. "Soon you will be with us," they seemed to whisper. The bike accelerated—100 kilometers per hour, 125, 150, 200.

The bike was climbing the narrow mountain road, and the cold air was reviving Josef and countering the effects of Labyrinth. As he reached the lookout point at the peak, his heart rate began to stabilize, and by the time he had brought the bike to a stop, the feeling of panic was subsiding.

The morning was beautiful. A fresh snow had fallen just before dawn, blanketing everything in glistening white; the sun shone brightly. Josef looked up; the sky was a perfect blue in a part of the world unsullied by pollution. Everything was light and bright, and the sunlight was glinting off the icy tops of the peaks. He thought that it resembled the light from the crystal prisms. For a fraction of a second, the scenery changed before his eyes, and he was at a lookout point overlooking peaks sculpted entirely from glimmering crystal prisms.

At that moment, the fog produced by the drug he had taken and his terrifying hallucinations evaporated. His mind was completely clear, his heart rate steady, his breathing calm. The biting cold of the air was invigorating as he surveyed the magnificent, glittering scenery before him. Whatever malevolence Afshin had infused into the prism when he had cursed it no longer had power over Josef's destiny. No vindictive spirits from the past were pursuing him—no tortured souls whispered in his ears now. The bright, cold, shimmering landscape was a profound contrast to the black furnace of torment he had seen in the prism. The latter was merely mischief wrought by a bitter old man—this was his present; this was reality. This was eternity—this pristine ice palace was his home, now and forever.

As he sat straddling his bike, suddenly Josef knew what to do. He would end things on his own terms—it was the only course that made any sense. Starting his bike, he pulled back onto the road and once again accelerated—100 kilometers per hour, 120, 200. He was racing up the narrowing road to the topmost point. The world below was reduced to a white blur as he reached the top and the bike sailed over the edge at almost 300 kilometers per hour.

Josef felt himself falling through the frozen air. Time seemed to stand still. He could not see the ground, but he could see the sunlight and the blue sky as he descended further and further down. The impact fractured his skull and pulverized his bones on the rocks below. His bike came to earth at almost the exact moment that he did. Within seconds the fuel tank exploded, consuming the bike and its owner in the flames.

Instantly, he was engulfed in darkness….

CHAPTER 35

Fred boarded the Branson Stream that made the flight from Dubai to New York in three hours. At the turn of the century when Richard Branson had built his spaceport at Las Cruces, New Mexico, to sell space flights to civilians, he had believed that the demand for the forty-five minute fifty-thousand-dollar flights would be sufficient to make his venture a commercial success. He soon discovered, however, that he had miscalculated, and he then decided to use the technology that his Virgin Industries had developed to produce a plane that made international travel faster and more convenient than any of his competitors. The resulting Branson Stream was an instant success.

Fred had never imagined that one day he would be in a position to fly on the Branson Stream. The tickets cost double the amount of those of other airlines, but the Sinclair brothers were generous, and they always provided him with the best accommodations. The attendant showed him to his seat—a large well-padded window lounger in putty-colored Italian leather. It was the ultimate in luxury, supporting his head, neck and back perfectly. The Branson Stream was designed with two seats to a row with a privacy screen between them so that every passenger enjoyed his own personal space.

Fred was glad to be going home. Although he had made several trips home, he had felt it was too dangerous to bring Annie to Dubai and so he had gone for several weeks at a time without seeing her. He missed her, and he was emotionally and physically drained. Josef was dead, and Fred had recovered all the evidence he had left behind of his massive crimes. He felt a shudder pass through his body as he thought about the heinous acts that Josef had committed. Fred was grateful that he had been able to play a major role in bringing to an end what might prove to be the most wide-spread killing spree that anyone had ever undertaken, but he had some regrets.

From the day of his arrival, Fred had felt such a burden for the people of the Middle East. There was great wealth, but there was also great poverty. Everywhere he looked he saw dust and dirt and relentless sun and endless sand. But more than that, he felt the overwhelming sadness and despair of a people who do not know Jesus. Work slaves from all over the planet labored for the world's most privileged classes. The poor had come to Dubai to find a better life and had been forced to live in filthy, crowded conditions where disease was rampant and the intense heat seemed to suck the life out of them. They had no means of escape from their subhuman living conditions, and the luxuries they observed as they bent their backs under the heavy loads that their masters imposed upon them were as unreal to them as a desert mirage that tantalizes the senses and then evaporates just when it appears to be within one's reach.

Fred had prayed for them every day that he had been in Dubai, and his prayer had always been that he would be able to reach them for Christ. He had prayed that God would send the greatest revival that the world had ever known and that it would begin in Dubai and spread across the Middle East "like a raging fire, consuming everything in its path." He had prayed that the revival would spread from the Middle East across the globe so that there would not be "one square centimeter of land on earth" where revival would not come. He had prayed that every living person would hear the gospel preached in his own language and that even those who were not searching for Christ would find Him.

As he sat looking out the window waiting for take-off, Fred felt like a failure. He had witnessed to everyone who would listen. Some had turned away in anger; others had listened politely; a few had seemed to be somewhat interested, but he had led only Walid to accept Jesus as his Savior. Yet, each day he had expected revival to begin. He had watched in vain for any sign that the Holy Spirit was lighting a fire in this lost land; now it was too late.

The engines roared to life, and the Branson Stream began to taxi down the runway. Fred turned his eyes to the window and watched the earth fall away beneath him as the huge plane gained altitude. Then he leaned back in his seat and closed his eyes. He had done all he could—all he knew to do—but he did not have the power to bring about revival. That was up to God.

At precisely that moment, three miles from the airport a small lizard scurried out from under the dry desert bush where he had been sleeping. He seemed to be disoriented as he turned to look at his former shelter. As the tiny creature watched, the small shrub burst into flame. It burned hotly for a long time, but it was not consumed. Hours later the flames still raged against the black nighttime sky as a gentle breeze caught the sparks and flung them upward in a golden shower that appeared to reach the very gates of heaven.

CHAPTER 36

The sunset over the ocean was a stunning kaleidoscope of crimson and gold hues. The few visible clouds filtered the light in such a way that the beams seemed to emanate from them and radiate across the sky. Below, the vast ocean reflected the same crimson hues and took on a strange, blood-like quality as far as the eye could see.

Demetri Kairos was making his way down a long series of marble steps that led to the shore. Behind him was a palatial estate constructed from white marble. An astute observer would have immediately recognized the Greek Parthenon, except that this building was in a state of perfect repair. On a marble terrace two steps above him his eight-year-old son ran eagerly. Demos bore an uncanny likeness to his father except that his skin was tanned a few shades darker from a summer spent playing on the shores of Labyrinth. He had the same silvery gray eyes that shone like the sea reflecting the clouds and eagerly took in every sight. His dark hair fell in soft waves against his neck. In his crisp white cotton shorts and shirt he looked more like an aspiring actor or child model than the future master of an uncharted island.

Demetri paused and waited for his son. "Why do you walk so quickly Father? Wait for me."

The father smiled at his son, "You must learn to keep up, Demos. The world moves quickly, and you must move even more quickly so that you can stay ahead of it." Lifting the boy over the marble railing that still separated them, he brought Demos to his side. "Can you keep up with me now?" Demos nodded affirmatively and together they made their way down the steps until they had reached the shore.

The sun was sinking so low now that it seemed to be setting into the water. The sky was losing its light, but the setting orb made the water appear still redder and more foreboding.

"Would you like to see some magic, Demos?"

"Yes, Father," Demos smiled broadly. Labyrinth was home to a great deal of magic, but Demos never tired of it.

"Then watch carefully," and his father pointed toward the water.

As they watched, the water began to displace before them as massive gray steel began to rise from the ocean.

Demos jumped up and down with excitement and then looked expectantly at his father, who watched and smiled but said nothing. As he watched, Demos saw what he was waiting for; as the object became more and more visible he could see the familiar image painted on the side—a fearsome beast unlike anything in nature. Its hideous form combined that of many creatures; it had seven heads and ten horns and each horn bore a crown. "It's our family crest!" Demos pointed at the image. Still his father said nothing.

The boy continued to gaze intently until the submarine had completely surfaced. The undersea boat was interesting, but he had seen it many times before, and it certainly was not magic. There must be something else, but nothing else emerged. After a while, Demos looked at his father, and said with disappointment in his voice, "It's only our submarine, Father. It's not magic." He continued to search his father's face for some explanation.

Demetri put his hand gently on the boy's head. "The magic is not the submarine, Demos. The magic is what the submarine has carried here to our island."

Now the boy looked both interested and confused. "What it is Father? What did it bring?"

"Our future—your future, my son. It is the most powerful magic the world has ever experienced—a Force to control every race, language, nationality and people group in the world. It is magic that controls people's minds and desires so that they will long to completely submit to it. It has chosen us, and it has come to us here to Labyrinth to live with us and teach us. For now it is in pieces, but later this evening the workers will take it from the vessel and bring it onto the shore. Then you and I will have it assembled here on Labyrinth. One day when the time is right, the magic will call you and send you far away from this island. It will give you the power to rule over all of the peoples of the world—the magic will make them your servants. Do you understand?"

"Yes, Father." The child's gray eyes glinted with excitement. Taking his father's hand, Demos watched as the last rays of light disappeared from the sky cloaking the ocean in blackness.

Epilogue

It was a rainy Saturday afternoon in Connecticut. The Sinclair brothers had planned to take their children to the zoo, but the weather had prevented their outing. Both wives had gone shopping, and Jarrod and Joshua were left to entertain the children. "Daddy! Tell us a story!" six-year-old Benjamin pleaded.

"Alright," Jarrod responded. "This is a story about your Uncle Joshua and me. When we were just about your age, our Sunday school teacher told us that the devil is powerful, and that if we weren't good he would get us!

"When we told Grandpa what she had said, he told us that we were Christian boys, and the devil can't get Christian boys. And then he told us something else—something very important. He said that the devil is not powerful; all power belongs to God and to Jesus. The devil uses force, but he has no power. Grandpa then told us that God's power is unlimited. He created everything there is in heaven and on earth. He has the power to protect us and to help us in every situation. There is nothing that is too hard for God because His power can both create and destroy. But the devil is different. He cannot create anything. He likes to destroy things—especially people's lives, but he has never created one single thing because force cannot create.

"Grandpa said that lots of things have force: floods, tornadoes, hurricanes, fires, earthquakes, but they are only able to destroy. Tornadoes have destroyed many towns, but you will never hear of one passing by and creating a town. The earth is filled with destructive forces, but those forces are nothing compared to God's power.

"Then Grandpa told us something that he wanted us to always remember. He said that as long as we have the power of God's Holy Spirit in us, the devil can never defeat us, and we never need to fear him. Grandpa said that one day God would call us to take a stand against the forces of Satan, and Grandpa was right; one day He did.

"But that happened a long time ago, long before the great fire had destroyed Doppelganger, long before Josef and his father had visited Cornucopia, long before we had suffered our great loss, on a cold January afternoon when snowflakes the size of goose feathers filled the sky and floated softly to the ground.

"Someday, when you are grown, God will call you to take a stand against Satan's forces. When that day comes, trust God to protect you. And whenever you feel afraid remember this: Whenever power and force collide, power always wins the fight."

ABOUT THE AUTHORS

Joyce and Alexandra Swann are mother and daughter. Joyce homeschooled her ten children from the first grade through master's degrees. She is a well-known author and speaker on the subject of homeschooling. For nearly a decade she was a popular columnist for *Practical Homeschooling* Magazine. She now blogs regularly on parenting, homeschooling, and Christian lifestyle issues.

Joyce and Alexandra have co-authored three other novels: *The Fourth Kingdom, The Twelfth Juror* and *The Chosen*. *The Fourth Kingdom* was a top four finalist in the *Christianity Today* 2011 book of the year awards. Joyce's personal story of her experiences raising and educating her family is chronicled in *Looking Backward: My Twenty-Five Years as a Homeschooling Mother,* published in February of 2011. Her novel, *The Warrior*, which tells the story of one woman's ten-year prayer vigil for a man she has never met, was released in May of 2012. She is also the author of two children's books, *Tales of Pig Isle* and *The McAloons*, which began as stories that she told to entertain her grandchildren.

Alexandra is author of *No Regrets: How Homeschooling Earned me a Master's Degree at Age Sixteen* and *Writing for Today.* For fifteen years she was self-employed in the financial services industry. She was the 2011 Chairwoman of the Board of the El Paso Hispanic Chamber of Commerce. Her novel *The Planner*, which is the prequel to *The Chosen*, was published in June of 2012.

Find these and other books by the Swanns at their website at http://www.frontier2000.net.

23431157R00193

Made in the USA
Charleston, SC
22 October 2013